Nine African Stories

Longman Imprint Books
General Editor: Michael Marland CBE

*Cassette available

LONGMAN IMPRINT BOOKS

Nine African Stories

Doris Lessing
with a specially written introduction by the author

Selected by
Michael Marland CBE BA
Headmaster, North Westminster School, London

Longman

Longman Group Limited
London

Associated companies, branches and representatives
throughout the world

The stories are selected from 'African Stories', Doris Lessing,
published by Michael Joseph Ltd 1964
This edition © Longman Group Ltd (formerly Longmans,
Green & Co. Ltd) 1968

This edition first published by Longman Group Ltd
by arrangement with Michael Joseph Ltd 1968

Sixth impression 1980

ISBN 0 582 23378 X

Printed in Hong Kong by
Commonwealth Printing Press Ltd

Photograph Acknowledgements

Photographs appear by permission of the following:
J. Allan Cash for pp. 253, 254, 255, 256, 257, 262, 266; Camera Press
for pp. 259, 261, 263, 264, 265; Central African Press Agency for p. 260;
Paul Popper for p. 258.

Contents

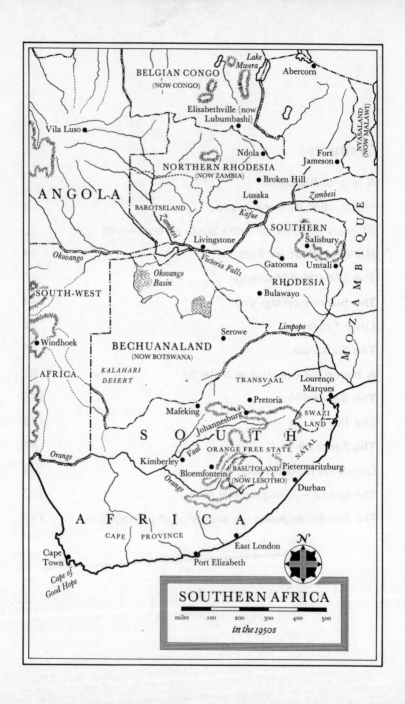

LAKE MWERU

BELGIAN CONGO
(NOW CONGO)

Abercorn

Elisabethville (now
Lubumbashi)

Vila Luso

Ndola

Fort
Jameson

NORTHERN RHODESIA
(NOW ZAMBIA)

ANGOLA

Broken Hill

BAROTSELAND

Zambesi

Lusaka

Zambesi

Kafue

SOUTHERN

Salisbury

NYASALAND
(NOW MALAWI)

Livingstone

Okovango

Victoria Falls

Gatooma

Umtali

SOUTH-WEST

Okovango
Basin

RHODESIA

Bulawayo

Windhoek

BECHUANALAND
(NOW BOTSWANA)

Serowe

Limpopo

AFRICA

KALAHARI
DESERT

TRANSVAAL

Lourenço
Marques

Mafeking

Pretoria

Johannesburg

SWAZI
LAND

SOUTH

Kimberley

Vaal

ORANGE FREE STATE

NATAL

Bloemfontein

Orange

BASUTOLAND
(NOW LESOTHO)

Pietermaritzburg

Durban

Orange

AFRICA

CAPE   PROVINCE

Cape
Town

East London

Port Elizabeth

N

Cape of
Good Hope

SOUTHERN AFRICA

miles   100   200   300   400   500

in the 1950s

Introduction

by Doris Lessing

These stories were written in the early 'fifties, after I came to Britain, except for *The Pig*, which was one of the first I wrote. Novels, stories, plays, can convey the truth about personal relations, emotions, and attitudes of which the people subject to them are perhaps unaware, or only partly aware: literature comes out of atmospheres, climates of opinion, everything that can not be described by the economic, the sociological approaches. You can read a hundred factual books or surveys about a country, or, for that matter, a factory or a farm, and you'll learn nothing of what a person experiencing that country, that factory, or farm feels or thinks. This collection of tales will tell you something about what it feels like to live in Rhodesia, and in the South African Republic—the two countries are similar in atmosphere and in political structure. The social conditions out of which they were written exist now. Things have worsened politically—both countries have become dictator-ships—and improved economically, but only slightly.

I am always being asked: "How is it possible? Why? What goes on?"—the implication being that the white people in the southern part of Africa are all mad—sometimes I think so myself—or wicked, deliberately cruel. They are of course no worse than you or I, but they are the rich and leisured class, or race, in a society where every privilege is for the whites, and it takes a strong character, or a naturally rebellious one, to fight the environment in which you have been brought up. Also, it is hard to see a society that you are a part of, dispassionately. There are people who regard the class system in Britain as crazy and inefficient, but most Britishers of whatever class are so used to it they take it for granted—can never understand how absurdly it strikes out-siders.

It is a sad truth that no matter how terrible a society is, there is only a minority who will fight it, or at least, only a

1

minority who will provide the leadership that the majority can follow. In Southern Africa the black people who resist are persecuted, imprisoned, exiled, or escape. The critical whites are in one way or another silenced or forced out. The opposition has been crushed—except for the few who stay and go on fighting. Braver people than these have never been. But there are now hundreds of people forbidden entry into South Africa and Rhodesia—I am one of them— people who have nothing in common except that one thing these two governments cannot tolerate: a critical attitude towards apartheid, towards white supremacy.

Well then, how is it all possible? For that you must go to the factual books, the histories. But perhaps a brief explanation about Rhodesia will help. When the white people conquered Rhodesia at the end of the last century, it was settled sparsely by African tribes, each of which regarded an area of territory as its own, boundaries marked out, as has been the case in Europe, by military conquest and defeat. These tribes differed as much from each other as do the French, the Germans, the British. Quite untrue, the saying that Africans are all alike. Inside a territory, a sub-section of a tribe occupied an area of land. They would build a village and cultivate some ground around it, but the site was chosen for the water and the supply of game—for they were hunters rather than farmers. After a time, when the earth was worked out, and the game had become scarce, they moved on a few miles and built another village. Around the first the game came back, the earth recovered, and the place was fit for use again. Such a village is described in *The Old Chief Mshlanga*, but with all the men gone, not hunting or to war, but to the white man's mines and farms. These people were neither migrant nor settled, but somewhere in between. Their tribal structure was complicated, their customs formalised, stable. What they understood and lived by was different from the white man's way; and what they held sacred was not understood by white men, who dismissed their beliefs as primitive.

A useful over simplification is that our way of life is individualistic, theirs, communal. For instance, a chief "owned" all the land of a tribe, or a clan, but this was because he *was* the clan or the tribe. He represented all the individuals in that tribe, which was administered by a council of elders where decisions were made communally, rather as the early Quakers took decisions, not by majority vote, but by not taking a decision at all, until everyone could agree to one. This feeling about the Chief is illustrated by what happens even now when a man from Barotseland (now part of Zambia) meets a countryman in London. He will ask: "Are the drums still beating?" This means, How is the Chief? What news from home? Because the Chief *is* the drums, a group of them, each one standing for a part of the country once conquered and then given equal representation. And one of the Chief's titles is "The Earth". So when such people praise or honour the Chief, they are wishing the whole country well, in his person.

It is so long since Britain had a society anything like this— I suppose the nearest to it was feudalism—that it is hard for us to imagine it. Hard to understand, too, how women were respected, in a complex system of rights and responsibilities all bound up with land, cattle, children. Not true at all the ignorant white man's gibe that a black woman was "nothing but a slave to her husband". A modern degeneration of the custom of *lobola*, or bride-price, appears in the story *A Home for the Highland Cattle*. The black people in it are rootless, placeless, belonging neither to the tribe nor to the white man's city, and there is no future for Theresa's child but what he, she, will have to fight for, make for himself, herself, with the prison door the likeliest one to open. But in the tribe as it used to be, still is in some parts, there were no orphanages, prisons, mental hospitals, old age homes—no institutions. The tribe absorbed the weak and the unfortunate, the Chief, representing everybody, being responsible for them. Our idea that misfits and the helpless should be channelled off out of sight of normal people, would have struck these "primitive" Africans as inhuman, irresponsible. But of course progress is changing all that. I remember a journalist friend of mine talking about a small town in Ghana, just after that country got independence. "I returned to X after five years and found that civilisation had set in—the finest building in the place was a prison."

A paradise on earth, the old Africa? Of course not. They were helpless against their physical environment, a violent one; victims of drought, storms, wild animals, and a primitive medicine. The witch-doctors were useful enough, as far as they went—and it is a great mistake to dismiss these men as nothing but magic-mongers—but they could not amputate a leg, or cure hookworm, bilharzia, leprosy, malaria, the diseases which are slowly being defeated by modern medicine. Every moment of the old life was a fight for survival. The story *A Sunrise on the Veld* was written out of a feeling of how grim a fight it must have been. The incident of the little buck being eaten by ants was told me by a white prospector, an old man who had spent all his life wandering over the veld. He said he had never been able to put the memory of it out of his mind. More important than the fight against nature, the tribes were continually at war, though their battles were not conducted with the refinements of beastliness that have been Europe's contribution to the art of war.

When the white man arrived, they saw themselves as civilisers. They knew nothing about the people they conquered and did not conceive it to be their duty to find out. Or, what they knew was put to their own uses. For instance, the men recruiting black labour for the mines took a look at the old custom that a girl would not marry a young man who had not proved himself in war or in the hunt; and they substituted for it the idea that a young man who had not worked in the mines was a "mompara", a fool—he had not proved himself a man. Very useful to the mine-owners. And very cynical.

This kind of attitude was not held by the first white visitors,

the explorers and the hunters, who met the black people
with respect and dignity. Their diaries make better reading
than any adventure story: accounts of expeditions into areas
where no white man had ever been. Try the diaries of Stanley,
Baines, and Selous the hunter*. After the explorers came the
missionaries, and they did not come as guests, but as
reformers. Their attitude can be summed up by an entry
written by one who had spent a long hard day in argument
with a Chief who thought his God was every bit as good as
the white man's God. The missionary was resting in a camp
across the river from the African village. All night he sat
up listening to the feasting, the dancing, the drumming,
the singing, the lovemaking from across the water, and
towards down he wrote: "These poor savages understand
nothing but joy and pleasure—they must be saved for Christ
at any cost." The diaries of the older Moffat and the
young Moffat, both missionaries, are available. They were
fine, brave and honourable men, but they were locked inside
a Victorian morality, a Victorian concept of duty.

The missionaries paved the way for the big mining
companies, who were given "concessions" to mine by the
Chiefs—Lobengula was one. The trouble was, it was incon-
ceivable to a black chief that land could be given away: it
was not his to give, it belonged to his people. He was giving
a present to a guest, as the custom was, in this case the
permission to dig for gold, which, inexplicably, the white
man found so important. He meant one thing by a conces-
sion, the white man another. Of course the white men knew
this, counted on it: they were not scoundrels, their crime
was ignorance, a lack of historical sense. And they were
bringing progress to unfortunate savages. Above all, they
did not understand the black man's code of honour which
is a powerful force in politics even now. During the strife
about ten years ago, over Northern Rhodesia (now Zambia)
getting independence, the black people felt sold out,

*The easiest one to find in a modern edition is *The Exploration Diaries of H. M.
Stanley*, ed. R. Stanley and A. Neame, London: 1961.

betrayed, because a treaty had been made with Queen Victoria, who had promised they would remain free men. They, Chiefs, free men, had made a treaty with another Chief, and the word of a Chief was a bond. That was how they saw it, felt it, most deeply. It is not, to put it mildly, how the modern political mind sees things.

And it was not what those Victorian mining men, half adventurers, half traders, understood. The black men watched their land being taken over by the mining companies, and their own people being pushed off it, used as cheap labour, as servants. They had been betrayed, they said. And the white men replied that the blacks were tricky, unreliable, and were going back on what they had promised. The whites, under their inspiring spirit Cecil Rhodes,* fought the blacks in a series of battles, and because they had modern arms—guns against spears—they won. They took the best land, and put the Africans into Reserves. Not all at once. *The Old Chief Mshlanga* describes an incident of the process: that was in the thirties. And today's *Guardian*, 26 April 1967, reports that a chief of a small poor tribe near the Portuguese border is fighting in the Courts in Rhodesia to stay on his land, where they are morally entitled to live because they occupied it long before the Europeans came. "Our land is regarded by European law as part of a vast European-owned ranch, so that we are squatters in the country which our forefathers occupied since before man can remember. Our ancestors are buried there. Their spirits are in these hills. . . ."

Many of the white people who live on "this vast European-owned ranch" left Britain with nothing but their courage and worked hard in poor and sometimes dangerous conditions to build their farms and mines—like some of the people in these tales. They got rich. Their children and grandchildren inherit a standard of comfort and leisure

---

*Cecil Rhodes (1853–1902) was an Englishman who went out to South Africa where he was one of the most important leaders in the extension of British territory, and later in the development of Rhodesia.

equalled by few in the world. But the price they pay for refusing to let the Africans live on equal terms, let alone giving them their own country back, is a steady narrowing of mind and understanding, so that I do not think any community anywhere can be as ignorant, provincial, limited as the white people of South Africa and Rhodesia. Their backwardness, their isolation, gets worse as they silence, kill, imprison the opposition. Goethe once said that "if you want to keep a man down in a ditch you must stay there with him". In a world which is increasingly refusing, at least in principle, to accept that poverty and ignorance are the inherent properties of races, these white people must close their minds to what is going on in the world.

It is a monstrous society. My father's farm was bought by him on a government scheme for "settling the land". Translated, this meant "settling it with white men". It was settled by black people already. He paid ten shillings an acre for it. He "owned" a couple of thousand acres, used thousands of acres of Government land (then unsettled, now settled by white people) that bordered his, for nothing. He grazed cattle on it. He cultivated about 300 acres of his land; the rest was left unused. He employed between 50 and a 100 black men, and their wages were 12s. 6d a month, with rations of maize meal, beans and a little meat. (Maize was introduced by the white people as a cheap filling food for the blacks.) The labourers came from the Reserves, Nyasaland, Portuguese territory. They built themselves a mud hut in the "compound". They were given a day to do this. *The Second Hut* describes how such a hut is built. They worked from six in the morning till six at night with an hour off at midday, seven days a week in the busy season. These were the conditions for the whole country: my father was a better, more humane employer than most. But no one can be more humane than an economic framework allows one to be.

Conditions have changed in the last thirty years. The average farm labourer will earn £3, or £4 a month, and rations that have improved to include more meat. These labourers are illiterate, illfed, in bad health, resentful and inefficient. *Little Tembi* describes how children were employed. They still are employed but now they may go to school for a couple of hours after the day's work. The "school" may be a corner of the barn, or the grading shed. Or on a "good" farm, the children may go to school all day, but the black teacher will have had four or five years education himself—be at the standard of a child of eleven or twelve in this country. In England we take education for granted. It is every child's right. In Rhodesia (and in many parts of Africa), parents, children, fight for what only a minority even now can get. Young men already employed, doing a ten-hour day of hard labour, travelling on foot or by bicycle seven miles, ten miles to work and back, will then go to nightschool to learn what children here learn before they are ten. Or parents poor beyond anything we can imagine, will build a classroom themselves for the children; or give up half their tiny income to pay for a child's schoolbooks.

All these stories had a basis, somewhere, in fact. *The Nuisance* was based on an incident that happened in our farm. *No Witchcraft for Sale* was suggested by what happened when a snake spat in my brother's eyes: the cook saved his sight, as I've described it, but the family in that story is not ours. *The Ant Heap* came out of a complex of experiences. Near our farm was such a mine with such a compound. Later I was told a tale of a white boy on a similar mine, and a boy of mixed parentage, and their difficult friendship. *A Home for the Highland Cattle* I wrote after watching a charming, liberal lady, newly immigrant to Rhodesia, who hated the society she found herself in—but eventually succumbed. She was not strong enough to fight it. The burning of the hut in *The Second Hut* happened more or less as described. None of these stories is "true" in the sense that things happened exactly as I've written them. Those of you who are learning to write stories will have found, perhaps, that the way to do it is to let yourself be attracted by an incident, an overheard remark, a face; and then allow this germ to grow, to accumulate around it memories, associations, things of a similar substance, until a whole is reached with a shape, a texture of its own, and very different from how it started off. If you describe something direct— that's reportage, journalism. Good journalism is fidelity to the fact and needs its own kind of discipline. What makes a story is the passivity, learning to wait, allowing the slow simmering process to take place—patience. For me, as for many other white people who lived in Africa, what accumulates and grows is the feeling of Africa itself, the love of the place. But perhaps too many white people have loved the country and too few the people who live in it. Perhaps this is why Africans do not find us very lovable. Admirable— perhaps; enviable, in some ways; but not likeable. "What a head has the white man", an African will exclaim. "But where is his heart?"

I remember one saying to me: "When God made the model for the white man, he used fine white earth, and then so astonished at the beauty of what he had made (this was said, of course, with a tongue kept firmly in his cheek) he forgot to put a heart in. That is why, when you talk to a white man, you have to talk to his head—there is nothing else you can talk to . . ."

DORIS LESSING
April 1967

Glossary

A handful of words which have long been part of the vocabulary of Rhodesia and South Africa may be unfamiliar to English readers. The words were originally introduced by the Dutch settlers into Afrikaans, that is the Dutch spoken in South Africa. These are the most common ones, used in many of the stories.

duiker, small antelope

bossboy, the leader of the native workers on a farm, rather like a foreman. He transmits the farmer's instructions. ("Boy" is an indication of the way in which native men are treated.)

kaffir, a member of the large group of South African tribes called the Bantu. It is also used for their language.

kopje, a small isolated hill.

kraal, a native village of huts clustered together.

mealie, the word most commonly used for maize. "Mealie pap" is a porridge-like mash made from the maize.

veld, open or only thinly forested grass country.

vlei, a natural hollow in the ground in which water collects during the rainy season only.

No Witchcraft for Sale

The Farquars had been childless for years when little Teddy was born; and they were touched by the pleasure of their servants, who brought presents of fowls and eggs and flowers to the homestead when they came to rejoice over the baby, exclaiming with delight over his downy golden head and his blue eyes. They congratulated Mrs Farquar as if she had achieved a very great thing, and she felt that she had—her smile for the lingering, admiring natives was warm and grateful.

Later, when Teddy had his first haircut, Gideon the cook picked up the soft gold tufts from the ground, and held them reverently in his hand. Then he smiled at the little boy and said: "Little Yellow Head." That became the native name for the child. Gideon and Teddy were great friends from the first. When Gideon had finished his work, he would lift Teddy on his shoulders to the shade of a big tree, and play with him there, forming curious little toys from twigs and leaves and grass, or shaping animals from wetted soil. When Teddy learned to walk it was often Gideon who crouched before him, clucking encouragement, finally catching him when he fell, tossing him up in the air till they both became breathless with laughter. Mrs Farquar was fond of the old cook because of his love for her child.

There was no second baby; and one day Gideon said: "Ah missus, missus, the Lord above sent this one; Little Yellow Head is the most good thing we have in our house." Because of that "we" Mrs Farquar felt a warm impulse towards her cook; and at the end of the month she raised his wages. He had been with her now for several years; he was one of the few natives who had his wife and children in the compound and never wanted to go home to this kraal, which was some hundreds of miles away. Sometimes a small piccanin who had been born the same time as Teddy, could be seen peering from the edge of the bush, staring in awe at the little white boy with his miraculous fair hair and northern blue eyes.

The two little children would gaze at each other with a wide, interested gaze, and once Teddy put out his hand curiously to touch the black child's cheeks and hair.

Gideon, who was watching, shook his head wonderingly, and said: "Ah, missus, these are both children, and one will grow up to be a Baas, and one will be a servant;" and Mrs Farquar smiled and said sadly, "Yes, Gideon, I was thinking the same." She sighed. "It is God's will," said Gideon, who was mission boy. The Farquars were very religious people; and this shared feeling about God bound servant and masters even closer together.

Teddy was about six years old when he was given a scooter, and discovered the intoxications of speed. All day he would fly around the homestead, in and out of flowerbeds, scattering squawking chickens and irritated dogs, finishing with a wide dizzying arc into the kitchen door. There he would cry: "Gideon, look at me!" And Gideon would laugh and say: "Very clever, Little Yellow Head." Gideon's youngest son, who was now a herdsboy, came especially up from the compound to see the scooter. He was afraid to come near it, but Teddy showed off in front of him. "Piccanin," shouted Teddy, "get out of my way!" And he raced in circles around the black child until he was frightened, and fled back to the bush.

"Why did you frighten him?" asked Gideon, gravely reproachful.

Teddy said defiantly: "He's only a black boy," and laughed. Then, when Gideon turned away from him without speaking, his face fell. Very soon he slipped into the house and found an orange and brought it to Gideon, saying: "This is for you." He could not bring himself to say he was sorry; but he could not bear to lose Gideon's affection either. Gideon took the orange unwillingly and sighed. "Soon you will be going away to school, Little Yellow Head," he said wonderingly, "and then you will be grown up." He shook his head gently and said, "And that is how our lives go." He seemed to be putting a distance between himself and

Teddy, not because of resentment, but in the way a person accepts something inevitable. The baby had lain in his arms and smiled up into his face: the tiny boy had swung from his shoulders had played with him by the hour. Now Gideon would not let his flesh touch the flesh of the white child. He was kind, but there was a grave formality in his voice that made Teddy pout and sulk away. Also, it made him into a man: with Gideon he was polite, and carried himself formally, and if he came into the kitchen to ask for something, it was in the way a white man uses towards a servant, expecting to be obeyed.

But on the day that Teddy came staggering into the kitchen with his fists to his eyes, shrieking with pain, Gideon dropped the pot full of hot soup that he was holding, rushed to the child, and forced aside his fingers. "A snake!" he exclaimed. Teddy had been on his scooter, and had come to a rest with his foot on the side of a big tub of plants. A tree-snake, hanging by its tail from the roof, had spat full into his eyes. Mrs Farquar came running when she heard the commotion. "He'll go blind," she sobbed, holding Teddy close against her. "Gideon, he'll go blind!" Already the eyes, with perhaps half an hour's sight left in them, were swollen up to the size of fists: Teddy's small white face was distorted by great purple oozing protuberances. Gideon said: "Wait a minute, missus, I'll get some medicine." He ran off into the bush.

Mrs Farquar lifted the child into the house and bathed his eyes with permanganate. She had scarcely heard Gideon's words; but when she saw that her remedies had no effect at all, and remembered how she had seen natives with no sight in their eyes, because of the spitting of a snake, she began to look for the return of her cook, remembering what she had heard of the efficacy of native herbs. She stood by the window, holding the terrified, sobbing little boy in her arms, and peered helplessly into the bush. It was not more than a few minutes before she saw Gideon come bounding back, and in his hand he held a plant.

"Do not be afraid, missus," said Gideon, "this will cure Little Yellow Head's eyes." He stripped the leaves from the plant, leaving a small white fleshy root. Without even washing it, he put the root in his mouth, chewed it vigorously, and then held the spittle there while he took the child forcibly from Mrs Farquar. He gripped Teddy down between his knees, and pressed the balls of his thumbs into the swollen eyes, so that the child screamed and Mrs Farquar cried out in protest: "Gideon, Gideon!" But Gideon took no notice. He knelt over the writhing child, pushing back the puffy lids till chinks of eyeball showed, and then he spat hard, again and again, into first one eye, and then the other. He finally lifted Teddy gently into his mother's arms, and said: "His eyes will get better." But Mrs Farquar was weeping with terror, and she could hardly thank him: it was impossible to believe that Teddy could keep his sight. In a couple of hours the swellings were gone; the eyes were inflamed and tender but Teddy could see. Mr and Mrs Farquar went to Gideon in the kitchen and thanked him over and over again. They felt helpless because of their gratitude: it seemed they could do nothing to express it. They gave Gideon presents for his wife and children, and a big increase in wages, but these things could not pay for Teddy's now completely cured eyes. Mrs Farquar said: "Gideon, God chose you as an instrument for His goodness," and Gideon said: "Yes, missus, God is very good."

Now, when such a thing happens on a farm, it cannot be long before everyone hears of it. Mr and Mrs Farquar told their neighbours and the story was discussed from one end of the district to the other. The bush is full of secrets. No one can live in Africa, or at least on the veld, without learning very soon that there is an ancient wisdom of leaf and soil and season—and, too, perhaps most important of all, of the darker tracts of the human mind—which is the black man's heritage. Up and down the district people were telling anecdotes, reminding each other of things that had happened to them.

"But I saw it myself, I tell you. It was a puff-adder bite. The kaffir's arm was swollen to the elbow, like a great shiny black bladder. He was groggy after half a minute. He was dying. Then suddenly a kaffir walked out of the bush with his hands full of green stuff. He smeared something on the place, and next day my boy was back at work, and all you could see was two small punctures in the skin."

This was the kind of tale they told. And, as always, with a certain amount of exasperation, because while all of them knew that in the bush of Africa are waiting valuable drugs locked in bark, in simple-looking leaves, in roots, it was impossible to ever get the truth about them from the natives themselves.

The story eventually reached town; and perhaps it was at a sundowner party, or some such function, that a doctor, who happened to be there, challenged it. "Nonsense," he said. "These things get exaggerated in the telling. We are always checking up on this kind of story, and we draw a blank every time."

Anyway, one morning there arrived a strange car at the homestead, and out stepped one of the workers from the laboratory in town, with cases full of test-tubes and chemicals.

Mr and Mrs Farquar were flustered and pleased and flattered. They asked the scientist to lunch, and they told the story all over again, for the hundredth time. Little Teddy was there too, his blue eyes sparkling with health, to prove the truth of it. The scientist explained how humanity might benefit if this new drug could be offered for sale; and the Farquars were even more pleased: they were kind, simple people, who liked to think of something good coming about because of them. But when the scientist began talking of the money that might result, their manner showed discomfort. Their feelings over the miracle (that was how they thought of it) were so strong and deep and religious, that it was distasteful to them to think of money. The scientist, seeing their faces, went back to his first point, which was the advancement of humanity. He was perhaps a trifle perfunctory: it was not the first time he had come salting the tail of a fabulous bush-secret.

Eventually, when the meal was over, the Farquars called Gideon into their living-room and explained to him that this baas, here, was a Big Doctor from the Big City, and he had come all that way to see Gideon. At this Gideon seemed afraid; he did not understand; and Mrs Farquar explained quickly that it was because of the wonderful thing he had done with Teddy's eyes that the Big Baas had come.

Gideon looked from Mrs Farquar to Mr Farquar, and then at the little boy, who was showing great importance because of the occasion. At last he said grudgingly: "The Big Baas wants to know what medicine I used?" He spoke incredulously, as if he could not believe his old friends could so betray him. Mr Farquar began explaining how a useful medicine could be made out of the root, and how it could be put on sale, and how thousands of people, black and white, up and down the continent of Africa, could be saved by the medicine when that spitting snake filled their eyes with poison. Gideon listened, his eyes bent on the ground, the skin of his forehead puckering in discomfort. When Mr Farquar had finished he did not reply. The scientist, who all this time had been leaning back in a big chair, sipping his coffee and smiling with sceptical good-humour, chipped in and explained all over again, in different words, about the making of drugs and the progress of science. Also, he offered Gideon a present.

There was silence after this further explanation, and then Gideon remarked indifferently that he could not remember the root. His face was sullen and hostile, even when he looked at the Farquars, whom he usually treated like old friends. They were beginning to feel annoyed; and this feeling annulled the guilt that had been sprung into life by Gideon's accusing manner. They were beginning to feel that he was unreasonable. But it was at that moment that they all realized he would never give in. The magical drug would remain where it was, unknown and useless except for the tiny scattering of Africans who had the knowledge, natives who might be digging a ditch for the municipality in a ragged shirt and a pair of patched shorts, but who were still born to healing, hereditary healers, being the nephews or sons of the old witch doctors whose ugly masks and bits of bone and all the uncouth properties of magic were the outward signs of real power and wisdom.

The Farquars might tread on that plant fifty times a day as they passed from house to garden, from cow kraal to mealie field, but they would never know it.

But they went on persuading and arguing, with all the force of their exasperation; and Gideon continued to say that he could not remember, or that there was no such root, or that it was the wrong season of the year, or that it wasn't the root itself, but the spit from his mouth that had cured Teddy's eyes. He said all these things one after another, and seemed not to care they were contradictory. He was rude and stubborn. The Farquars could hardly recognize their gentle, lovable old servant in this ignorant, perversely obstinate African, standing there in front of them with lowered eyes, his hands twitching his cook's apron, repeating over and over whichever one of the stupid refusals that first entered his head.

And suddenly he appeared to give in. He lifted his head, gave a long, blank angry look at the circle of whites, who seemed to him like a circle of yelping dogs pressing around him, and said: "I will show you the root."

They walked single file away from the homestead down a kaffir path. It was a blazing December afternoon, with the sky full of hot rain-clouds. Everything was hot: the sun was like a bronze tray whirling overhead, there was a heat shimmer over the fields, the soil was scorching underfoot, the dusty wind blew gritty and thick and warm in their faces. It was a terrible day, fit only for reclining on a verandah with iced drinks, which is where they would normally have been at that hour.

From time to time, remembering that on the day of the snake it had taken ten minutes to find the root, someone asked: "Is it much further, Gideon?" And Gideon would answer over his shoulder, with angry politeness: "I'm looking for the root, baas." And indeed, he would frequently bend sideways and trail his hand among the grasses with a gesture that was insulting in its perfunctoriness. He walked them through the bush along unknown paths for two hours, in that melting destroying heat, so that the sweat trickled coldly down them and their heads ached. They were all quite silent: the Farquars because they were angry, the scientist because he was being proved right again; there was no such plant. His was a tactful silence.

At last, six miles from the house, Gideon suddenly decided they had had enough; or perhaps his anger evaporated at that moment. He picked up, without an attempt at looking anything but casual, a handful of blue flowers from the grass, flowers that had been growing plentifully all down the paths they had come.

He handed them to the scientist without looking at him, and marched off by himself on the way home, leaving them to follow him if they chose.

When they got back to the house, the scientist went to the kitchen to thank Gideon: he was being very polite, even though there was an amused look in his eyes. Gideon was not there. Throwing the flowers casually into the back of his car, the eminent visitor departed on his way back to his laboratory.

Gideon was back in his kitchen in time to prepare dinner, but he was sulking. He spoke to Mrs Farquar like an unwilling servant. It was days before they liked each other again.

The Farquars made enquiries about the root from their labourers. Sometimes they were answered with distrustful stares. Sometimes the natives said: "We do not know. We have never heard of the root." One, the cattle boy, who had been with them a long time, and had grown to trust them a little said: "Ask your boy in the kitchen. Now, there's a doctor for you. He's the son of a famous medicine man who used to be in these parts, and there's nothing he cannot cure." Then he added politely: "Of course, he's not as good as the whiteman's doctor, we know that, but he's good for us."

After some time, when the soreness had gone from between the Farquars and Gideon, they began to joke: "When are you going to show us the snake-root, Gideon?" And he would laugh and shake his head, saying, a little uncomfortably: "But I did show you, missus, have you forgotten?"

Much later, Teddy, as a schoolboy, would come into the kitchen and say: "You old rascal, Gideon! Do you remember that time you tricked us all by making us walk miles all over the veld for nothing? It was so far my father had to carry me!"

And Gideon would double up with polite laughter. After much laughing, he would suddenly straighten himself up, wipe his old eyes, and look sadly at Teddy, who was grinning mischievously at him across the kitchen: "Ah, Little Yellow Head, how you have grown! Soon you will be grown up with a farm of your own . . ."

The Old Chief Mshlanga

They were good, the years of ranging the bush over her father's farm which, like every white farm, was largely unused, broken only occasionally by small patches of cultivation. In between, nothing but trees, the long sparse grass, thorn and cactus and gully, grass and outcrop and thorn. And a jutting piece of rock which had been thrust up from the warm soil of Africa unimaginable eras of time ago, washed into hollows and whorls by sun and wind that had travelled so many thousands of miles of space and bush, would hold the weight of a small girl whose eyes were sightless for anything but a pale willowed river, a pale gleaming castle—a small girl singing: "Out flew the web and floated wide, the mirror cracked from side to side . . ."

Pushing her way through the green aisles of the mealie stalks, the leaves arching like cathedrals veined with sunlight far overhead, with the packed red earth underfoot, a fine lace of red-starred witchweed would summon up a black bent figure croaking premonitions: the Northern witch, bred of cold Northern forests, would stand before her among the mealie fields, and it was the mealie fields that faded and fled, leaving her among the gnarled roots of an oak, snow falling thick and soft and white, the wood-cutter's fire glowing red welcome through crowding tree trunks.

A white child, opening its eyes curiously on a sun suffused landscape, a gaunt and violent landscape, might be supposed to accept it as her own, to take the msasa trees and the thorn trees as familiars, to feel her blood running free and responsive to the swing of the seasons.

This child could not see a msasa tree, or the thorn, for what they were. Her books held tales of alien fairies, her rivers ran slow and peaceful, and she knew the shape of the leaves of an ash or an oak, the names of the little creatures that lived in English streams, when the words "the veld" meant strangeness, though she could remember nothing else.

Because of this, for many years, it was the veld that seemed unreal; the sun was a foreign sun, and the wind spoke a strange language.

The black people on the farm were as remote as the trees and the rocks. They were an amorphous black mass, mingling and thinning and massing like tadpoles, faceless, who existed merely to serve, to say "Yes, Baas," take their money and go. They changed season by season, moving from one farm to the next, according to their outlandish needs, which one did not have to understand, coming from perhaps hundreds of miles North or East, passing on after a few months—where? Perhaps even as far away as the fabled gold mines of Johannesburg, where the pay was so much better than the few shillings a month and the double handful of mealie meal twice a day which they earned in that part of Africa.

The child was taught to take them for granted: the servants in the house would come running a hundred yards to pick up a book if she dropped it. She was called "Nkosikaas"— Chieftainess, even by the black children her own age.

Later, when the farm grew too small to hold her curiosity, she carried a gun in the crook of her arm and wandered miles a day, from vlei to vlei, from kopje to kopje, accompanied by two dogs: the dogs and the gun were an armour against fear. Because of them she never felt fear.

If a native came into sight along the kaffir paths half a mile away, the dogs would flush him up a tree as if he were a bird. If he expostulated (in his uncouth language which was by itself ridiculous) that was cheek. If one was in a good mood, it could be a matter for laughter. Otherwise one passed on, hardly glancing at the angry man in the tree.

On the rare occasions when white children met together they could amuse themselves by hailing a passing native in order to make a buffoon of him; they could set the dogs on him and watch him run; they could tease a small black child as if he were a puppy—save that they would not throw stones and sticks at a dog without a sense of guilt.

Later still, certain questions presented themselves in the child's mind; and because the answers were not easy to accept, they were silenced by an even greater arrogance of manner.

It was even impossible to think of the black people who worked about the house as friends, for if she talked to one of them, her mother would come running anxiously: "Come away; you mustn't talk to natives."

It was this instilled consciousness of danger, of something unpleasant, that made it easy to laugh out loud, crudely, if a servant made a mistake in his English or if he failed to understand an order—there is a certain kind of laughter that is fear, afraid of itself.

One evening, when I was about fourteen, I was walking down the side of a mealie field that had been newly ploughed, so that the great red clods showed fresh and tumbling to the vlei beyond, like a choppy red sea; it was that hushed and listening hour, when the birds send long sad calls from tree to tree, and all the colours of earth and sky and leaf are deep and golden. I had my rifle in the curve of my arm, and the dogs were at my heels.

In front of me, perhaps a couple of hundred yards away, a group of three Africans came into sight around the side of a big antheap. I whistled the dogs close in to my skirts and let the gun swing in my hand, and advanced, waiting for them to move aside, off the path, in respect for my passing. But they came on steadily, and the dogs looked up at me for the command to chase. I was angry. It was "cheek" for a native not to stand off a path, the moment he caught sight of you.

In front walked an old man, stooping his weight on to a stick, his hair grizzled white, a dark red blanket slung over his shoulders like a cloak. Behind him came two young men, carrying bundles of pots, assegais, hatchets.

The group was not a usual one. They were not natives seeking work. These had an air of dignity, of quietly following their own purpose. It was the dignity that checked my tongue. I walked quietly on, talking softly to the growling dogs, till I was ten paces away. Then the old man stopped, drawing his blanket close.

"'Morning, Nkosikaas," he said, using the customary greeting for any time of the day.

"Good morning," I said. "Where are you going?" My voice was a little truculent.

The old man spoke in his own language, then one of the young men stepped forward politely and said in careful English: "My Chief travels to see his brothers beyond the river."

A Chief! I thought, understanding the pride that made the old man stand before me like an equal—more than an equal, for he showed courtesy, and I showed none.

The old man spoke again, wearing dignity like an inherited garment, still standing ten paces off, flanked by his entourage, not looking at me (that would have been rude) but directing his eyes somewhere over my head at the trees.

"You are the little Nkosikaas from the farm of Baas Jordan?"

"That's right," I said.

"Perhaps your father does not remember," said the interpreter for the old man, "but there was an affair with some goats. I remember seeing you when you were . . ." The young man held his hand at knee level and smiled.

We all smiled.

"What is your name?" I asked.

"This is Chief Mshlanga," said the young man.

"I will tell my father that I met you," I said.

The old man said: "My greetings to your father, little Nkosikaas."

"Good morning," I said politely, finding the politeness difficult, from lack of use.

"'Morning, little Nkosikaas," said the old man, and stood aside to let me pass.

I went by, my gun hanging awkwardly, the dogs sniffing

and growling, cheated of their favourite game of chasing natives like animals.

Not long afterwards I read in an old explorer's book the phrase: "Chief Mshlanga's country." It went like this: "Our destination was Chief Mshlanga's country, to the north of the river; and it was our desire to ask his permission to prospect for gold in his territory."

The phrase "ask his permission" was so extraordinary to a white child, brought up to consider all natives as things to use, that it revived those questions, which could not be suppressed: they fermented slowly in my mind.

On another occasion one of those old prospectors who still move over Africa looking for neglected reefs, with their hammers and tents, and pans for sifting gold from crushed rock, came to the farm and, in talking of the old days, used that phrase again: "This was the Old Chief's country," he said. "It stretched from those mountains over there way back to the river, hundreds of miles of country." That was his name for our district: "The Old Chief's Country"; he did not use our name for it—a new phrase which held no implication of usurped ownership.

As I read more books about the time when this part of Africa was opened up, not much more than fifty years before, I found Old Chief Mshlanga had been a famous man, known to all the explorers and prospectors. But then he had been young; or maybe it was his father or uncle they spoke of—I never found out.

During that year I met him several times in the part of the farm that was traversed by natives moving over the country. I learned that the path up the side of the big red field where the birds sang was the recognized highway for migrants. Perhaps I even haunted it in the hope of meeting him: being greeted by him, the exchange of courtesies, seemed to answer the questions that troubled me.

Soon I carried a gun in a different spirit; I used it for shooting food and not to give me confidence. And now the dogs learned better manners. When I saw a native approaching, we offered and took greetings; and slowly that other landscape in my mind faded, and my feet struck directly on the African soil, and I saw the shapes of tree and hill clearly, and the black people moved back, as it were, out of my life: it was as if I stood aside to watch a slow intimate dance of landscape and men, a very old dance, whose steps I could not learn.

But I thought: this is my heritage, too; I was bred here; it is my country as well as the black man's country; and there is plenty of room for all of us, without elbowing each other off the pavements and roads.

It seemed it was only necessary to let free that respect I felt when I was talking with old Chief Mshlanga, to let both black and white people meet gently, with tolerance for each other's differences: it seemed quite easy.

Then, one day, something new happened. Working in our house as servants were always three natives: cook, houseboy, garden boy. They used to change as the farm natives changed: staying for a few months, then moving on to a new job, or back home to their kraals. They were thought of as "good" or "bad" natives; which meant: how did they behave as servants? Were they lazy, efficient, obedient, or disrespectful? If the family felt good-humoured, the phrase was: "What can you expect from raw black savages?" If we were angry, we said: "These damned niggers, we would be much better off without them."

One day, a white policeman was on his rounds of the district, and he said laughingly: "Did you know you have an important man in your kitchen?"

"What!" exclaimed my mother sharply. "What do you mean?"

"A Chief's son." The policeman seemed amused. "He'll boss the tribe when the old man dies."

"He'd better not put on a Chief's son act with me," said my mother.

When the policeman left, we looked with different eyes
at our cook: he was a good worker, but he drank too much
at week-ends—that was how we knew him.

He was a tall youth, with very black skin, like black
polished metal, his tightly-growing black hair parted white
man's fashion at one side, with a metal comb from the store
stuck into it; very polite, very distant, very quick to obey
an order. Now it had been pointed out, we said: "Of course,
you can see. Blood always tells."

My mother became strict with him now she knew about
his birth and prospects. Sometimes, when she lost her
temper, she would say: "You aren't the Chief yet, you
know." And he would answer her very quietly, his eyes on
the ground: "Yes, Nkosikaas."

One afternoon he asked for a whole day off, instead of
the customary half-day, to go home next Sunday.

"How can you go home in one day?"

"It will take me half an hour on my bicycle," he
explained.

I watched the direction he took; and the next day I went
off to look for this kraal; I understood he must be Chief
Mshlanga's successor: there was no other kraal near enough
our farm.

Beyond our boundaries on that side the country was new
to me. I followed unfamiliar paths past kopjes that till now
had been part of the jagged horizon, hazed with distance.
This was Government land, which had never been cultivated
by white men; at first I could not understand why it was
that it appeared, in merely crossing the boundary, I had
entered a completely fresh type of landscape. It was a
wide green valley, where a small river sparkled, and vivid
water-birds darted over the rushes. The grass was thick and
soft to my calves, the trees stood tall and shapely.

I was used to our farm, whose hundreds of acres of harsh
eroded soil bore trees that had been cut for the mine furnaces
and had grown thin and twisted, where the cattle had
dragged the grass flat, leaving innumerable criss-crossing

trails that deepened each season into gullies, under the force of the rains.

This country had been left untouched, save for prospectors whose picks had struck a few sparks from the surface of the rocks as they wandered by; and for migrant natives whose passing had left, perhaps, a charred patch on the trunk of a tree where their evening fire had nestled.

It was very silent: a hot morning with pigeons cooing throatily, the midday shadows lying dense and thick with clear yellow spaces of sunlight between and in all that wide green park-like valley, not a human soul but myself.

I was listening to the quick regular tapping of a woodpecker when slowly a chill feeling seemed to grow up from the small of my back to my shoulders, in a constricting spasm like a shudder, and at the roots of my hair a tingling sensation began and ran down over the surface of my flesh, leaving me goosefleshed and cold, though I was damp with sweat. Fever? I thought; then uneasily, turned to look over my shoulder; and realized suddenly that this was fear. It was extraordinary, even humiliating. It was a new fear. For all the years I had walked by myself over this country I had never known a moment's uneasiness; in the beginning because I had been supported by a gun and the dogs, then because I had learnt an easy friendliness for the Africans I might encounter.

I had read of this feeling, how the bigness and silence of Africa, under the ancient sun, grows dense and takes shape in the mind, till even the birds seem to call menacingly, and a deadly spirit comes out of the trees and the rocks. You move warily, as if your very passing disturbs something old and evil, something dark and big and angry that might suddenly rear and strike from behind. You look at groves of entwined trees, and picture the animals that might be lurking there; you look at the river running slowly, dropping from level to level through the vlei, spreading into pools where at night the buck come to drink, and the crocodiles rise and drag them by their soft noses into underwater caves.

Fear possessed me. I found I was turning round and round, because of that shapeless menace behind me that might reach out and take me; I kept glancing at the files of kopjes which, seen from a different angle, seemed to change with every step so that even known landmarks, like a big mountain that had sentinelled my world since I first became conscious of it, showed an unfamiliar sunlit valley among its foothills. I did not know where I was. I was lost. Panic seized me. I found I was spinning round and round, staring anxiously at this tree and that, peering up at the sun which appeared to have moved into an eastern slant, shedding the sad yellow light of sunset. Hours must have passed! I looked at my watch and found that this state of meaningless terror had lasted perhaps ten minutes.

The point was that it was meaningless. I was not ten miles from home: I had only to take my way back along the valley to find myself at the fence; away among the foothills of the kopjes gleamed the roof of a neighbour's house, and a couple of hours walking would reach it. This was the sort of fear that contracts the flesh of a dog at night and sets him howling at the full moon. It had nothing to do with what I thought or felt; and I was more disturbed by the fact that I could become its victim than of the physical sensation itself: I walked steadily on, quietened, in a divided mind, watching my own pricking nerves and apprehensive glances from side to side with a disgusted amusement. Deliberately I set myself to think of this village I was seeking, and what I should do when I entered it—if I could find it, which was doubtful, since I was walking aimlessly and it might be anywhere in the hundreds of thousands of acres of bush that stretched about me. With my mind on that village, I realised that a new sensation was added to the fear: loneliness. Now such a terror of isolation invaded me that I could hardly walk; and if it were not that I came over the crest of a small rise and saw a village below me, I should have turned and gone home. It was a cluster of thatched huts in a clearing among trees. There were neat patches of mealies and pumpkins and millet, and cattle grazed under some trees at a distance. Fowls scratched among the huts, dogs lay sleeping on the grass, and goats friezed a kopje that jutted up beyond a tributary of the river lying like an enclosing arm round the village.

As I came close I saw the huts were lovingly decorated with patterns of yellow and red and ochre mud on the walls; and the thatch was tied in place with plaits of straw.

This was not at all like our farm compound, a dirty and neglected place, a temporary home for migrants who had no roots in it.

And now I did not know what to do next. I called a small black boy, who was sitting on a log playing a stringed gourd, quite naked except for the strings of blue beads round his neck, and said: "Tell the Chief I am here." The child stuck his thumb in his mouth and stared shyly back at me.

For minutes I shifted my feet on the edge of what seemed a deserted village, till at last the child scuttled off, and then some women came. They were draped in bright cloths, with brass glinting in their ears and on their arms. They also stared, silently; then turned to chatter among themselves.

I said again: "Can I see Chief Mshlanga?" I saw they caught the name; they did not understand what I wanted. I did not understand myself.

At last I walked through them and came past the huts and saw a clearing under a big shady tree, where a dozen old men sat cross-legged on the ground, talking. Chief Mshlanga was leaning back against the tree, holding a gourd in his hand, from which he had been drinking. When he saw me, not a muscle of his face moved, and I could see he was not pleased: perhaps he was afflicted with my own shyness, due to being unable to find the right forms of courtesy for the occasion. To meet me, on our own farm, was one thing; but I should not have come here. What had I expected? I could not join them socially: the thing was unheard of. Bad enough that I, a white girl, should be walking the veld alone as a white man might: and this part of the bush where only Government officials had the right to move.

Again I stood, smiling foolishly, while behind me stood the groups of brightly-clad, chattering women, their faces alert with curiosity and interest, and in front of me sat the old men, with old lined faces, their eyes guarded, aloof. It was a village of ancients and children and women. Even the two young men who kneeled beside the Chief were not those I had seen with him previously: the young men were all away working on the white men's farms and mines, and the Chief must depend on relatives who were temporarily on holiday for his attendants.

"The small white Nkosikaas is far from home," remarked the old man at last.

"Yes," I agreed, "it is far." I wanted to say: "I have come to pay you a friendly visit, Chief Mshlanga." I could not say it. I might now be feeling an urgent helpless desire to get to know these men and women as people, to be accepted by them as a friend, but the truth was I had set out in a spirit of curiosity: I had wanted to see the village that one day our cook, the reserved and obedient young man who got drunk on Sundays, would one day rule over.

"The child of Nkosi Jordan is welcome," said Chief Mshlanga.

"Thank you," I said, and could think of nothing more to say. There was a silence, while the flies rose and began to buzz around my head; and the wind shook a little in the thick green tree that spread its branches over the old men.

"Good morning," I said at last. "I have to return now to my home."

"'Morning, little Nkosikaas," said Chief Mshlanga.

I walked away from the indifferent village, over the rise past the staring amber-eyed goats, down through the tall stately trees into the great rich green valley where the river meandered and the pigeons cooed tales of plenty and the woodpecker tapped softly.

The fear had gone; the loneliness had set into stiff-necked stoicism; there was now a queer hostility in the landscape, a cold, hard, sullen indomitability that walked with me, as strong as a wall, as intangible as smoke; it seemed to say to me: you walk here as a destroyer. I went slowly homewards, with an empty heart: I had learned that if one cannot call a country to heel like a dog, neither can one dismiss the past with a smile in an easy gush of feeling, saying: I could not help it, I am also a victim.

I only saw Chief Mshlanga once again.

One night my father's big red land was trampled down by small sharp hooves, and it was discovered that the culprits were goats from Chief Mshlanga's kraal. This had happened once before, years ago.

My father confiscated all the goats. Then he sent a message to the old Chief that if he wanted them he would have to pay for the damage.

He arrived at our house at the time of sunset one evening, looking very old and bent now, walking stiffly under his regally-draped blanket, leaning on a big stick. My father sat himself down in his big chair below the steps of the house; the old man squatted carefully on the ground before him, flanked by his two young men.

The palaver was long and painful, because of the bad English of the young man who interpreted, and because my father could not speak dialect, but only kitchen kaffir.

From my father's point of view, at least two hundred pounds worth of damage had been done to the crop. He knew he could not get the money from the old man. He felt he was entitled to keep the goats. As for the old Chief, he kept repeating angrily: "Twenty goats! My people cannot lose twenty goats! We are not rich, like the Nkosi Jordan, to lose twenty goats at once."

My father did not think of himself as rich, but rather as very poor. He spoke quickly and angrily in return, saying that the damage done meant a great deal to him, and that he was entitled to the goats.

At last it grew so heated that the cook, the Chief's son, was called from the kitchen to be interpreter, and now my father spoke fluently in English, and our cook translated rapidly so that the old man could understand how very angry my father was. The young man spoke without emotion, in a mechanical way, his eyes lowered, but showing how he felt his position by a hostile uncomfortable set of the shoulders.

It was now in the late sunset, the sky a welter of colours, the birds singing their last songs, and the cattle, lowing peacefully, moving past us towards their sheds for the night. It was the hour when Africa is most beautiful; and here was this pathetic, ugly scene, doing no one any good.

At last my father stated finally: "I'm not going to argue about it. I am keeping the goats."

The old Chief flashed back in his own language: "That means that my people will go hungry when the dry season comes."

"Go to the police, then," said my father, and looked triumphant.

There was, of course, no more to be said.

The old man sat silent, his head bent, his hands dangling helplessly over his withered knees. Then he rose, the young men helping him, and he stood facing my father. He spoke once again, very stiffly; and turned away and went home to his village.

"What did he say?" asked my father of the young man, who laughed uncomfortably and would not meet his eyes.

"What did he say?" insisted my father.

Our cook stood straight and silent, his brows knotted together. Then he spoke. "My father says: All this land, this land you call yours, is his land, and belongs to our people."

Having made this statement, he walked off into the bush after his father, and we did not see him again.

Our next cook was a migrant from Nyasaland, with no expectations of greatness.

Next time the policeman came on his rounds he was told this story. He remarked: "That kraal has no right to be there; it should have been moved long ago. I don't know why no one has done anything about it. I'll have a chat to the Native Commissioner next week. I'm going over for tennis on Sunday, anyway."

Some time later we heard that Chief Mshlanga and his people had been moved two hundred miles east, to a proper native reserve; the Government land was going to be opened up for white settlement soon.

I went to see the village again, about a year afterwards. There was nothing there. Mounds of red mud, where the huts had been, had long swathes of rotting thatch over them, veined with the red galleries of the white ants. The pumpkin vines rioted everywhere, over the bushes, up the lower branches of trees so that the great golden balls rolled underfoot and dangled overhead: it was a festival of pumpkins. The bushes were crowding up, the new grass sprang vivid green.

The settler lucky enough to be allotted the lush warm valley (if he chose to cultivate this particular section) would find, suddenly, in the middle of a mealie field, the plants were growing fifteen feet tall, the weight of the cobs dragging at the stalks, and wonder what unsuspected vein of richness he had struck.

A Sunrise on the Veld

Every night that winter he said aloud into the dark of the pillow: Half-past four! Half-past four! till he felt his brain had gripped the words and held them fast. Then he fell asleep at once, as if a shutter had fallen; and lay with his face turned to the clock so that he could see it first thing when he woke.

It was half-past four to the minute, every morning. Triumphantly pressing down the alarm-knob of the clock, which the dark half of his mind had outwitted, remaining vigilant all night and counting the hours as he lay relaxed in sleep, he huddled down for a last warm moment under the clothes, playing with the idea of lying abed for this once only. But he played with it for the fun of knowing that it was a weakness he could defeat without effort; just as he set the alarm each night for the delight of the moment when he woke and stretched his limbs, feeling the muscles tighten, and thought: Even my brain—even that! I can control every part of myself.

Luxury of warm rested body, with the arms and legs and fingers waiting like soldiers for a word of command! Joy of knowing that the precious hours were given to sleep voluntarily!—for he had once stayed awake three nights running, to prove that he could, and then worked all day, refusing even to admit that he was tired; and now sleep seemed to him a servant to be commanded and refused.

The boy stretched his frame full-length, touching the wall at his head with his hands, and the bedfoot with his toes; then he sprung out, like a fish leaping from water. And it was cold, cold.

He always dressed rapidly, so as to try and conserve his night-warmth till the sun rose two hours later; but by the time he had on his clothes his hands were numbed and he could scarcely hold his shoes. These he could not put on for fear of waking his parents, who never came to know how early he rose.

As soon as he stepped over the lintel, the flesh of his soles contracted on the chilled earth, and his legs began to ache with cold. It was night: the stars were glittering, the trees standing black and still. He looked for signs of day, for the greying of the edge of a stone, or a lightening in the sky where the sun would rise, but there was nothing yet. Alert as an animal he crept past the dangerous window, standing poised with his hand on the sill for one proudly fastidious moment, looking in at the stuffy blackness of the room where his parents lay.

Feeling for the grass-edge of the path with his toes, he reached inside another window further along the wall, where his gun had been set in readiness the night before. The steel was icy, and numbed fingers slipped along it, so that he had to hold it in the crook of his arm for safety. Then he tiptoed to the room where the dogs slept, and was fearful that they might have been tempted to go before him; but they were waiting, their haunches crouched in reluctance at the cold, but ears and swinging tails greeting the gun ecstatically. His warning undertone kept them secret and silent till the house was a hundred yards back: then they bolted off into the bush, yelping excitedly. The boy imagined his parents turning in their beds and muttering: Those dogs again! before they were dragged back in sleep; and he smiled scornfully. He always looked back over his shoulder at the house before he passed a wall of trees that shut it from sight. It looked so low and small, crouching there under a tall and brilliant sky. Then he turned his back on it, and on the frowsting sleepers, and forgot them.

He would have to hurry. Before the light grew strong he must be four miles away; and already a tint of green stood in the hollow of a leaf, and the air smelled of morning and the stars were dimming.

He slung the shoes over his shoulder, veld skoen that were crinkled and hard with the dews of a hundred mornings. They would be necessary when the ground became too hot to bear. Now he felt the chilled dust push up between his toes, and he let the muscles of his feet spread and settle into the shapes of the earth; and he thought: I could walk a hundred miles on feet like these! I could walk all day, and never tire!

He was walking swiftly through the dark tunnel of foliage that in daytime was a road. The dogs were invisibly ranging the lower travelways of the bush, and he heard them panting. Sometimes he felt a cold muzzle on his leg before they were off again, scouting for a trail to follow. They were not trained, but free-running companions of the hunt, who often tired of the long stalk before the final shots, and went off on their own pleasure. Soon he could see them, small and wild-looking in a wild strange light, now that the bush stood trembling on the verge of colour, waiting for the sun to paint earth and grass afresh.

The grass stood to his shoulders; and the trees were showering a faint silvery rain. He was soaked; his whole body was clenched in a steady shiver.

Once he bent to the road that was newly scored with animal trails, and regretfully straightened, reminding himself that the pleasure of tracking must wait till another day.

He began to run along the edge of a field, noting jerkily how it was filmed over with fresh spiderweb, so that the long reaches of great black clods seemed netted in glistening grey. He was using the steady lope he had learned by watching the natives, the run that is a dropping of the weight of the body from one foot to the next in a slow balancing movement that never tires, nor shortens the breath; and he felt the blood pulsing down his legs and along his arms, and the exultation and pride of body mounted in him till he was shutting his teeth hard against a violent desire to shout his triumph.

Soon he had left the cultivated part of the farm. Behind him the bush was low and black. In front was a long vlei, acres of long pale grass that sent back a hollowing gleam of light to a satiny sky. Near him thick swathes of grass

were bent with the weight of water, and diamond drops
sparkled on each frond.

The first bird woke at his feet and at once a flock of them
sprang into the air calling shrilly that day had come; and
suddenly, behind him, the bush woke into song, and he
could hear the guinea-fowl calling far ahead of him. That
meant they would now be sailing down from their trees into
thick grass, and it was for them he had come: he was too
late. But he did not mind. He forgot he had come to shoot.
He set his legs wide, and balanced from foot to foot,
and swung his gun up and down in both hands horizontally, in a kind of improvised exercise, and let his head
sink back till it was pillowed in his neck muscles, and
watched how above him small rosy clouds floated in a lake
of gold.

Suddenly it all rose in him: it was unbearable. He leapt
up into the air, shouting and yelling wild, unrecognizable
noises. Then he began to run, not carefully, as he had before,
but madly, like a wild thing. He was clean crazy, yelling
mad with the joy of living and a superfluity of youth. He
rushed down the vlei under a tumult of crimson and gold,
while all the birds of the world sang about him. He ran in
great leaping strides, and shouted as he ran, feeling his
body rise into the crisp rushing air and fall back surely on
to sure feet; and thought briefly, not believing that such
a thing could happen to him, that he could break his ankle
any moment, in this thick tangled grass. He cleared bushes
like a duiker, leaped over rocks; and finally came to a dead
stop at a place where the ground fell abruptly away below
him to the river. It had been a two-mile-long dash through
waist-high growth, and he was breathing hoarsely and could
no longer sing. But he poised on a rock and looked down
at stretches of water that gleamed through stooping trees,
and thought suddenly, I am fifteen! Fifteen! The words
came new to him; so that he kept repeating them wonderingly, with swelling excitement; and he felt the years of his
life with his hands, as if he were counting marbles, each

one hard and separate and compact, each one a wonderful shining thing. That was what he was: fifteen years of this rich soil, and this slow-moving water, and air that smelt like a challenge whether it was warm and sultry at noon, or as brisk as cold water, like it was now.

There was nothing he couldn't do, nothing! A vision came to him, as he stood there, like when a child hears the word 'eternity' and tries to understand it, and time takes possession of the mind. He felt his life ahead of him as a great and wonderful thing, something that was his; and he said aloud, with the blood rising to his head: all the great men of the world have been as I am now, and there is nothing I can't become, nothing I can't do; there is no country in the world I cannot make part of myself, if I choose. I contain the world. I can make of it what I want. If I choose, I can change everything that is going to happen: it depends on me, and what I decide now.

The urgency, and the truth and the courage of what his voice was saying exulted him so that he began to sing again, at the top of his voice, and the sound went echoing down the river gorge. He stopped for the echo, and sang again: stopped and shouted. That was what he was!—he sang, if he chose; and the world had to answer him.

And for minutes he stood there, shouting and singing and waiting for the lovely eddying sound of the echo; so that his own new strong thoughts came back and washed round his head, as if someone were answering him and encouraging him; till the gorge was full of soft voices clashing back and forth from rock to rock over the river. And then it seemed as if there was a new voice. He listened, puzzled, for it was not his own. Soon he was leaning forward, all his nerves alert, quite still: somewhere close to him there was a noise that was no joyful bird, nor tinkle of falling water, nor ponderous movement of cattle.

There it was again. In the deep morning hush that held his future and his past, was a sound of pain, and repeated over and over: it was a kind of shortened scream, as if someone, something, had no breath to scream. He came to himself, looked about him, and called for the dogs. They did not appear: they had gone off on their own business, and he was alone. Now he was clean sober, all the madness gone. His heart beating fast, because of that frightened screaming, he stepped carefully off the rock and went towards a belt of trees. He was moving cautiously, for not so long ago he had seen a leopard in just this spot.

At the edge of the trees he stopped and peered, holding his gun ready; he advanced, looking steadily about him, his eyes narrowed. Then, all at once, in the middle of a step, he faltered, and his face was puzzled. He shook his head impatiently, as if he doubted his own sight.

There, between two trees, against a background of gaunt black rocks, was a figure from a dream, a strange beast that was horned and drunken-legged, but like something he had never even imagined. It seemed to be ragged. It looked like a small buck that had black ragged tufts of fur standing up irregularly all over it, with patches of raw flesh beneath . . . but the patches of rawness were disappearing under moving black and came again elsewhere; and all the time the creature screamed, in small gasping screams, and leaped drunkenly from side to side, as if it were blind.

Then the boy understood: it *was* a buck. He ran closer, and again stood still, stopped by a new fear. Around him the grass was whispering and alive. He looked wildly about, and then down. The ground was black with ants, great energetic ants that took no notice of him, but hurried and scurried towards the fighting shape, like glistening black water flowing through the grass.

And, as he drew in his breath and pity and terror seized him, the beast fell and the screaming stopped. Now he could hear nothing but one bird singing, and the sound of the rustling whispering ants.

He peered over at the writhing blackness that jerked convulsively with the jerking nerves. It grew quieter. There were small twitches from the mass that still looked vaguely like the shape of a small animal.

It came into his mind that he should shoot it and end its pain; and he raised the gun. Then he lowered it again. The buck could no longer feel; its fighting was a mechanical protest of the nerves. But it was not that which made him put down the gun. It was a swelling feeling of rage and misery and protest that expressed itself in the thought; if I had not come it would have died like this: so why should I interfere? All over the bush things like this happen; they happen all the time; this is how life goes on, by living things dying in anguish. He gripped the gun between his knees and felt in his own limbs the myriad swarming pain of the twitching animal that could no longer feel, and set his teeth, and said over and over again under his breath: I can't stop it. I can't stop it. There is nothing I can do.

He was glad that the buck was unconscious and had gone past suffering so that he did not have to make a decision to kill it even when he was feeling with his whole body: this is what happens, this is how things work.

It was right—that was what he was feeling. *It was right and nothing could alter it.*

The knowledge of fatality, of what has to be, had gripped him and for the first time in his life; and he was left unable to make any movement of brain or body, except to say: "Yes, yes. That is what living is." It had entered his flesh and his bones and grown in to the furthest corners of his brain and would never leave him. And at that moment he could not have performed the smallest action of mercy, knowing as he did, having lived on it all his life, the vast unalterable, cruel veld, where at any moment one might stumble over a skull or crush the skeleton of some small creature.

Suffering, sick, and angry, but also grimly satisfied with his new stoicism, he stood there leaning on his rifle, and watched the seething black mound grow smaller. At his feet, now, were ants trickling back with pink fragments in their mouths, and there was a fresh acid smell in his nostrils. He sternly controlled the uselessly convulsing muscles of his empty stomach, and reminded himself: the ants must eat too! At the same time he found that the tears were streaming down his face, and his clothes were soaked with the sweat of that other creature's pain.

The shape had grown small. Now it looked like nothing recognizable. He did not know how long it was before he saw the blackness thin, and bits of white showed through, shining in the sun—yes, there was the sun, just up, glowing over the rocks. Why, the whole thing could not have taken longer than a few minutes.

He began to swear, as if the shortness of the time was in itself unbearable, using the words he had heard his father say. He strode forward, crushing ants with each step, and brushing them off his clothes, till he stood above the skeleton, which lay sprawled under a small bush. It was clean-picked. It might have been lying there years, save that on the white bone were pink fragments of gristle. About the bones ants were ebbing away, their pincers full of meat.

The boy looked at them, big black ugly insects. A few were standing and gazing up at him with small glittering eyes.

"Go away!" he said to the ants, very coldly. "I am not for you— not just yet, at any rate. Go away." And he fancied that the ants turned and went away.

He bent over the bones and touched the sockets in the skull; that was where the eyes were, he thought incredulously, remembering the liquid dark eyes of a buck. And then he bent the slim foreleg bone, swinging it horizontally in his palm.

That morning, perhaps an hour ago, this small creature had been stepping proud and free through the bush, feeling the chill on its hide even as he himself had done, exhilarated by it. Proudly stepping the earth, tossing its horns, frisking a pretty white tail, it had sniffed the cold morning air. Walking like kings and conquerors it had moved through this free-held bush, where each blade of grass grew for it alone, and where the river ran pure sparkling water for its slaking.

And then—what had happened? Such a swift surefooted thing could surely not be trapped by a swarm of ants?

The boy bent curiously to the skeleton. Then he saw that the back leg that lay uppermost and strained out in the tension of death, was snapped midway in the thigh, so that broken bones jutted over each other uselessly. So that was it! Limping into the ant-masses it could not escape, once it had sensed the danger. Yes, but how had the leg been broken? Had it fallen, perhaps? Impossible, a buck was too light and graceful. Had some jealous rival horned it?

What could possibly have happened? Perhaps some Africans had thrown stones at it, as they do, trying to kill it for meat, and had broken its leg. Yes, that must be it.

Even as he imagined the crowd of running, shouting natives, and the flying stones, and the leaping buck, another picture came into his mind. He saw himself, on any one of these bright ringing mornings, drunk with excitement, taking a snap shot at some half-seen buck. He saw himself with the gun lowered, wondering whether he had missed or not; and thinking at last that it was late, and he wanted his breakfast, and it was not worth while to track miles after an animal that would very likely get away from him in any case.

For a moment he would not face it. He was a small boy again, kicking sulkily at the skeleton, hanging his head, refusing to accept the responsibility.

Then he straightened up, and looked down at the bones with an odd expression of dismay, all the anger gone out of him. His mind went quite empty: all around him he could see trickles of ants disappearing into the grass. The whispering noise was faint and dry, like the rustling of a cast snakeskin.

At last he picked up his gun and walked homewards. He was telling himself half defiantly that he wanted his breakfast. He was telling himself that it was getting very hot, much too hot to be out roaming the bush.

Really, he was tired. He walked heavily, not looking where he put his feet. When he came within sight of his home he stopped, knitting his brows. There was something he had to think out. The death of that small animal was a thing that concerned him, and he was by no means finished with it. It lay at the back of his mind uncomfortably.

Soon, the very next morning, he would get clear of every-body and go to the bush and think about it.

Little Tembi

Jane McCluster, who had been a nurse before she married, started a clinic on the farm within a month of arriving. Though she had been born and brought up in town, her experience of natives was wide, for she had been a sister in the native wards of the city hospital, by choice, for years; she liked nursing natives, and explained her feeling in the words: "They are just like children, and appreciate what you do for them." So, when she had taken a thorough diagnosing kind of look at the farm natives, she exclaimed, "Poor things!" and set about turning an old dairy into a dispensary. Her husband was pleased; it would save money in the long run by cutting down illness in the compound.

Willie McCluster who had also been born and raised in South Africa was nevertheless unmistakably and determinedly Scottish. His accent might be emphasized for loyalty's sake, but he had kept all the fine qualities of his people unimpaired by a slowing and relaxing climate. He was shrewd, vigorous, earthy, practical and kind. In appearance he was largely built, with a square bony face, a tight mouth, and eyes whose fierce blue glance was tempered by the laughter wrinkles about them. He became a farmer young having planned the step for years: he was not one of those who drift on to the land because of discontent with an office, or because of failure, or vague yearnings towards "freedom". Jane, a cheerful and competent girl who knew what she wanted, trifled with her numerous suitors with one eye on Willie, who wrote her weekly letters from the farming college in the Transvaal. As soon as his four years training were completed, they married.

They were then twenty-seven, and felt themselves well-equipped for a useful and enjoyable life. Their house was planned for a family. They would have been delighted if a baby had been born the old-fashioned nine months after marriage. As it was, a baby did not come; and when two years had passed Jane took a journey into the city to see a doctor. She was not so much unhappy as indignant to find she needed an operation before she could have children. She did not associate illness with herself, and felt as if the whole thing were out of character. But she submitted to the operation, and to waiting a further two years before starting a family, with her usual practical good sense. But it subdued her a little. The uncertainty preyed on her, in spite of herself; and it was because of her rather wistful, disappointed frame of mind at this time that her work in the clinic became so important to her. Whereas, in the beginning, she had dispensed medicines and good advice as a routine, every morning for a couple of hours after breakfast, she now threw herself into it, working hard keeping herself at full stretch, trying to attack causes rather than symptoms.

The compound was the usual farm compound of insanitary mud and grass huts; the diseases she had to deal with were caused by poverty and bad feeding.

Having lived in the country all her life, she did not make the mistake of expecting too much; she had that shrewd, ironical patience that achieves more with backward people than any amount of angry idealism.

First she chose an acre of good soil for vegetables, and saw to the planting and cultivating herself. One cannot overthrow the customs of centuries in a season, and she was patient with the natives who would not at first touch food they were not used to. She persuaded and lectured. She gave the women of the compound lessons in cleanliness and baby care. She drew up diet sheets and ordered sacks of citrus from the big estates; in fact, it was not long before it was Jane who organized the feeding of Willie's two-hundred-strong labour force, and he was glad to have her help. Neighbours laughed at them; for it is even now customary to feed natives on maize meal only, with an occasional slaughtered ox for a feasting; but there was no doubt Willie's natives were healthier than most and he got far more work out of them. On cold winter mornings Jane would stand dispensing cans of hot cocoa from a petrol drum with a slow fire burning under it to the natives before they went to the fields; and if a neighbour passed and laughed at her, she set her lips and good-humouredly: "It's good sound commonsense, that's what it is. Besides—poor things, poor things!" Since the McClusters were respected in the district, they were humoured in what seemed a ridiculous eccentricity.

But it was not easy, not easy at all. It was of no use to cure hook-worm-infested feet that would become reinfected in a week, since none wore shoes; nothing could be done about bilharzia, when all the rivers were full of it; and the natives continued to live in the dark and smoky huts.

But the children could be helped; Jane most particularly loved the little black piccanins.* She knew that fewer children died in her compound than in any for miles around, and this was her pride. She would spend whole mornings explaining to the women about dirt and proper feeding; if a child became ill, she would sit up all night with it, and cried bitterly if it died. The name for her among the natives was The Goodhearted One. They trusted her. Though mostly they hated and feared the white man's medicines,† they let Jane have her way, because they felt she was prompted by kindness; and day by day the crowds of natives waiting for medical attention became larger. This filled Jane with pride; and every morning she made her way to the big stone-floored, thatched building at the back of the house that smelled always of disinfectant and soap, accompanied by the houseboy who helped her, and spent there many hours helping the mothers and the children and the labourers who had hurt themselves at work.

Little Tembi was brought to her for help at the time when she knew she could not hope to have a child of her own for at least two years. He had what the natives call "the hot

piccanin: a small child—a word used with affection.

†This story was written in 1950. [*Author's note.*]

weather sickness." His mother had not brought him soon enough, and by the time Jane took him in her arms he was a tiny wizened skeleton, loosely covered with harsh greyish skin, the stomach painfully distended "He will die," moaned the mother from outside the clinic door with that fatalistic note that always annoyed Jane. "Nonsense!" she said briskly—even more briskly because she was so afraid he would.

She laid the child warmly in a lined basket, and the houseboy and she looked grimly into each other's faces. Jane said sharply to the mother, who was whimpering helplessly from the floor where she squatted with her hands to her face: "Stop crying. That doesn't do any good. Didn't I cure your first child when he had the same trouble?" But that other little boy had not been nearly as sick as this one.

When Jane had carried the basket into the kitchen, and set it beside the fire for warmth, she saw the same grim look on the cook boy's face as she had seen on the houseboy's—and could feel on her own. "This child is *not* going to die," she said to herself. "I won't let it! I won't let it." It seemed to her that if she could pull little Tembi through, the life of the child she herself wanted so badly would be granted her.

She sat beside the basket all day, willing the baby to live, with medicines on the table beside her, and the cookboy and the houseboy helping her where they could. At night the mother came from the compound with her blanket; and the two women kept vigil together. Because on the fixed, imploring eyes of the black woman Jane was even more spurred to win through; and the next day and the next, and through the long nights, she fought for Tembi's life even when she could see from the faces of the house natives that they thought she was beaten. Once, towards dawn of one night when the air was cold and still, the little body chilled to the touch and there seemed no breath in it, Jane held it close to the warmth of her own breast murmuring fiercely over and over again: You *will* live, you *will* live—and when the sun rose the infant was breathing deeply and its feet were pulsing in her hand.

When it became clear that he would not die, the whole house was pervaded with a feeling of happiness and victory. Willie came to see the child, and said affectionately to Jane: "Nice work, old girl. I never thought you'd do it." The cookboy and the houseboy were warm and friendly towards Jane, and brought her gratitude presents of eggs and ground meal. As for the mother, she took her child in her arms with trembling joy and wept as she thanked Jane.

Jane herself, though exhausted and weak, was too happy to rest or sleep: she was thinking of the child she would have. She was not a superstitious person, and the thing could not be described in such terms: she felt that she had thumbed her nose at death, that she had sent death slinking from her door in defeat, and now she would be strong to make life, fine strong children of her own; she could imagine them springing up beside her, lovely children conceived from her own strength and power against sneaking death.

Little Tembi was brought by his mother up to the house every day for a month, partly to make sure he would not relapse, partly because Jane had grown to love him. When he was quite well, and no longer came to the clinic, Jane would ask the cookboy after him, and sometimes sent a message that he should be fetched to see her. The native woman would then come smiling to the back door with the little Tembi on her back and her older child at her skirts, and Jane would run down the steps, smiling with pleasure, waiting impatiently as the cloth was unwound from the mother's back, revealing Tembi curled there, thumb in mouth, with great black solemn eyes, his other hand clutching the stuff of his mother's dress for security. Jane would carry him indoors to show Willie. "Look," she would say tenderly, "Here's my little Tembi. Isn't he a sweet little piccanin?"

He grew into a fat shy little boy, staggering uncertainly from his mother's arms to Jane's. Later, when he was strong on his legs, he would run to Jane and laugh as she caught him up. There was always fruit or sweets for him when he visited the house, always a hug from Jane and a good-humoured, amused smile from Willie.

He was two years old when Jane said to his mother: "When the rains come this year I shall also have a child." And the two women, forgetting the difference in colour, were happy together because of the coming children: the black woman was expecting her third baby.

Tembi was with his mother when she came to visit the cradle of the little white boy. Jane held out her hand to him and said: "Tembi, how are you?" Then she took her baby from the cradle and held it out, saying: "Come and see my baby, Tembi." But Tembi backed away, as if afraid, and began to cry. "Silly Tembi" said Jane affectionately; and sent the houseboy to fetch some fruit as a present. She did not make the gift herself, as she was holding her child.

She was absorbed by this new interest, and very soon found herself pregnant again. She did not forget little Tembi, but thought of him rather as he had been, the little toddler whom she had loved wistfully when she was childless. Once she caught sight of Tembi's mother walking along one of the farm roads, leading a child by the hand and said: "But where's Tembi?" Then she saw the child was Tembi. She greeted him; but afterwards said to Willie: "Oh dear, it's such a pity when they grow up, isn't it?" "He could hardly be described as grown-up," said Willie, smiling indulgently at her where she sat with her two infants on her lap. "You won't be able to have them climbing all over you when we've a dozen," he teased her—they had decided to wait another two years and then have some more; Willie came from a family of nine children. "Who said a dozen?" exclaimed Jane tartly, playing up to him. "Why not?" asked Willie. "We can afford it." "How do you think I can do everything?" grumbled Jane pleasantly. For she was very busy. She had not let the work at the clinic lapse; it was still she who did the ordering and planning of the labourers' food; and she looked after her children without help—she did not even have the customary native nanny. She could not really be blamed for losing touch with little Tembi.

He was brought to her notice one evening when Willie was having the usual weekly discussion with the bossboy over the farm work. He was short of labour again and the rains had been heavy and the lands were full of weeds. As fast as the gangs of natives worked through a field it seemed that the weeds were higher than ever. Willie suggested that it might be possible to take some of the older children from their mothers for a few weeks. He already employed a gang of piccanins, of between about nine and fifteen years old, who did lighter work; but he was not sure that all the available children were working. The bossboy said he would see what he could find.

As a result of this discussion Willie and Jane were called one day to the front door by a smiling cookboy to see Little Tembi, now about six years old, standing proudly beside his father, who was also smiling. "Here is a man to work for you," said Tembi's father to Willie, pushing forward Tembi, who jibbed like a little calf, standing with his head lowered and his fingers in his mouth. He looked so tiny, standing all by himself, that Jane exclaimed compassionately: "But, Willie, he's just a baby still!" Tembi was quite naked, save for a string of blue beads cutting into the flesh of his fat stomach. Tembi's father explained that his older child, who was eight, had been herding the calves for a year now, and that there was no reason why Tembi should not help him.

"But I don't need two herdboys for the calves," protested Willie. And then, to Tembi: "And now, my big man, what money do you want?" At this Tembi dropped his head still lower, twisted his feet in the dust, and muttered: "Five shillings." "Five shillings a month!" exclaimed Willie indignantly. "What next! Why, the ten-year-old piccanins get that much." And then, feeling Jane's hand on his arm, he said hurriedly: "Oh, all right, four and sixpence. He can help his big brother with the calves." Jane, Willie, the cookboy and Tembi's father stood laughing sympathetically as Tembi lifted his head, stuck out his stomach even further, and swaggered off down the path, beaming with pride. "Well," sighed Jane, "I never would have thought it. Little Tembi! Why, it seems only the other day . . ."

Tembi, promoted to a loincloth, joined his brother with the calves; and as the two children ran alongside the animals, everyone turned to look smiling after the tiny black child, strutting with delight, and importantly swishing the twig his father had cut him from the bush as if he were a full-grown driver with his team of beasts.

The calves were supposed to stay all day near the kraal; when the cows had been driven away to the grazing, Tembi and his brother squatted under a tree and watched the calves, rising to run, shouting, if one attempted to stray. For a year Tembi was apprentice to the job; and then his brother joined the gang of older piccanins who worked with the hoe. Tembi was then seven years old, and responsible for twenty calves, some standing higher than he. Normally a much older child had the job; but Willie was chronically short of labour, as all the farmers were, and he needed every pair of hands he could find, for work in the fields.

"Did you know your Tembi is a proper herdsboy now?" Willie said to Jane, laughing, one day. "What!" exclaimed Jane. "That baby! Why, it's absurd." She looked jealously at her own children, because of Tembi; she was the kind of woman who hates to think of her children growing up. But she now had three, and was very busy indeed. She forgot the little black boy.

Then one day a catastrophe happened. It was very hot, and Tembi fell asleep under the trees. His father came up to the house, uneasily apologetic, to say that some of the calves had got into the mealie field and trampled down the plants. Willie was angry. It was that futile, simmering anger that cannot be assuaged, for it is caused by something that cannot be remedied: children had to herd the calves because adults were needed for more important work, and one could not be really angry with a child of Tembi's age. Willie had Tembi fetched to the house, and gave him a stern lecture about the terrible thing he had done. Tembi was crying when he turned away; he stumbled off to the compound with his father's hand resting on his shoulder, because the tears were streaming so fast he could not have directed his own steps. But in spite of the tears, and his contrition, it all happened again not very long afterwards. He fell asleep in the drowsily-warm shade, and when he woke, towards evening, all the calves had strayed into the fields and flattened acres of mealies. Unable to face punishment he ran away, crying, into the bush. He was found that night by his father who cuffed him lightly round the head for running away.

And now it was a very serious matter indeed. Willie was angry. To have happened once—that was bad, but forgivable. But twice, and within a month! He did not at first summon Tembi, but had a consultation with his father. "We must do something he will not forget, as a lesson," said Willie. Tembi's father said the child had already been punished. "You have beaten him?" asked Willie. But he knew that Africans do not beat their children, or so seldom it was not likely that Tembi had really been punished. "You say you have beaten him?" he insisted; and saw, from the way the man turned away his eyes and said, "Yes, baas," that it was not true. "Listen," said Willie. "Those calves straying must have cost me about thirty pounds. There's nothing I can do. I can't get it back from Tembi, can I? And now I'm going to stop it happening again." Tembi's father did not reply. "You will fetch Tembi up here, to the house and cut a switch from the bush, and I will give him a beating." "Yes, baas," said Tembi's father, after a pause.

When Jane heard of the punishment she said: "Shame! Beating my little Tembi . . ."

When the hour came, she took away her children so that they would not have such an unpleasant thing in their memories. Tembi was brought up to the verandah, clutching his father's hand and shivering with fear. Willie said he did not like the business of beating; he considered it necessary, however, and intended to go through with it. He took the long light switch from the cookboy, who had cut it from the bush, since Tembi's father had come without it, and ran the sharply-whistling thing loosely through the air to frighten Tembi. Tembi shivered more than ever, and pressed his face against his father's thighs. "Come here, Tembi." Tembi did not move; so his father lifted him close to Willie. "Bend down." Tembi did not bend down, so his father bent him down, hiding the small face against his own legs. Then Willie glanced smilingly but uncomfortably at the cookboy, the houseboy and Tembi's father, who were all regarding him with stern, unresponsive faces, and swished the wand backwards and forwards over Tembi's back; he wanted them to see he was only trying to frighten Tembi for the good of his upbringing. But they did not smile at all. Finally Willie said in an awful, solemn voice: "Now, Tembi!" And then, having made the occasion solemn and angry, he switched Tembi lightly, three times, across the buttocks, and threw the switch away into the bush. "Now you will never do it again, Tembi, will you?" he said. Tembi stood quite still, shuddering, in front of him, and would not meet his eyes. His father gently took his hand and led him away back home.

"Is it over?" asked Jane, appearing from the house. "I didn't hurt him," said Willie crossly. He was annoyed, because he felt the black men were annoyed with him. "They want to have it both ways," he said. "If the child is old enough to earn money, then he's old enough to be responsible. Thirty pounds!"

"I was thinking of our little Freddie," said Jane emotionally. Freddie was their first child. Willie said impatiently: "And what's the good of thinking of him?" "Oh no good,

Willie. No good at all," agreed Jane tearfully. "It does seem awful, though. Do you remember him, Willie? Do you remember what a sweet little thing he was?" Willie could not afford to remember the sweetness of the baby Tembi at that moment; and he was displeased with Jane for reminding him; there was a small constriction of feeling between them for a little while, which soon dissolved, for they were good friends, and were in the same mind about most things.

The calves did not stray again. At the end of the month, when Tembi stepped forward to take his four shillings and sixpence wages, Willie smiled at him and said: "Well, Tembi, and how are things with you?" "I want more money," said Tembi boldly. "Wha-a-at!" exclaimed Willie, astounded. He called to Tembi's father, who stepped out of the gang of waiting Africans, to hear what Willie wanted to say. "This little rascal of yours lets the cattle stray twice, and then says he wants more money." Willie said this loudly, so that everyone could hear; and there was laughter from the labourers. But Tembi kept his head high, and said defiantly: "Yes, baas, I want more money." "You'll get your bottom tanned," said Willie, only half-indignant: and Tembi went off sulkily, holding his silver in his hand, with amused glances following him.

He was now about seven, very thin and lithe, though he still carried his protuberant stomach before him. His legs were flat and spindly, and his arms broader below the elbow than above. He was not crying now, nor stumbling. His small thin shape was straight, and—so it seemed—angry. Willie forgot the incident.

But next month the child again stood his ground and argued stubbornly for an increase. Willie raised him to five and sixpence, saying resignedly that Jane had spoiled him. Tembi bit his lips in triumph, and as he walked off gave little joyous skipping steps, finally breaking into a run as he reached the trees. He was still the youngest of the working children, and was now earning as much as some three or four years older then he: this made them grumble, but it was recognized, because of Jane's attitude, that he was a favourite.

Now, in the normal run of things, it would have been a year, at least, before he got any more money. But the very month following, he claimed the right to another increase. This time the listening natives made sounds of amused protest; the lad was forgetting himself. As for Willie, he was really annoyed. There was something insistent, something demanding, in the child's manner that was almost impertinent. He said sharply: "If you don't stop this nonsense, I'll tell your father to teach you a lesson where it hurts." Tembi's eyes glowed angrily, and he attempted to argue, but Willie dismissed him curtly, turning to the next labourer.

A few minutes later Jane was fetched to the back door by the cook, and there stood Tembi, shifting in embarrassment from foot to foot, but grinning at her eagerly. "Why, Tembi . . ." she said vaguely. She had been feeding the children, and her mind was filled with thoughts of bathing and getting them to bed—thoughts very far from Tembi. Indeed, she had to look twice before she recognized him, for she carried always in the back of her mind the picture of that sweet fat black baby who bore, for her, the name Tembi. Only his eyes were the same: large dark glowing eyes, now imploringly fixed on her. "Tell the boss to give me more money," he beseeched.

Jane laughed kindly. "But, Tembi, how can I do that? I've nothing to do with the farm. You know that."

"Tell him, missus. Tell him, my missus," he beseeched.

Jane felt the beginnings of annoyance. But she chose to laugh again, and said, "Wait a minute, Tembi." She went inside and fetched from the children's supper table some slices of cake, which she folded into a piece of paper and thrust into Tembi's hand. She was touched to see the child's face spread into a beaming smile: he had forgotten about the wages, the cake did as well or better. "Thank you, thank you," he said; and, turning, scuttled off into the trees.

And now Jane was given no chance of forgetting Tembi. He would come up to the house on a Sunday with quaint little mud toys for the children, or with the feather from a brilliant bird he had found in the bush; even a handful of wild flowers tied with wisps of grass. Always Jane welcomed him, talked to him, and rewarded him with small gifts. Then she had another child, and was very busy again. Sometimes she was too occupied to go herself to the back door. She would send her servant with an apple or a few sweets.

Soon after, Tembi appeared at the clinic one morning with his toe bound up. When Jane removed the dirty bit of cloth, she saw a minute cut, the sort of thing no native, whether child or adult, would normally take any notice of at all. But she bound it properly for him, and even dressed it good-naturedly when he appeared again, several days later. Then, only a week afterwards, there was a small cut on his finger. Jane said impatiently: "Look here, Tembi, I don't run this clinic for nonsense of this kind." When the child stared up at her blankly, those big dark eyes fixed on her with an intensity that made her uncomfortable, she directed the houseboy to translate the remark into dialect, for she thought Tembi had not understood. He said, stammering: "Missus, my missus, I come to see you only." But Jane laughed and sent him away. He did not go far. Later, when all the other patients had gone; she saw him standing a little way off, looking hopefully at her. "What *is* it?" she asked, a little crossly, for she could hear the new baby crying for attention inside the house.

"I want to work for you," said Tembi. "But, Tembi, I don't need another boy. Besides, you are too small for housework. When you are older, perhaps." "Let me look after the children." Jane did not smile, for it was quite usual to employ small piccanins as nurses for children not much younger than themselves. She might even have considered it, but she said: "Tembi, I have just arranged for a nanny to come and help me. Perhaps later on. I'll remember you, and if I need someone to help the nanny I'll send for you.

First you must learn to work well. You must work well with the calves and not let them stray; and then we'll know you are a good boy, and you can come to the house and help me with the children."

Tembi departed on this occasion with lingering steps, and some time later Jane, glancing from the window, saw him standing at the edge of the bush gazing towards the house. She despatched the houseboy to send him away, saying that she would not have him loitering round the house doing nothing.

Jane, too, was now feeling that she had "spoiled" Tembi, that he had "got above himself."

And now nothing happened for quite a long time.

Then Jane missed her diamond engagement ring. She used often to take it off when doing household things; so that she was not at first concerned. After several days she searched thoroughly for it but it could not be found. A little later a pearl brooch was missing. And there were several small losses, a spoon used for the baby's feeding, a pair of scissors, a silver christening mug. Jane said crossly to Willie that there must be a poltergeist. "I had the thing in my hand and when I turned round it was gone. It's just silly. Things don't vanish like that." "A black poltergeist, perhaps," said Willie. "How about the cook?" "Don't be ridiculous," said Jane, a little too quickly. "Both the houseboys have been with us since we came to the farm." But suspicion flared in her, nevertheless. It was a well-worn maxim that no native, no matter how friendly, could be trusted; scratch any one of them, and you found a thief. Then she looked at Willie, understood that he was feeling the same, and was as ashamed of his feelings as she was. The houseboys were almost personal friends. "Nonsense," said Jane firmly. "I don't believe a word of it." But no solution offered itself, and things continued to vanish.

One day Tembi's father asked to speak to the boss. He untied a piece of cloth, laid it on the ground—and there were all the missing articles. "But not Tembi, *surely*," protested Jane. Tembi's father, awkward in his embarrassment, explained that he had happened to be passing the cattle kraals, and had happened to notice the little boy sitting on his antheap, in the shade, playing with his treasures. "Of course he had no idea of their value," appealed Jane. "It was just because they were so shiny and glittering." And indeed, as they stood there, looking down at the lamplight glinting on the silver and the diamonds, it was easy to see how a child could be fascinated. "Well, and what are we going to do?" asked Willie practically. Jane did not reply directly to the question; she exclaimed helplessly: "Do you realise that the little imp must have been watching me doing things round the house for weeks, nipping in when my back was turned for a moment—he must be quick as a snake." "Yes, but what are we going to do?" "Just give him a good talking-to," said Jane, who did not know why she felt so dismayed and lost. She was angry; but far more distressed—there was something ugly and persistent in this planned, deliberate thieving, that she could not bear to associate with little Tembi, whom she had saved from death.

"A talking-to won't do any good," said Willie. Tembi was whipped again; this time properly, with no nonsense about making the switch whistle for effect. He was made to expose his bare bottom across his father's knees, and when he got up, Willie said with satisfaction: "He's not going to be comfortable sitting down for a week." "But, Willie, there's blood," said Jane. For as Tembi walked off stiffly, his legs straddled apart from the pain, his fists thrust into his streaming eyes, reddish patches appeared on the stuff of his trousers. Willie said angrily: "Well, what do you expect me to do—make him a present of it and say: How clever of you?"

"But *blood*, Willie!"

"I didn't know I was hitting so hard," admitted Willie. He examined the long flexible twig in his hands, before throwing it away, as if surprised at its effectiveness. "That

must have hurt," he said doubtfully. "Still, he deserved
it. Now stop crying, Jane. He won't do that again."

But Jane did not stop crying. She could not bear to think
of the beating; and Willie, no matter what he said, was
uncomfortable when he remembered it. They would have
been pleased to let Tembi slip from their minds for a while,
and have him reappear later, when there had been time
for kindness to grow in them again.

But it was not a week before he demanded to be made
nurse to the children: he was now big enough, he said; and
Jane had promised. Jane was so astonished she could not
speak to him. She went indoors, shutting the door on him;
and when she knew he was still lingering there for speech
with her, sent out the houseboy to say she was not having a
thief as nurse for her children.

A few weeks later he asked again; and again she refused.
Then he took to waylaying her every day, sometimes several
times a day: "Missus, my missus, let me work near you,
let me work near you." Always she refused, and always she
grew more angry.

At last, the sheer persistence of the thing defeated her.
She said: "I won't have you as a nurse, but you can help me
with the vegetable garden." Tembi was sullen, but he
presented himself at the garden next day, which was not
the one near the house, but the fenced patch near the compound, for the use of the natives. Jane employed a garden
boy to run it, telling him when was the time to plant, explaining about compost and the proper treatment of soil. Tembi
was to help him.

She did not often go to the garden; it ran of itself. Sometimes, passing, she saw the beds full of vegetables were
running to waste; this meant that a new batch of Africans
were in the compound, natives who had to be educated
afresh to eat what was good for them. But now she had had
her last baby, and employed two nannies in the nurseries,
she felt free to spend more time at the clinic and at the
garden. Here she made a point of being friendly to Tembi.

She was not a person to bear grudges, though a feeling that he was not to be trusted barred him as a nurse. She would talk to him about her own children, and how they were growing, and would soon be going to school in the city. She would talk to him about keeping himself clean, and eating the right things; how he must earn good money so that he could buy shoes to keep his feet from the germ-laden dust; how he must be honest, always tell the truth and be obedient to the white people. While she was in the garden he would follow her around, and hoe trailing forgotten in his hand, his eyes fixed on her. "Yes, missus; yes, my missus," he repeated continually. And when she left, he would implore: "When are you coming again? Come again soon, my missus." She took to bringing him her own children's books, when they were too worn for use in the nursery. "You must learn to read, Tembi," she would say. "Then, when you want to get a job, you will earn more wages if you can say: "Yes, missus, I can read and write." You can take messages on the telephone then, and write down orders so that you don't forget them." "Yes, missus," Tembi would say, reverently taking the books from her. When she left the garden, she would glance back, always a little uncomfortably, because of Tembi's intense devotion, and see him kneeling on the rich red soil, framed by the bright green of the vegetables, knitting his brows over the strange coloured pictures and the unfamiliar print.

This went on for about two years. She said to Willie: "Tembi seems to have got over that funny business of his. He's really useful in that garden. I don't have to tell him when to plant things. He knows as well as I do. And he goes round the huts in the compound with the vegetables, persuading the natives to eat them." "I bet he makes a bit on the side," said Willie, chuckling. "Oh no. Willie, I'm sure he wouldn't do that."

And, in fact, he didn't. Tembi regarded himself as an apostle of the white man's way of life. He would say earnestly, displaying the baskets of carefully displayed vegetables to the native women: "The Good-hearted One says it is right we should eat these things. She says eating them will save us from sickness." Tembi achieved more than Jane had done in years of propaganda.

He was nearly eleven when he began giving trouble again. Jane sent her two elder children to boarding-school, dismissed her nannies, and decided to engage a piccanin to help with the children's washing. She did not think of Tembi; but she engaged Tembi's younger brother.

Tembi presented himself at the back door, as of old, his eyes flashing, his body held fine and taut, to protest. "Missus, missus you promised I should work for you." "But Tembi, you are working for me, with the vegetables." "Missus, my missus, you said when you took a piccanin for the house, that piccanin would be me." But Jane did not give way. She still felt as if Tembi were on probation. And the demanding, insistent, impatient thing in Tembi did not seem to her a good quality to be near her children. Besides, she liked Tembi's little brother, who was a softer, smiling, chubby Tembi, playing good-naturedly with the children in the garden when he had finished the washing and ironing. She saw no reason to change, and said so.

Tembi sulked. He no longer took baskets of green stuff from door to door in the compound. And he did as little work as he need without actually neglecting it. The spirit had gone out of him.

"You know," said Jane half indignantly, half amused, to Willie: "Tembi behaves as if he had some sort of claim on us."

Quite soon, Tembi came to Willie and asked to be allowed to buy a bicycle. He was then earning ten shillings a month, and the rule was that no native earning less than fifteen shillings could buy a bicycle. A fifteen-shilling native would keep five shillings of his wages, give ten to Willie, and undertake to remain on the farm till the debt was paid. That might take two years, or even longer. "No,"

said Willie. "And what does a piccanin like you want with
a bicycle? A bicycle is for big men."

Next day, their eldest child's bicycle vanished from the
house, and was found in the compound leaning against
Tembi's hut. Tembi had not even troubled to conceal the
theft; and when he was called for an interview kept silent.
At last he said: "I don't know why I stole it. I don't know."
And he ran off, crying, into the trees.

"He must go," said Willie finally, baffled and angry.

"But his father and mother and the family live in our
compound," protested Jane.

"I'm not having a thief on the farm," said Willie. But
getting rid of Tembi was more than dismissing a thief: it
was pushing aside a problem that the McClusters were not
equipped to handle. Suddenly Jane knew that when she no
longer saw Tembi's burning, pleading eyes, it would be
a relief; though she said guiltily: "Well, I suppose he can
find work on one of the farms nearby."

Tembi did not allow himself to be sacked so easily. When
Willie told him he burst into passionate tears, like a very
small child. Then he ran round the house and banged his
fists on the kitchen door till Jane came out. "Missus, my
missus, don't let the baas send me away." "But Tembi, you
must go, if the boss says so." "I work for you, missus, I'm
your boy, let me stay. I'll work for you in the garden and
I won't ask for any more money." "I'm sorry, Tembi," said
Jane. Tembi gazed at her while his face hollowed into
incredulous misery: he had not believed she would not take
his part. At this moment his little brother came round the
corner of the house carrying Jane's youngest child, and
Tembi flew across and flung himself on them, so that the
little black child staggered back, clutching the white infant
to himself with difficulty. Jane flew to rescue her baby, and
then pulled Tembi off his brother, who was bitten and
scratched all over his face and arms.

"That finishes it," she said coldly. "You will be off this
farm in an hour, or the police will chase you off."

They asked Tembi's father, later, if the lad had found work; the reply was that he was garden boy on a neighbouring farm. When the McClusters saw these neighbours they asked after Tembi, but the reply was vague: on this new farm Tembi was just another labourer without a history.

Later still, Tembi's father said there had been "trouble" and that Tembi had moved to another farm, many miles away. Then, no one seemed to know where he was; it was said he had joined a gang of boys moving south to Johannesburg for work on the gold mines.

The McClusters forgot Tembi. They were pleased to be able to forget him. They thought of themselves as good masters; they had a good name with their labourers for kindness and fair dealing; while the affair of Tembi left something hard and unassimilable in them, like a grain of sand in a mouthful of food. The name "Tembi" brought uncomfortable emotions with it; and there was no reason why it should, according to their ideas of right and wrong. So at last they did not even remember to ask Tembi's father what had become of him: he had become another of those natives who vanish from one's life after seeming to be such an intimate part of it.

It was about four years later that the robberies began again. The McClusters' house was the first to be rifled. Someone climbed in one night and took the following articles: Willie's big winter coat, his stick, two old dresses belonging to Jane, a quantity of children's clothing and an old and battered child's tricycle. Money left lying in a drawer was untouched. "What extraordinary things to take," marvelled the McClusters. For except for Willie's coat, there was nothing of value. The theft was reported to the police, and a routine visit was made to the compound. It was established that the thief must be someone who knew the house, for the dogs had not barked at him; and that it was not an experienced thief, who would certainly have taken money and jewellery.

Because of this, the first theft was not connected with

the second, which took place at a neighbouring farmhouse. There, money and watches and a gun were stolen. And there were more thefts in the district of the same kind. The police decided it must be a gang of thieves, not the ordinary pilferer, for the robberies were so clever and it seemed as if several people had planned them. Watchdogs were poisoned; times were chosen when servants were out of the house; and on two occasions someone had entered through bars so closely set together that no one but a child could have forced his way through.

The district gossiped about the robberies; and because of them, the anger lying dormant between white and black, always ready to flare up, deepened in an ugly way. There was hatred in the white people's voices when they addressed their servants, that futile anger, for even if their personal servants were giving information to the thieves, what could be done about it? The most trusted servant could turn out to be a thief. During these months when the unknown gang terrorized the district, unpleasant things happened; people were fined more often for beating their natives; a greater number of labourers than usual ran away over the border to Portuguese territory; the dangerous, simmering anger was like heat growing in the air. Even Jane found herself saying one day: "Why do we do it? Look how I spend my time nursing and helping these natives! What thanks do I get? They aren't grateful for anything we do for them."

This question of gratitude was in every white person's mind during that time.

As the thefts continued, Willie put bars in all the windows of the house, and bought two large fierce dogs. This annoyed Jane, for it made her feel confined and a prisoner in her own home.

To look at a beautiful view of mountains and shaded green bush through bars, robs the sight of joy; and to be greeted on her way from house to storerooms by the growling of hostile dogs who treated everyone, black and white, as an enemy, became daily more exasperating. They bit everyone who came near the house, and Jane was afraid for her children. However, it was not more than three weeks after they were bought that they were found lying stretched in the sun, quite dead, foam at their mouths and their eyes glazing. They had been poisoned. "It looks as if we can expect another visit," said Willie crossly; for he was by now impatient of the whole business. "However," he said impatiently, "if one chooses to live in a damned country like this, one has to take the consequences." It was an exclamation that meant nothing, that could not be taken seriously by anyone. During that time, however, a lot of settled and contented people were talking with prickly anger about "the damned country." In short, their nerves were on edge.

Not long after the dogs were poisoned, it became necessary for Willie to make the trip into town, thirty miles off. Jane did not want to go; she disliked the long, hot, scurrying day in the streets. So Willie went by himself.

In the morning, Jane went to the vegetable garden with her younger children. They played around the water-butt, by themselves, while she staked out a new row of beds; her mind was lazily empty, her hands working quickly with twine and wooden pegs. Suddenly, however, an extraordinary need took her to turn around sharply, and she heard herself say: "Tembi!" She looked wildly about her; afterwards it seemed to her she had heard him speak her name. It seemed to her that she would see a spindly earnest-faced black child kneeling behind her between the vegetable beds poring over a tattered picture book. Time slipped and swam together; she felt confused; and it was only by looking determinedly at her two children that she regained a knowledge of how long it had been since Tembi followed her around this garden.

When she got back to the house, she sewed on the verandah. Leaving her chair for a moment to fetch a glass of water, she found her sewing basket had gone. At first she could not believe it. Distrusting her own senses, she searched the place for her basket, which she knew very well had been on the verandah not a few moments before. It meant that a native was lingering in the bush, perhaps a couple of hundred yards away, watching her movements. It wasn't a pleasant thought. An old uneasiness filled her, and again the name "Tembi" rose into her mind. She took herself into the kitchen and said to the cookboy: "Have you heard anything of Tembi recently." But there had been no news, it seemed. He was "at the gold mines." His parents had not heard from him for years.

"But why a sewing basket?" muttered Jane to herself, incredulously. "Why take such a risk for so little? It's insane."

That afternoon, when the children were playing in the garden and Jane was asleep on her bed, someone walked quietly into the bedroom and took her big garden hat, her apron, and the dress she had been wearing that morning. When Jane woke and discovered this, she began to tremble, half with anger, half with fear. She was alone in the house, and she had the prickling feeling of being watched. As she moved from room to room, she kept glancing over her shoulders behind the angles of wardrobe and cupboard, and fancied that Tembi's great imploring eyes would appear there, as unappeasable as a dead person's eyes, following her.

She found herself watching the road for Willie's return. If Willie had been there, she could have put the responsibility on to him and felt safe: Jane was a woman who depended very much on that invisible support a husband gives. She had not known, before that afternoon, just how much she depended on him; and this knowledge—which it seemed the thief shared—made her unhappy and restless. She felt that she should be able to manage this thing by herself, instead of waiting helplessly for her husband. I must do something, I must do something, she kept repeating.

It was a long, warm, sunny afternoon. Jane, with all her nerves standing to attention, waited on the verandah, shading her eyes as she gazed along the road for Willie's car. The waiting preyed on her. She could not prevent her eyes from returning again and again to the bush immediately in front of the house, which stretched for mile on mile, a low, dark scrubby green, darker because of the lengthening shadows of approaching evening. An impulse pulled her to her feet, and she marched towards the bush through the garden. At its edge she stopped, peering everywhere for those dark and urgent eyes, and called "Tembi, Tembi." There was no sound. "I won't punish you, Tembi," she implored. "Come here to me." She waited, listening delicately, for the slightest movement of branch or dislodged pebble. But the bush was silent under the sun; even the birds were drugged by the heat; and the leaves hung without trembling. "Tembi!" she called again; at first peremptorily, and then with a quaver in her voice. She knew very well that he was there, flattening himself behind some tree or bush, waiting for her to say the right word, to find the right things to say, so that he could trust her. It maddened her to think he was so close, and she could no more reach him than she could lay her hands on a shadow. Lowering her voice persuasively she said: "Tembi, I know you are there. Come here and talk to me. I won't tell the police. Can't you trust me, Tembi?"

Not a sound, not the whisper of a reply. She tried to make her mind soft and blank, so that the words she needed would appear there, ready for using. The grass was beginning to shake a little in the evening breeze, and the hanging leaves tremored once or twice; there was a warm mellowing of the light that meant the sun would soon sink; a red glow showed on the foliage, and the sky was flaring high with light. Jane was trembling so she could not control her limbs; it was a deep internal trembling, welling up from inside, like a wound bleeding invisibly. She tried to steady herself. She said: This is silly. I can't be afraid of little Tembi! How could I be? She made her voice firm and loud and said:

"Tembi, you are being very foolish. What's the use of stealing things like a stupid child? You can be clever about stealing for a little while, but sooner or later the police will catch you and you will go to prison. You don't want that, do you? Listen to me, now. You come out now and let me see you; and when the boss comes I'll explain to him and I'll say you are sorry, and you can come back and work for me in the vegetable garden. I don't like to think of you as a thief, Tembi. Thieves are bad people." She stopped. The silence settled around her; she felt the silence like a coldness, as when a cloud passes overhead. She saw that the shadows were thick about her and the light had gone from the leaves, that had a cold grey look. She knew Tembi would not come out to her now. She had not found the right things to say. "You are a silly little boy," she announced to the still listening bush. "You make me very angry, Tembi." And she walked very slowly back to the house, holding herself calm and dignified, knowing that Tembi was watching her, with some plan in his mind she could not conjecture.

When Willie returned from town, tired and irritable as he always was after a day of traffic, and interviewing people, and shopping, she told him carefully, choosing her words, what had happened. When she told how she had called to Tembi from the verges of the bush, Willie looked gently at her and said: "My dear, what good do you think that's going to do?" "But Willie, it's all so awful . . ." Her lips began to tremble luxuriously, and she allowed herself to weep comfortably on his shoulder. "You don't know it is Tembi," said Willie. "Of course it's Tembi. Who else could it be? The silly little boy. My silly little Tembi . . ."

She could not eat. After supper she said suddenly: "He'll come here tonight. I'm sure of it." "Do you think he will?" said Willie seriously, for he had a great respect for Jane's irrational knowledge. "Well, don't worry, we'll be ready for him." "If he'd only let me talk to him," said Jane. "Talk to him!" said Willie. "Like hell! I'll have him in prison.

That's the only place for him." "But, *Willie* ..." Jane protested, knowing perfectly well that Tembi must go to prison.

It was then not eight o'clock. "I'll have my gun beside the bed," planned Willie. "He stole a gun, didn't he, from the farm over the river? He might be dangerous." Willie's blue eyes were alight; he was walking up and down the room, his hands in his pockets, alert and excited: he seemed to be enjoying the idea of capturing Tembi, and because of this Jane felt herself go cold against him. It was at this moment that there was a sound from the bedroom next door. They sprang up, and reached the entrance together. There stood Tembi, facing them, his hands dangling empty at his sides. He had grown taller, but still seemed the same lithe, narrow child, with the thin face and great eloquent eyes. At the sight of those eyes Jane said weakly: "Willie ..."

Willie, however, marched across to Tembi and took that unresisting criminal by the arm. "You young rascal," he said angrily, but in a voice appropriate, not to a dangerous thief, who had robbed many houses, but rather to a naughty child caught pilfering fruit. Tembi did not reply to Willie: his eyes were fixed on Jane. He was trembling; he looked no more than a boy.

"Why didn't you come when I called you?" asked Jane. "You are so foolish, Tembi."

"I was afraid, missus," said Tembi, in a voice just above a whisper. "But I said I wouldn't tell the police," said Jane.

"Be quiet, Jane," ordered Willie. "Of course we're calling the police. What are you thinking of?" As if feeling the need to remind himself of this important fact, he said: "After all, the lad's a criminal."

"I'm not a bad boy," whispered Tembi imploringly to Jane. "Missus, my missus, I'm not a bad boy."

But the thing was out of Jane's hands; she had relinquished it to Willie.

Willie seemed uncertain what to do. Finally he strode

purposefully to the wardrobe, and took his rifle from it,
and handed it to Jane. "You stay here," he ordered. "I'm
calling the police on the telephone." He went out, leaving
the door open, while Jane stood there holding the big gun,
and waiting for the sound of the telephone.

She looked helplessly down at the rifle, set it against
the bed, and said in a whisper: "Tembi, why did you steal?"
Tembi hung his head and said: "I don't know, missus."
"But you must know." There was no reply. The tears poured
down Tembi's cheeks.

"Tembi, did you like Johannesburg?" There was no reply.
"How long were you there?" "Three years, missus." "Why
did you come back?" "They put me in prison, missus."
"What for?" "I didn't have a pass." "Did you get out of
prison?" "No, I was there one month and they let me go."
"Was it you who stole all the things from the houses around
here?" Tembi nodded, his eyes cast down to the floor.

Jane did not know what to do. She repeated firmly to
herself: "This is a dangerous boy, who is quite unscrupulous,
and very clever," and picked up the rifle again. But the
weight of it, a cold hostile thing, made her feel sorry. She set
it down sharply. "Look at me, Tembi," she whispered. Outside, in the passage, Willie was saying in a firm confident
voice: "Yes, Sergeant, we've got him here. He used to work
for us, years ago. Yes."

"Look, Tembi," whispered Jane quickly. "I'm going out
to the room. You must run away quickly. How did you get
in?" This thought came to her for the first time. Tembi
looked at the window. Jane could see how the bars had been
forced apart, so that a very slight person could squeeze in,
sideways. "You must be strong," she said. "Now, there isn't
any need to go out that way. Just walk out of that door,"
she pointed at the door to the living-room, "and go through
into the verandah, and run into the bush. Go to another
district and get yourself an honest job and stop being a
thief. I'll talk to the baas. I'll tell him to tell the police we
made a mistake, *Now then, Tembi* . . ." she concluded

urgently, and went into the passage, where Willie was at the telephone, with his back to her.

He lifted his head, looked at her incredulously, and said: "Jane, you're crazy." Into the telephone he said: "Yes, come quickly." He set down the receiver, turned to Jane and said: "You know he'll do it again, don't you?" He ran back to the bedroom.

But there had been no need to run. There stood Tembi, exactly where they had left him, his fists in his eyes, like a small child.

"I told you to run away," said Jane angrily.

"He's nuts," said Willie.

And now, just as Jane had done, Willie picked up the rifle, seemed to feel foolish holding it, and set it down again.

Willie sat on the bed and looked at Tembi with the look of one who has been outwitted. "Well, I'm damned," he said. "It's got me beat, this has."

Tembi continued to stand there in the centre of the floor, hanging his head and crying. Jane was crying too. Willie was getting angrier, more and more irritable. Finally he left the room, slamming the door, and saying: "God damn it, everyone is mad."

Soon the police came, and there was no more doubt about what should be done. Tembi nodded at every question: he admitted everything. The handcuffs were put on him, and he was taken away in the police car.

At last Willie came back into the bedroom, where Jane lay crying on the bed. He patted her on the shoulder and said: "Now stop it. The thing is over. We can't do anything."

Jane sobbed out: "He's only alive because of me. That's what's so awful. And now he's going to prison."

"They don't think anything of prison. It isn't a disgrace as it is for us."

"But he is going to be one of those natives who spend all their lives in and out of prison."

"Well, what of it?" said Willie. With the gentle, controlled exasperation of a husband, he lifted Jane and offered her his handkerchief. "Now stop it, old girl," he reasoned. "Do stop it. I'm tired. I want to go to bed. I've had hell up and down those damned pavements all day, and I've got a heavy day tomorrow with the tobacco." He began pulling off his boots.

Jane stopped crying, and also undressed. "There's something horrible about it all," she said restlessly. "I can't forget it." And finally, "What did he *want*, Willie? What is it he was *wanting*, all this time?"

The Nuisance

Two narrow tracks, one of them deepened to a smooth dusty groove by the incessant padding of bare feet, wound from the farm compound to the old well through half a mile of tall blonde grass that was soiled and matted because of the nearness of the clustering huts: the compound had been on that ridge for twenty years.

The native women with their children used to loiter down the track, and their shrill laughter and chattering sounded through the trees as if one might suddenly have come on a flock of brilliant noisy parrots. It seemed as if fetching water was more of a social event to them than a chore. At the well itself they would linger half the morning, standing in groups to gossip, their arms raised in that graceful, eternally moving gesture to steady glittering or rusted petrol tins balanced on head-rings woven of grass; kneeling to slap bits of bright cloth on slabs of stone blasted long ago from the depths of earth. Here they washed and scolded and dandled their children. Here they scrubbed their pots. Here they sluiced themselves and combed their hair.

Coming upon them suddenly there would be sharp exclamations; a glimpse of soft brown shoulders and thighs withdrawing to the bushes, or annoyed and resentful eyes. It was their well. And while they were there, with their laughter, and gossip and singing, their folded draperies, bright armbands, earthenware jars and metal combs, grouped in attitudes of head-slowed indolence, it seemed as if the bellowing of distant cattle, drone of tractor, all the noises of the farm, were simply lending themselves to form a background to this antique scene: Women, drawing water at the well.

When they left the ground would be scattered with the bright-pink fleshy skins of the native wild-plum which contracts the mouth shudderingly with its astringency, or with the shiny green fragments of the shells of kaffir oranges.

Without the women the place was ugly, paltry. The windlass, coiled with greasy rope, propped for safety with a forked stick, was sheltered by a tiny cock of thatch that threw across the track a long, intensely black shadow. For the rest, veld; the sere, flattened, sun-dried veld.

They were beautiful, these women. But she whom I thought of vaguely as "The cross-eyed one", offended the sight. She used to lag behind the others on the road, either by herself, or in charge of the older children. Not only did she suffer from a painful squint, so that when she looked towards you it was with a confused glare of white eyeball; but her body was hideous. She wore the traditional dark-patterned blue stuff looped at the waist, and above it her breasts were loose, flat crinkling triangles.

She was a solitary figure at the well, doing her washing unaided and without laughter. She would strain at the windlass during the long slow ascent of the swinging bucket that clanged sometimes far below, against the sides of naked rock until at that critical moment when it hung vibrating at the mouth of the well, she would set the weight of her shoulder in the crook of the handle and with a fearful snatching movement bring the water to safety. It would slop over, dissolving in a shower of great drops that fell tinkling to disturb the surface of that tiny, circular, dully-gleaming mirror which lay at the bottom of the plunging rock tunnel. She was clumsy. Because of her eyes her body lumbered.

She was the oldest wife of "The Long One", who was our most skilful driver.

"The Long One" was not so tall as he was abnormally thin. It was the leanness of those driven by inner restlessness. He could never keep still. His hands plucked at pieces of grass, his shoulder twitched to a secret rhythm of the nerves. Set a-top of that sinewy narrow, taut body was a narrow head, with wide-pointed ears, which gave him an appearance of alert caution. The expression of the face was always violent, whether he was angry, laughing, or—most usually—sardonically critical. He had a tongue that was feared by every labourer on the farm. Even my father would smile ruefully after an altercation with his driver and say: "He's a man, that native. One must respect him, after all. He never lets you get away with anything."

In his own line he was an artist—his line being cattle. He handled oxen with a delicate brutality that was fascinating and horrifying to watch. Give him a bunch of screaming, rearing three-year-olds, due to take their first taste of the yoke, and he would fight them for hours under a blistering sun with the sweat running off him, his eyes glowing with a wicked and sombre satisfaction. Then he would use his whip, grunting savagely as the lash cut down into flesh, his tongue stuck calculatingly between his teeth as he measured the exact weight of the blow. But to watch him handle a team of sixteen fat tamed oxen was a different thing. It was like watching a circus act; there was the same suspense in it: it was a matter of pride to him that he did not need to use the whip. This did not by any means imply that he wished to spare the beasts pain, not at all, he liked to feed his pride on his own skill. Alongside the double line of ponderous cattle that strained across acres of heavy clods, danced, raved and screamed the Long One, with his twelve-foot-long lash circling in black patterns over their backs; and though his threatening yells were the yells of an inspired mad-man, and the heavy whip could be heard clean across the farm, so that on a moonlight night when they were ploughing late it sounded like the crack and whine of a rifle, never did the dangerous metal-tipped lash so much as touch a hair of their hides. If you examined the oxen as they were outspanned, they might be exhausted, driven to staggering-point, so that my father had to remonstrate, but there was never a mark on them.

"He knows how to handle oxen, but he can't handle his women."

We gave our natives labels such as that, since it was impossible ever to know them as their fellows knew them, in the round. That phrase summarized for us what the Long One offered in entertainment during the years he was with us. Coming back to the farm, after an absence, one would say in humorous anticipation: "And what has the Long One been up to now, with his harem?"

There was always trouble with his three wives. He used to come up to the house to discuss with my father, man to man, how the youngest wife was flirting with the bossboy from the neighbouring compound, six miles off; or how she had thrown a big pot of smoking mealie-pap at the middle wife, who was jealous of her.

We grew accustomed to the sight of the Long One standing at the back door, at the sunset hour, when my father held audience after work. He always wore long khaki trousers that slipped down over thin bony hips and went bare-chested, and there would be a ruddy gleam on his polished black skin, and his spindly gesticulating form would be outlined against a sea of fiery colours. At the end of his tale of complaint he would relapse suddenly into a pose of resignation that was self-consciously weary. My father used to laugh until his face was wet and say: "That man is a natural-born comedian. He would have been on the stage if he had been born another colour."

But he was no buffoon. He would play up to my father's appreciation of the comic, but he would never play the ape, as some Africans did, for our amusement. And he was certainly no figure of fun to his fellows. That same thing in him that sat apart, watchfully critical, even of himself, gave his humour its mordancy, his tongue its sting. And he was terribly attractive to his women. I have seen him slouch down the road on his way from one team to another, his whip trailing behind in the dust, his trousers sagging in folds from hip-bone to ankle, his eyes broodingly directed in front of him, merely nodding as he passed a group of women among whom might be his wives. And it was as if he had lashed them with that whip. They would bridle and writhe; and then call provocatively after him, but with a note of real anger, to make him notice them. He would not so much as turn his head.

When the real trouble started, though, my father soon got tired of it. He liked to be amused, not seriously implicated in his labourers' problems. The Long One took to coming up not occasionally, as he had been used to do, but every evening. He was deadly serious, and very bitter. He wanted my father to persuade the old wife, the cross-eyed one, to go back home to her own people. The woman was driving him crazy. A nagging woman in your house was like having a flea on your body; you could scratch but it always moved to another place, and there was no peace till you killed it.

"But you can't send her back, just because you are tired of her."

The Long One said his life had become insupportable. She grumbled, she sulked, she spoilt his food.

"Well, then your other wives can cook for you."

But it seemed there were complications. The two younger women hated each other, but they were united in one thing, that the old wife should stay, for she was so useful. She looked after the children; she did the hoeing in the garden; she picked relishes from the veld. Besides, she provided endless amusement with her ungainliness. She was the eternal butt, the fool, marked by fate for the entertainment of the whole-limbed and the comely.

My father referred at this point to a certain handbook on native lore, which stated definitively that an elder wife was entitled to be waited on by a young wife, perhaps as compensation for having to give up the pleasures of her lord's favour. The Long One and his ménage cut clean across this amiable theory. And my father, being unable to find a prescribed remedy (as one might look for a cure for a disease in a pharmacopoeia) grew angry. After some weeks of incessant complaint from the Long One he was told to hold his tongue and manage his women himself. That evening the man stalked furiously down the path, muttering to himself between teeth clenched on a grass-stem, on his way home to his two giggling younger wives and the ugly sour-faced old woman, the mother of his elder children, the drudge of his household and the scourge of his life.

It was some weeks later that my father asked casually one day: "And by the way, Long One, how are things with you? All right again?"

And the Long One answered simply: "Yes, baas. She's gone away."

"What do you mean, gone away?"

The Long One shrugged. She had just gone. She had left suddenly, without saying anything to anyone.

Now, the woman came from Nyasaland, which was days and days of weary walking away. Surely she hadn't gone by herself? Had a brother or an uncle come to fetch her? Had she gone with a band of passing Africans on their way home?

My father wondered a little, and then forgot about it. It wasn't his affair. He was pleased to have his most useful native back at work with an unharassed mind. And he was particularly pleased that the whole business was ended before the annual trouble over the water-carrying.

For there were two wells. The new one, used by ourselves, had fresh sparkling water that was sweet in the mouth; but in July of each year it ran dry. The water of the old well had a faintly unpleasant taste and was pale brown, but there was always plenty of it. For three or four months of the year, depending on the rains, we shared that well with the compound.

Now, the Long One hated fetching water three miles, four times a week, in the water-cart. The women of the compound disliked having to arrange their visits to the well so as not to get in the way of the water-carriers. There was always grumbling.

This year we had not even begun to use the old well when complaints started that the water tasted bad. The big baas must get the well cleaned.

My father said vaguely that he would clean the well when he had time.

Next day there came a deputation from the women of the compound. Half a dozen of them stood at the back door, arguing that if the well wasn't cleaned soon, all their children would be sick.

"I'll do it next week," he promised, with bad grace.

The following morning the Long One brought our first load of the season from the old well; and as we turned the taps on the barrels a foetid smell began to pervade the house. As for drinking it, that was out of the question.

"Why don't you keep the cover on the well?" my father said to the women, who were still loitering resentfully at the back door. He was really angry. "Last time the well was cleaned there were fourteen dead rats and a dead snake. We never get things in our well because we remember to keep the lid on."

But the women appeared to consider the lid being on, or off, was an act of God, and nothing to do with them.

We always went down to watch the well-emptying, which had the fascination of a ritual. Like the mealie-shelling, or the first rains, it marked a turning-point in the year. It seemed as if a besieged city were laying plans for the conservation of supplies. The sap was falling in tree and grass-root; the sun was with drawing high, high, behind a veil of smoke and dust; the fierce dryness of the air was a new element, parching foliage as the heat cauterized it. The well-emptying was an act of faith, and of defiance. For a whole afternoon there would be no water on the farm at all. One well was completely dry. And this one would be drained, dependent on the mysterious ebbing and flowing of underground rivers. What if they should fail us? There was an anxious evening, every year; and in the morning, when the Long One stood at the back door and said, beaming, that the bucket was bringing up fine new water, it was like a festival.

But this afternoon we could not stick it out. The smell was intolerable. We saw the usual complement of bloated rats, laid out on the stones around the well, and there was even the skeleton of a small buck that must have fallen in the dark. Then we left, along the road that was temporarily a river whose source was that apparently endless succession of buckets filled by greyish, evil water.

It was the Long One himself that came to tell us the news. Afterwards we tried to remember what look that always expressive face wore as he told it.

It seemed that in the last bucket but one had floated a human arm, or rather the fragments of one. Piece by piece they had fetched her up, the Cross-eyed Woman, his own first wife. They recognized her by her bangles. Last of all, the Long One went down to fetch up her head, which was missing.

"I thought you said your wife had gone home?" said my father.

"I thought she had. Where else could she have gone?"

"Well," said my father at last, disgusted by the whole thing, "if she had to kill herself, why couldn't she hang herself on a tree, instead of spoiling the well?"

"She might have slipped and fallen," said the Long One.

My father looked up at him suddenly. He started for a few moments. Then: "Ye-yes," he said, "I suppose she might."

Later, we talked about the thing, saying how odd it was that natives should commit suicide; it seemed almost like an impertinence, as if they were claiming to have the same delicate feelings as ours.

But later still, apropos of nothing in particular, my father was heard to remark: "Well, I don't know, I'm damned if I know, but in any case he's a damned good driver."

A Home for the Highland Cattle

These days, when people emigrate, it is not so much in search of sunshine, or food, or even servants. It is fairly safe to say that the family bound for Australia, or wherever it may be, has in its mind a vision of a nice house, or a flat, with maybe a bit of garden. I don't know how things were a hundred or fifty years ago. It seems from books, that the colonizers and adventurers went sailing off to a new fine life, a new country, opportunities, and so forth. Now all they want is a roof over their heads.

An interesting thing, this: how is it that otherwise reasonable people come to believe that this same roof, that practically vanishing commodity, is freely obtainable just by packing up and going to another country? After all, headlines like World Housing Shortage are common to the point point of tedium; and there is not a brochure or pamphlet issued by immigration departments that does not say (though probably in small print, throwing it away as it were) that it is undesirable to leave home, without first making sure of a place to live.

Marina Giles left England with her husband in just this frame of mind. They had been living where they could, sharing flats and baths, and kitchens, for some years. If someone remarked enviously: "They say that in Africa the sky is always blue," she was likely to reply absentmindedly: "Yes, and won't it be nice to have a proper house after all these years."

They arrived in Southern Rhodesia, and there was a choice of an immigrants' camp, consisting of mud huts with a common water supply, or a hotel; and they chose the hotel, being what is known as people of means. That is to say, they had a few hundred pounds, with which they had intended to buy a house as soon as they arrived. It was quite possible to buy a house, just as it is in England, provided one gives up all idea of buying a home one likes, and at a reasonable price. For years Marina had been inspecting houses. They fell into two groups, those she liked, and those she could afford. Now Marina was a romantic, she had not yet fallen into that passive state of mind which accepts (as nine-tenths of the population do) that one should find a corner to live anywhere, and then arrange one's whole life around it, schooling for one's children, one's place of work, and so on. And since she refused to accept it, she had been living in extreme discomfort, exclaiming: "Why should we spend all the capital we are ever likely to have tying ourselves down to a place we detest!" Nothing could be more reasonable, on the face of it.

But she had not expected to cross an ocean, enter a new and indubitably romantic-sounding country, and find herself in exactly the same position.

The city, seen from the air, is half-buried in trees. Sixty years ago, this was all bare veld; and even now it appears not as if the veld encloses an area of buildings and streets, but rather as if the houses have forced themselves up, under and among the trees. Flying low over it, one sees greenness, growth, then the white flash of a high building, the fragment of a street that has no beginning or end, for it emerges from trees, and is at once reabsorbed by them. And yet it is a large town, spreading wide and scattered, for here there is no problem of space: pressure scatters people outwards, it does not force them perpendicularly. Driving through it from suburb to suburb, is perhaps fifteen miles—some of the important cities of the world are not much less; but if one asks a person who lives there what the population is, he will say ten thousand, which is very little. Why do so small a number of people need so large a space? The inhabitant will probably shrug, for he has never wondered. The truth is that there are not ten thousand, but more likely 150,000, but the others are black, which means that they are not considered. The blacks do not so much *live* here, as squeeze themselves in as they can—all this is very confusing for the newcomer, and it takes quite a time to adjust oneself.

Perhaps every city has one particular thing by which it is

known, something which sums it up, both for the people who live in it, and those who have never known it, save in books or legend. Three hundred miles south, for instance, old Lobengula's kraal had the Big Tree. Under its branches sat the betrayed, sorrowful, magnificent King in his rolls of black fat and beads and gauds, watching his doom approach in the white people's advance from the south, and dispensing life and death according to known and honoured customs. That was only sixty years ago. . .

This town has The Kopje. When the Pioneers were sent north, they were told to trek on till they reached a large and noble mountain they could not possibly mistake; and there they must stop and build their city. Twenty miles too soon, due to some confusion of mind, or perhaps to understandable exhaustion, they stopped near a small and less shapely hill. This has rankled ever since. Each year, when the ceremonies are held to honour those pioneers, and the vision of Rhodes who sent them forth, the thought creeps in that this is not really what the Founder intended . . . Standing there, at the foot of that kopje, the speech-makers say: Sixty years look what we have accomplished in sixty years. And in the mind of the listeners springs a vision of that city we all dream of, the planned and shapely city without stain or slum—the city that could in fact have been created in those sixty years.

The town spread from the foot of this hill. Around it are the slums, the narrow and crooked streets where the coloured people eke out their short swarming lives among decaying brick and tin. Five minutes walk to one side, and the street peters out in long soiled grass, above which a power chimney pours black smoke and where an old petrol tin lies in a gulley, so that a diving hawk swerves away and up, squawking, scared out of his nature by a flash of sunlight. Ten minutes the other way is the business centre the dazzling white blocks of concrete, modern buildings like modern buildings the world over. Here are the imported clothes the glass windows full of cars from America, the neon lights, the counters full of pamphlets advertising flights Home—wherever one's home might be. A few blocks further on, and the business part of the town is left behind. This was once the smart area. People who have grown with the city will drive through here on a Sunday afternoon, and, looking at the bungalows raised on their foundations and ornamented with iron scrollwork, will say: In 1910 there was nothing beyond this house but bare veld.

Now, however, there are more houses, small and ugly houses until all at once we are in the 'thirties, with tall houses, eight to a block, like very big soldiers standing to attention in a small space. The verandahs have gone. Tiny balconies project like eyelids, the roofs are like bowler hats, rimless. Exposed to the blistering sun these houses crowd together without invitation to shade or coolness, for they were not planned for this climate, and until the trees grow, and the creepers spread, they are extremely uncomfortable. (Though, of course, very smart.) Beyond these? The veld gain wastes of grass clotted with the dung of humans and animals, a vlei that is crossed and criss-crossed by innumerable footpaths where the Africans walk in the afternoon from suburb to suburb stopping to snatch a mouthful of water in cupped palms from pot-holes filmed with iridescent oil, for safety against mosquitoes.

Over the vlei (which is rapidly being invaded by building, so that soon there will be no open spaces left) is a new suburb. Now, this is something quite different. Where the houses, only twenty minutes walk away, stood eight to a block, now there are twenty tiny, flimsy little houses, and the men who planned them had in mind the cheap houses along the ribbon roads of England. Small patches of roofed cement, with room, perhaps, for a couple of chairs, call themselves verandahs. There is a hall a couple of yards square—for otherwise where should one hang one's hat? Each little house is divided into rooms so small that there is no space to move from one wall to the other without circling a table or stumbling over a chair. And white walls, glaring white walls, so that one's eyes turn in relief to the trees.

The trees—these houses are intolerable unless foliage softens and hides them. Any new owner, moving in, says wistfully: It won't be so bad when the shrubs grow up. And they grow very quickly. It is an extraordinary thing that this town, which must be one of the most graceless and inconvenient in existence, considered simply as an association of streets and buildings, is so beautiful that no one fails to fall in love with it at first sight. Every street is lined and double-lined with trees, every house screened with brilliant growth. It is a city of gardens.

Marina was at first enchanted. Then her mood changed. For the only houses they could afford were in those mass-produced suburbs, that were spreading like measles as fast as materials could be imported to build them. She said to Philip: "In England, we did not buy a house because we did not want to live in a suburb. We uproot ourselves, come to a reputedly exotic and wild country, and the only place we can afford to live is another suburb. I'd rather be dead."

Philip listened. He was not as upset as she was. They were rather different. Marina was that liberally-minded* person produced so plentifully in England during the 'thirties, while Philip was a scientist, and put his faith in techniques, rather than in the inherent decency of human beings. He was, it is true, in his own way an idealist, for he had come to this continent in a mood of fine optimism. England, it seemed to him, did not offer opportunities to young men equipped, as he was, with enthusiasm and so much training. Things would be different overseas. All that was necessary was a go-ahead Government prepared to vote sufficient money to Science—this was just common sense. (Clearly, a new country was likely to have more common sense than an old one.) He was prepared to make gardens flourish

---

* *Liberal* is the word given not only to the political party of that name (when it is used with a capital 'L'), but also to the ideas of removing privileges in society and making life freer and thus better.

where deserts had been. Africa appeared to him eminently
suitable for this treatment; and the more he saw of it,
those first few weeks, the more enthusiastic he became.

But he soon came to understand that in the evenings,
when he propounded these ideas to Marina, her mind was
elsewhere. It seemed to him bad luck that they should be
in this hotel, which was uncomfortable, with bad food, and
packed by fellow-immigrants all desperately searching for
that legendary roof. But a house would turn up sooner or
later—he had been convinced of this for years. He would
not have objected to buying one of those suburban houses.
He did not like them, certainly, but he knew quite well that
it was not the house, as such, that Marina revolted against.
And this feeling we all have about the suburbs! How we
dislike the thought of being just like the fellow next door!
Bad luck, when the whole world rapidly fills with suburbs,
for what is a British Colony but a sort of highly-flavoured
suburb to England itself? Somewhere in the back of Marina's
mind has been a vision of herself and Philip living in a
group of amiable people, pleasantly interested in the arts,
who read the *New Statesman* week by week, and held that
discreditable phenomena like the colour bar and the black-
white struggle could be solved by sufficient goodwill . . . a
delightful picture.

Temporarily Philip turned his mind from thoughts of
blossoming deserts, and so on, and tried another approach.
Perhaps they could buy a house through one of the Schemes
for Immigrants? He would return from this Housing Board
or that, and say in a worried voice: "There isn't a hope
unless one has three children." At this, Marina was likely
to become depressed; for she still held the old-fashioned
view that before one has children, one should have a house
to put them in.

"It's all very well for you," said Marina. "As far as I can
see you'll be spending half your time gallivanting in your
lorry from one end of the country to the other, visiting native
reserves, and having a lovely time. I don't *mind*, but I have

to make some sort of life for myself while you do it." Philip looked rather guilty: for in fact he was away three or four days a week, on trips with fellow experts, and Marina would be very often left alone.

"Perhaps we could find somewhere temporary, while we wait for a house to turn up?" he suggested.

This offered itself quite soon. Philip heard from a man he met casually that there was a flat available for three months, but he wouldn't swear to it, because it was only an overheard remark at a sundowner party—Philip followed the trail, clinched the deal and returned to Marina. "It's only for three months," he comforted her.

138 Cecil John Rhodes Vista was in that part of the town built before the sudden expansion in the 'thirties. These were all old houses, unfashionable, built to no important recipe, but according to the whims of the first owners. On one side of 138 was a house whose roof curved down, Chinese fashion, built on a platform for protection against ants, with wooden steps. Its walls were of wood and it was possible to hear feet tramping over the wooden floors even in the street outside. The other neighbour was a house whose walls were invisible under a mass of golden shower—thick yellow clusters, like smoky honey, dripped from roof to ground. The houses opposite were hidden by massed shrubs.

From the street, all but the roof of 138 was screened by a, tall and straggling hedge. The sidewalks were dusty grass, scattered with faggots of dogs' dirt, so that one had to walk carefully. Outside the gate was a great clump of bamboo reaching high into the sky, and all the year round weaver-birds' nests, like woven-grass cricket balls, dangled there bouncing and swaying in the wind. Near it reached the angled brown sticks of the frangipani, breaking into white and a creamy pink, as if a young coloured girl held armfuls of blossom. The street itself was double-lined with trees, first jacaranda, fine green lace against the blue sky, and behind heavy dark masses of the cedrilatoona. All the way down the street were bursts of colour, a drape of purple bougainvillaea, the sparse scarlet flowers of the hibiscus. It was very beautiful, very peaceful.

Once inside the unkempt hedge, 138 was exposed as a shallow brick building, tin-roofed, like an elongated barn, that occupied the centre of two building stands, leaving plenty of space for front and back yards. It had a history. Some twenty years back, some enterprising businessman had built the place, ignoring every known rule of hygiene, in the interests of economy. By the time the local authorities had come to notice its unfitness to exist, the roof was on. There followed a series of court cases. An exhausted judge had finally remarked that there was a housing shortage; and on this basis the place was allowed to remain.

It was really eight semi-detached houses, stuck together in such a way that, standing before the front door of any one, it was possible to see clear through the two rooms which composed each, to the back yard, where washing flapped over the woodpile. A verandah enclosed the front of the building: eight short flights of steps, eight front doors, eight windows—but these windows illuminated the front rooms only. The back room opened into a porch that was screened in by dull green mosquito gauze; and in this way the architect had achieved the really remarkable feat of producing, in a country continually drenched by sunlight, rooms in which it was necessary to have the lights burning all day.

The back yard, a space of bare dust enclosed by parallel hibiscus hedges, was a triumph of individualism over communal living. Eight separate wood piles, eight clotheslines, eight short paths edged with brick leading to the eight lavatories that were built side by side like segments of chocolate, behind an enclosing tin screen: the locks (and therefore the keys) were identical, for the sake of cheapness, a system which guaranteed strife among the inhabitants. On either side of the lavatories were two rooms, built

as a unit. In these four rooms lived eight native servants.
At least, officially there were eight, in practice for more.

When Marina, a woman who took her responsibilities
seriously as has been indicated, looked inside the room
which her servant shared with the servant from next door,
she exclaimed helplessly "Dear me, how awful!" The room
was very small. The brick walls were unplastered, the tin
of the roof bare, focussing the sun's intensity inwards all
day, so that even while she stood on the threshold, she began
to feel a little faint, because of the enclosed heat. The floor
was cement, and the blankets that served as beds lay directly
on it. No cupboards or shelves: these were substituted by a
string stretching from corner to corner. Two small, high
windows, whose glass was cracked and pasted with paper.
On the walls were pictures of the English royal family,
torn out of illustrated magazines, and of various female
film stars, mostly unclothed.

"Dear me," said Marina again, vaguely. She was
feeling very guilty, because of this squalor. She came out
of the room with relief, wiping the sweat from her face, and
looked around the yard. Seen from the back, 138 Cecil John
Rhodes Vista was undeniably picturesque. The yard, enclosed by low, scarlet-flowering hibiscus hedges, was of
dull red earth; the piles of grey wood were each surrounded
by a patch of scattered chips, yellow, orange, white. The
colourful washing lines swung and danced. The servants,
in their crisp white, leaned on their axes, or gossiped.
There was a little black nurse-girl seated on one of the logs.
under a big tree, with a white child in her arms. A delightful
scene; it would have done as it was for the opening number
of a musical comedy. Marina turned her back on it; and with
her stern reformer's eye looked again at the end of the yard.
In the spaces between the lavatories and the servants' rooms
stood eight rubbish cans, each covered by its cloud of flies,
and exuding a stale, sour smell. She walked through them
into the sanitary lane. Now, if one drives down the streets

of such a city, one sees the trees, the gardens, the flowering hedges: the streets form neat squares. Squares (one might suppose) filled with blossoms and greenness, in which the houses are charmingly arranged. But each block is divided down the middle by a sanitary lane, a dust lane, which is lined by rubbish cans, and in this the servants have their social life. Here they go for a quick smoke in the middle of the day's work; here they meet their friends, or flirt with the women who sell vegetables. It is as if, between each of the streets of the white man's city, there is a hidden street, ignored, forgotten. Marina, emerging into it, found it swarming with gossiping and laughing Africans. They froze, gave her a long suspicious stare, and all at once seemed to vanish, escaping into their respective back yards. In a moment she was alone.

She walked slowly back across the yard to her back door, picking her way among the soft litter from the wood piles, ducking her head under the flapping clothes. She was watched, cautiously, by the servants, who were suspicious of this sudden curiosity about their way of life—experience had taught them to be suspicious. She was watched, also, by several of the women, through their kitchen windows. They saw a small Englishwoman, with a neat and composed body, pretty fair hair, and a pink and white face under a large straw hat, which she balanced in position with a hand clothed in a white glove. She moved delicately and with obvious distaste through the dust, as if at any moment she might take wings and fly away altogether.

When she reached her back steps, she stopped and called: "Charlie! Come here a moment, please." It was a high voice, a little querulous. When they heard the accents of that voice, saw the white glove, and noted that *please*, the watching women found all their worst fears confirmed.

A young African emerged from the sanitary lane where he had been gossiping (until interrupted by Marina's appearance) with some passing friends. He ran to his new mistress. He wore white shorts, a scarlet American-style shirt, tartan socks which were secured by mauve suspenders, and white tennis shoes. He stopped before her with a polite smile, which almost at once spread into a grin of pure friendliness. He was an amiable and cheerful young man by temperament. This was Marina's first morning in her new home, and she was already conscious of the disproportion between her strong pity for her servant, and that inveterately cheerful face.

She did not, of course, speak any native language, but Charlie spoke English.

"Charlie, how long have you been working here?"

"Two years, madam."

"Where do you come from?"

"Madam?"

"Where is your home?"

"Nyasaland."

"Oh." For this was hundreds of miles north.

"Do you go home to visit your family?"

"Perhaps this year, madam."

"I see. Do you like it here?"

"Madam?" A pause; and he involuntarily glanced back over the rubbish cans at the sanitary lane. He hoped that his friends, who worked on the other side of the town, and whom he did not often see, would not get tired of waiting for him. He hoped, too, that this new mistress (whose politeness to him he did not trust) was not going to choose this moment to order him to clean the silver or do the washing. He continued to grin, but his face was a little anxious, and his eyes rolled continually backwards at the sanitary lane.

"I hope you will be happy working for me," said Marina.

"Oh, yes, madam," he said at once, disappointedly; for clearly she was going to tell him to work.

"If there is anything you want, you must ask me. I am new to the country, and I may make mistakes."

He hesitated, handling the words in his mind. But they were difficult, and he let them slip. He did not think in terms

of countries, of continents. He knew the white man's town—
this town. He knew the veld. He knew the village from which
he came. He knew, from his educated friends, that there
was "a big water" across which the white men came in ships:
he had seen pictures of ships in old magazines, but this
"big water" was confused in his mind with the great lake
in his own country. He understood that these white people
came from places called England, Germany, Europe, but
these were names to him. Once, a friend of his who had
been three years to a mission school had said that Africa
was one of several continents, and had shown him a tattered
sheet of paper—one half of the map of the world—saying:
Here is Africa, here is England, here is India. He pointed
out Nyasaland, a tiny strip of country, and Charlie felt
confused and diminished, for Nyasaland was what he knew,
and it seemed to him so vast. Now, when Marina used the
phrase "this country" Charlie saw, for a moment, this flat
piece of paper, tinted pink and green and blue—the world.
But from the sanitary lane came shouts of laughter—again
he glanced anxiously over his shoulder; and Marina was
conscious of a feeling remarkably like irritation. "Well,
you may go," she said formally; and saw his smile flash
white right across his face. He turned, and ran back across
the yard like an athlete, clearing the woodpile, then the
rubbish cans, in a series of great bounds, and vanished
behind the lavatories. Marina went inside her "flat" with
what was, had she known it, an angry frown. "Disgraceful."
she muttered, including in this condemnation the bare
room in which this man was expected to fit his life, the
dirty sanitary lane bordered with stinking rubbish cans,
and also his unreasonable cheerfulness.

Inside, she forgot him in her own discomfort. It was a
truly shocking place. The two small rooms were so made
that the inter-leading door was in the centre of the wall.
They were more like passages than rooms. She switched
on the light in what would be the bedroom, and put her

hands to her cheek, for it stung where the sun had caught her unaccustomed skin through the chinks of the straw of her hat. The furniture was really beyond description! Two iron bedsteads, on either side of the door, a vast chocolate-brown wardrobe, whose door would not properly shut, one dingy straw mat that slid this way and that over the slippery boards as one walked on it. And the front room! If possible, it was even worse. An enormous cretonne-covered sofa, like a solidified flower bed, a hard and shiny table stuck in the middle of the floor, so that one must walk carefully around it, and four straight, hard chairs, ranged like soldiers against the wall. And the pictures—she did not know such pictures still existed. There was a desert scene, done in coloured cloth, behind glass; a motto in woven straw, also framed in glass, saying: *Welcome all who come in here, Good luck to you and all good cheer.*

There was also a very large picture of highland cattle. Half a dozen of these shaggy and ferocious creatures glared down at her from where they stood knee-deep in sunset-tinted pools. One might imagine that pictures of highland cattle no longer existed outside of Victorian novels, or re-mote suburban boarding-houses—but no, here they were. Really, why bother to emigrate?

She almost marched over and wrenched that picture from the wall. A curious inhibition prevented her. It was, though she did not know it, the spirit of the building. Some time later she heard Mrs Black, who had been living for years in the next flat with her husband and three children, remark grimly: "My front door handle has been stuck for weeks, but I'm not going to mend it. If I start doing the place up, it means I'm here for ever." Marina recognized her own feeling when she heard these words. It accounted for the fact that while the families here were all respectable, in the sense that they owned cars, and could expect a regular monthly income, if one looked through the neglected hedge it was impossible not to conclude that every person in the building was born sloven or slut. No one really lived here. They might have been here for years, without prospect of anything better, but they did not live here.

There was one exception, Mrs Pond, who painted her walls and mended what broke. It was felt she let everyone else down. In front of *her* steps a narrow path edged with brick led to her segment of yard, which was perhaps two feet across, in which lilies and roses were held upright by trellis work, like a tall, green sandwich standing at random in the dusty yard.

Marina thought: Well, what's the point? I'm not going to *live* here. The picture could stay. Similarly, she decided there was no sense in unpacking her nice curtains or her books. And the furniture might remain as it was, for it was too awful to waste effort on it. Her thoughts returned to the servants' rooms at the back: it was a disgrace. The whole system was disgraceful . . .

At this point, Mrs Pond knocked perfunctorily and entered. She was a short, solid woman, tied in at the waist, like a tight sausage, by the string of her apron. She had hard red cheeks, a full, hard bosom, and energetic red hands. Her eyes were small and inquisitive. Her face was ill-tempered, perhaps because she could not help knowing she was disliked. She was used to the disapproving eyes of her fellow tenants, watching her attend to her strip of "garden"; or while she swept the narrow strip across the back yard that was her path from the back door to her lavatory. There she stood, every morning, among the washing and the woodpiles, wearing a pink satin dressing-gown trimmed with swansdown, among the clouds of dust stirred up by her yard broom, returning defiant glances for the disapproving ones; and later she would say: "Two rooms is quite enough for a woman by herself. I'm quite satisfied."

She had no right to be satisfied, or at any rate, to say so . . .

But for a woman contented with her lot, there was a look in those sharp eyes which could too easily be diagnosed as envy; and when she said, much too sweetly: "You are an old friend of Mrs Skinner, maybe?" Marina recognized, with the exhaustion that comes to everyone who has lived too long in overfull buildings, the existence of conspiracy. "I have never met Mrs Skinner," she said briefly. "She said she was coming here this morning, to make arrangements."

Now, arrangements had been made already, with Philip; and Marina knew Mrs Skinner was coming to inspect herself; and this thought irritated her.

"She is a nice lady," said Mrs Pond. "She's my friend. We two have been living here longer than anyone else." Her voice was sour. Marina followed the direction of her eyes, and saw a large white door set into the wall. A built-in cupboard, in fact. She had already noted that cupboard as the only sensible amenity the "flat" possessed.

"That's a nice cupboard," said Mrs Pond.

"Have all the flats got built-in cupboards?"

"Oh, no. Mrs Skinner had this put in special last year. She paid for it. Not the landlord. You don't catch the landlord paying for anything."

"I see," said Marina.

"Mrs Skinner promised me this flat," said Mrs Pond.

Marina made no reply. She looked at her wrist-watch. It was a beautiful gesture; she even felt a little guilty because of the pointedness of it; but Mrs Pond promptly said: "It's eleven o'clock. The clock just struck."

"I must finish the unpacking," said Marina.

Mrs Pond seated herself on the flowery sofa, and re-marked: "There's always plenty to do when you move in. That cupboard will save you plenty of space. Mrs Skinner kept her linen in it. I was going to put all my clothes in. You're Civil Service, so I hear?"

"Yes," said Marina. She could not account for the grudging tone of that last, apparently irrelevant question. She did not know that in this country the privileged class was the Civil Service, or considered to be. No aristocracy, no class distinctions—but alas, one must have something to hate, and the Civil Service does as well as anything. She added: "My husband chose this country rather than the Gold Coast, because it seems the climate is better, even though the pay is bad."

This remark was received with the same sceptical smile that she would have earned in England had she been tactless enough to say to her charwoman: Death duties spell the doom of the middle classes.

"You have to be in the Service to get what's going," said Mrs Pond, with what she imagined to be a friendly smile. "The Service gets all the plums." And she glanced at the cupboard.

"I think," said Marina icily, "that you are under some misapprehension. My husband happened to hear of this flat by chance."

"There were plenty of people waiting for this flat," said Mrs Pond reprovingly. "The lady next door, Mrs Black, would have been glad of it. And she's got three children, too. You have no children, perhaps?"

"Mrs Pond, I have no idea at all why Mrs Skinner gave us this flat when she had promised it to Mrs Black . . ."

"Oh, no, she had promised it to me. It was a faithful promise."

At this moment another lady entered the room without knocking. She was an ample, middle-aged person, in tight corsets, with rigidly-waved hair, and a sharp, efficient face that was now scarlet from heat. She said peremptorily: "Excuse me for coming in without knocking, but I can't get used to a stranger being here when I've lived here so long." Suddenly she saw Mrs Pond, and at once stiffened into aggression. "I see you have already made friends with Mrs Pond," she said, giving that lady a glare.

Mrs Pond was standing, hands on hips, in the traditional attitude of combat; but she squeezed a smile on to her face and said: "I'm making acquaintance."

"Well," said Mrs Skinner, dismissing her, "I'm going to discuss business with my tenant."

Mrs Pond hesitated. Mrs Skinner gave her a long, quelling stare. Mrs Pond slowly deflated, and went to the door. From the verandah floated back the words: "When people make promises they should keep them, that's what I say, instead of giving it to people new to the country, and civil servants . . ."

Mrs Skinner waited until the loud and angry voice faded, and then said briskly: "If you take my advice, you'll have nothing to do with Mrs Pond, she's more trouble than she's worth."

Marina now understood that she owed this flat to the fact that this highly-coloured lady decided to let it to a stranger simply in order to spite all her friends in the building who hoped to inherit that beautiful cupboard, if only for three months. Mrs Skinner was looking suspiciously around her; she said at last: "I wouldn't like to think my things weren't looked after."

"Naturally not," said Marina politely.

"When I spoke to your husband we were rather in a hurry. I hope you will make yourself comfortable, but I don't want to have anything altered."

Marina maintained a polite silence.

Mrs Skinner marched to the inbuilt cupboard, opened it, and found it empty. "I paid a lot of money to have this fitted," she said in an aggrieved voice.

"We only came in yesterday," said Marina. "I haven't unpacked yet."

"You'll find it very useful," said Mrs Skinner. "I paid for it myself. Some people would have made allowances in the rent."

"I think the rent is quite high enough," said Marina, joining battle at last.

Clearly, this note of defiance was what Mrs Skinner had been waiting for. She made use of the familiar weapon: "There are plenty of people who would have been glad of it, I can tell you."

"So I gather."

"I could let it tomorrow."

"But," said Marina, in the high formal voice, "you have in fact let it to us, and the lease has been signed, so there is no more to be said, is there?"

Mrs Skinner hesitated, and finally contented herself by repeating: "I hope my furniture will be looked after. I said in the lease nothing must be altered."

Suddenly Marina found herself saying: "Well, I shall of course move the furniture to suit myself, and hang my own pictures."

"This flat is let furnished, and I'm very fond of my pictures."

"But you will be away, won't you?" This, a sufficiently crude way of saying: "But it is we who will be looking at the pictures, and not you," misfired completely, for Mrs Skinner merely said: "Yes, I like my pictures, and I don't like to think of them being packed."

Marina looked at the highland cattle and, though not half an hour before she had decided to leave it, said now: "I should like to take that one down."

Mrs Skinner clasped her hands together before her, in a pose of simple devotion, compressed her lips, and stood staring mournfully up at the picture. "That picture means a lot to me. It used to hang in the parlour when I was a child, back Home: It was my granny's picture first. When I married Mr Skinner, my mother packed it and sent it especial over the sea, knowing how I was fond of it. It's moved with me everywhere I've been. I wouldn't like to think of it being treated bad, I wouldn't really."

"Oh, very well," said Marina, suddenly exhausted. What, after all, did it matter?

Mrs Skinner gave her a doubtful look: was it possible she had won her point so easily? "You must keep an eye on Charlie," she went on. "The number of times I've told him he'd poke his broom-handle through that picture . . ."

Hope flared in Marina. There was an extraordinary amount of glass. It seemed that the entire wall was surfaced by angry, shaggy cattle. Accidents did happen . . .

"You must keep an eye on Charlie, anyway. He never does a   stroke more than he has to. He's bred bone lazy. You'd better keep an eye on the food too. He steals. I had to have the police to him only last month, when I lost my garnet brooch. Of course he swore he hadn't taken it, but I've never laid my hands on it since. My husband gave him a good hiding, but Master Charlie came up smiling, as usual."

Marina, revolted by this tale, raised her eyebrows dis-approvingly. "Indeed?" she said, in her coolest voice.

Mrs Skinner looked at her, as if to say: "What are you making that funny face for?" she remarked: "They're all born thieves and liars. You shouldn't trust them further than you can kick them. I'm warning you. Of course, you're new here. Only last week a friend was saying, I'm surprised at you letting to people just from England, they always spoil the servants, with their ideas, and I said: 'Oh, Mr Giles is a sensible man, I trust him,' " This last was said pointedly.

"I don't think," remarked Marina coldly, "that you would be well-advised to trust my husband to give people 'hidings'." She delicately isolated this word. "I rather feel, in similar circumstance that even if he did, he would first make sure whether the man had, in fact, stolen the brooch."

Mrs Skinner disentangled this sentence and in due course gave Marina a distrustful stare. "Well," she said, "it's too late now, and everyone has his way, but of course this is my furniture, and if it is stolen or damaged, you are respon-sible.

"That, I should have thought, went without saying," said Marina.

They shook hands, with formality, and Mrs Skinner went out. She returned from the verandah twice, first to say that Marina must not forget to fumigate the native quarters once a month if she didn't want livestock brought into her own flat . . . ("Not that I care if they want to live with lice, dirty creatures, but you have to protect yourself . . ."); and the second time to say that after you've lived in a place for years, it was hard to leave it, even for a holiday, and she was really regretting the day she let it at all. She gave Marina a final accusing and sorrowful look, as if the flat had been stolen from her, and this time finally departed. Marina was left in a mood of defiant anger, looking at the highland cattle picture which had assumed, during this exchange, the look of a battle-ground. "Really," she said aloud to herself. "Really! One might have thought that one would be entitled to pack away a picture, if one rents a place . . ."

Two days later she got a note from Mrs Skinner, saying that she hoped Marina would be happy in the flat, she must remember to keep an eye on Mrs Pond, who was a real trouble-maker, and she must remember to look after the picture—Mrs Skinner positively could not sleep for worrying about it.

Since Marina had decided she was not living here, there was comparatively little unpacking to be done. Things were stored. She had more than ever the appearance of a migrating bird who dislikes the twig it has chosen to alight on, but is rather too exhausted to move to another.

But she did read the advertisement columns every day, which were exactly like those in the papers back home. The *accommodation wanted* occupied a full column, while the *accommodation offered* usually did not figure at all. When houses were advertised they usually cost between five and twelve thousand—Marina saw some of them. They were very beautiful; if one had five thousand pounds, what a happy life one might lead—but the same might be said of any country. She also paid another visit to one of the new suburbs, and returned shuddering. "What!" she exclaimed to Philip. "Have we emigrated in order that I may spend the rest of life gossiping and taking tea with women like Mrs Black and Mrs Skinner?"

"Perhaps they aren't all like that," he suggested absent-mindedly. For he was quite absorbed in his work. This country was fascinating! He was spending his days in his Government lorry, rushing over hundreds of miles of veld, visiting native reserves and settlements. Never had soil been so misused! Thousands of acres of it, denuded, robbed, fit for nothing, cattle and human beings crowded together—the solution, of course, was perfectly obvious. All one had to do was—and if the Government had any sense—

Marina understood that Philip was acclimatised. One does not speak of the "Government" with that particular mixture of affection and exasperation unless one feels at home. But she was not at all at home. She found herself playing with the idea of buying one of those revolting little houses. After all, one has to live somewhere . . .

Almost every morning, in 138, one might see a group of women standing outside one or other of the flats, debating how to rearrange the rooms. The plan of the building being so eccentric, no solution could possibly be satisfactory, and as soon as everything had been moved around, it was bound to be just as uncomfortable as before. "If I move the bookcase behind the door, then perhaps . . . " Or: "It might be better if I put it into the bathroom . . ."

The problem was: Where should one eat? If the dining-table was in the front room, then the servant had to come through the bedroom with the food. On the other hand, if one had the front room as bedroom, then visitors had to walk through it to the dining-room. Marina kept Mrs Skinner's arrangement. On the back porch which was the width of a passage, stood a collapsible card-table. When it was set up, Philip sat crouched under the window that opened inwards over his head, while Marina shrank sideways into the bathroom door as Charlie came past with the vegetables. To serve food, Charlie put on a starched white coat, red fez, and white cotton gloves. In between courses he stood just behind them, in the kitchen door, while Marina and Philip ate in state, if discomfort.

Marina found herself becoming increasingly sensitive to what she imagined was his attitude of tolerance. It seemed ridiculous that the ritual of soup, fish, and sweet, silver and glass and fish-knives should continue under such circumstances. She began to wonder how it all appeared to this young man, who, as soon as his meat was finished, took an enormous pot of mealie porridge off the stove and retired with it to his room, where he started it (eating with his fingers and squatting on the floor) with the servant from next door, and any of his friends or relatives who happened to be out of work at the time.

That no such thoughts entered the heads of the other inhabitants was clear; and Marina could understand how necessary it was to banish them as quickly as possible. On the other hand . . .

There was something absurd in a system which allowed a healthy young man to spend his life in her kitchen, so that she might do nothing. Besides, it was more trouble than it was worth. Before she and Philip rose, Charlie walked around the outside of the building, and into the front room, and cleaned it. But as the wall was thin and he energetic, they were awakened every morning by the violent banging of his broom and the scraping of furniture. On the other hand, if it were left till they woke up, where should Marina sit while he cleaned it? On the bed, presumably, in the dark bedroom, till he had finished? It seemed to her that she spent half her time arranging her actions so that she might not get in Charlie's way while he cleaned or cooked. But she had learned better than to suggest doing her own work. On one of Mrs Pond's visits, she had spoken with disgust of certain immigrants from England, who had so far forgotten what was due to their position as white people as to dispense with servants. Marina felt it was hardly worth while upsetting Mrs Pond for such a small matter. Particularly, of course, as it was only for three months . . .

But upset Mrs Pond she did, and almost immediately.

When it came to the end of the month, when Charlie's wages were due, and she laid out the twenty shillings he earned. She was filled with guilt. She really could not pay him such an idiotic sum for a whole month's work. But were twenty-five shillings, or thirty any less ridiculous? She paid him twenty-five and saw him beam with amazed surprise. He had been planning to ask for a rise. Since this woman was easy-going, and he naturally optimistic; but to get a rise without asking for it, and then a full five shillings! Why it had taken him three months of hard bargaining with Mrs Skinner to get raised from seventeen and sixpence to nineteen shillings. "Thank you, madam," he said hastily; grabbing the money as if at any moment she might change her mind and take it back later that same day, she saw that he was wearing a new pair of crimson satin garters, and felt rather annoyed. Surely those five shillings might have been more sensibly spent? What these unfortunate people needed was an education in civilized values—but before she could pursue the thought, Mrs Pond entered, looking aggrieved.

It appeared that Mrs Pond's servant had also demanded a rise from his nineteen shillings. If Charlie could earn twenty-five shillings, why not he? Marina understood that Mrs Pond was speaking for all the women in the building.

"You shouldn't spoil them," she said. "I know you are from England, and all that, but . . ."

"It seems to me they are absurdly underpaid," said Marina.

"Before the war they were lucky to get ten bob. They're never satisfied."

"Well, according to the cost-of-living index, the value of money has halved," said Marina. But as even the Government had not come to terms with this official and indisputable fact, Mrs Pond could not be expected to, and she said crossly: "All you people are the same, you come here with your fancy ideas."

Marina was conscious that every time she left her rooms, she was followed by resentful eyes. Besides, she was feeling a little ridiculous. Crimson satin garters, really!

She discussed the thing with Philip, and decided that payment in kind was more practical. She arranged that Charlie should be supplied, in addition to a pound of

meat twice a week, with vegetables. Once again Mrs Pond
came on a deputation of protest. All the natives in the
building were demanding vegetables. "They aren't used
to it," she complained. "Their stomachs aren't like ours.
They don't need vegetables. You're just putting ideas into
their heads."

"According to the regulations," Marina pointed out
in that high clear voice, "Africans should be supplied with
vegetables."

"Where did you get that from?" said Mrs Pond suspiciously.

Marina produced the regulations, which Mrs Pond read
in grim silence. "The Government doesn't have to pay for
it," she pointed out, very aggrieved. And then, "They're
getting out of hand, that's what it is. There'll be trouble,
you mark my words . . ."

Marina completed her disgrace on the day when she
bought a second-hand iron bedstead and installed it in
Charlie's room. That her servant should have to sleep on
the bare cement floor, wrapped in a blanket, this she could
no longer tolerate. As for Charlie, he accepted his good
fortune fatalistically. He could not understand Marina.
She appeared to feel guilty about telling him to do the
simplest thing, such as clearing away cobwebs he had forgotten. Mrs Skinner would have docked his wages, and Mr
Skinner cuffed him. This woman presented him with a new
bed on the day that he broke her best cut-glass bowl.

He bought himself some new ties, and began swaggering
around the back yard among the other servants, whose
attitude towards him was as one might expect; one did not
expect justice from the white man, whose ways were in-
comprehensible, but there should be a certain proportion:
why should Charlie be the one to chance on an employer
who presented him with a fine bed, extra meat, vegetables,
and gave him two afternoons off a week instead of one?
They looked unkindly at Charlie, as he swanked across the
yard in his fine new clothes; they might even shout sarcastic

remarks after him. But Charlie was too good-natured and friendly a person to relish such a situation. He made a joke of it, in self-defence, as Marina soon learned.

She had discovered that there was no need to share the complicated social life of the building in order to find out what went on. If, for instance, Mrs Pond had quarrelled with a neighbour over some sugar that had not been returned, so that all the women were taking sides, there was no need to listen to Mrs Pond herself to find the truth. Instead, one went to the kitchen window overlooking the back yard, hid oneself behind the curtain, and peered out at the servants.

There they stood, leaning on their axes, or in the intervals of pegging the washing, a group of laughing and gesticulating men, who were creating the new chapter in that perpetually unrolling saga, the extraordinary life of the white people, their masters, in 138 Cecil John Rhodes Vista . . .

February, Mrs Pond's servant, stepped forward, while the others fell back in a circle around him, already grinning appreciatively. He thrust out his chest, stuck out his chin, and over a bad-tempered face he stretched his mouth in a smile so poisonously ingratiating that his audience roared and slapped their knees with delight. He was Mrs Pond, one could not mistake it. He minced over to an invisible person, put on an attitude of supplication, held out his hand, received something in it. He returned to the centre of the circle, and looked at what he held with a triumphant smile. In one hand he held an invisible cup, with the other he spooned in invisible sugar. He was Mrs Pond, drinking her tea, with immense satisfaction, in small dainty sips. Then he belched, rubbed his belly, smacked his lips. Entering into the game another servant came forward, and acted a falsely amiable woman: hands on hips the jutting elbows, the whole angry body showing indignation, but the face was smiling. February drew himself up, nodded and smiled, turned himself about, lifted something from the air behind him, and began pouring it out: sugar, one could positively hear it trickling. He took the container, and handed it proudly to the waiting visitor. But just as it was taken from him, he changed his mind. A look of agonized greed came over his face, and he withdrew the sugar. Hastily turning himself back, throwing furtive glances over his shoulder, he poured back some of the sugar, then, slowly, as if it hurt to do it, he forced himself round, held out the sugar, and again—just as it left his hand, he grabbed it and poured back just a little more. The other servants were rolling with laughter, as the two men faced each other in the centre of the yard, one indignant, but still polite, screwing up his eyes at the returned sugar, as if there were too small a quantity to be seen, while February held it out at arm's length, his face contorted with the agony it caused him to return it at all. Suddenly the two sprang together, faced each other like a pair of angry hens, and began screeching and flailing their arms.

"February!" came a shout from Mrs Pond's flat, in her loud, shrill voice, "February, I told you to do the ironing!"

"Madam!" said February, in his politest voice. He walked backwards to the steps, his face screwed up in a grimace of martyred suffering; as he reached steps, his body fell into the pose of a willing servant, and he walked hastily into the kitchen, where Mrs Pond was waiting for him.

But the other servants remained, unwilling to drop the game. There was a moment of indecision. They glanced guiltily at the back of the building: perhaps some of the other women were watching? No, complete silence. It was mid-morning, the sun poured down, the shadows lay deep under the big tree, the sap crystallized into little rivulets like burnt toffee on the wood chips, and sent a warm fragrance mingling into the odours of dust and warmed foliage. For the moment, they could not think of anything to do, they might as well go on with the wood-chopping. One yawned, another lifted his axe and let it fall into a log of wood, where it was held, vibrating. He plucked the handle, and it thrummed like a deep guitar note. At once, delightedly, the men gathered around the embedded axe. One twanged it, and the others began to sing. At first Marina was unable to make out the words. Then she heard:

> *There's a man who comes to our house,*
> *When poppa goes away,*
> *Poppa comes back, and . . .*

The men were laughing, and looking at No. 4 of the flats, where a certain lady was housed whose husband worked on the railways. They sang it again:

> *There's a man who comes to this house,*
> *Every single day,*
> *The baas come back, and*
> *The man goes away . . .*

Marina found that she was angry. Really! The thing had turned into another drama. Charlie, her own servant, was driving an imaginary engine across the yard, chuff chuff, like a child, while two of the others, seated on a log of wood were—really, it was positively obscene!

Marina came away from the window, and reasoned with herself. She was using, in her mind, one of the formulae of the country: *What can one expect?*

At this moment, while she was standing beside the kitchen table, arguing with her anger, she heard the shrill cry: "Peas! Nice potatoes! Cabbage! Ver' chip!"

Yes, she needed vegetables. She went to the back door. There stood a native woman, with a baby on her back, carefully unslinging the sacks of vegetables which she had supported over her shoulder. She opened the mouth of one, displaying the soft mass of green pea-pods.

"How much?"

"Only one sheeling," said the woman hopefully.

"What!" began Marina, in protest; for this was twice what the shops charged. Then she stopped. Poor woman. No woman should have to carry a heavy child on her back, and great sacks of vegetables from house to house, street

E

to street, all day—"Give me a pound," she said. Using a tin cup, the woman ladled out a small quantity of peas. Marina nearly insisted on weighing them; then she remembered how Mrs Pond brought her scales out to the backdoor, on these occasions, shouting abuse at the vendor, if there was short weight. She took in the peas, and brought out a shilling. The woman, who had not expected this, gave Marina a considering look and fell into the pose of a suppliant. She held out her hands, palms upwards, her head bowed, and murmured: "Present, missus, present for my baby."

Again Marina hesitated. She looked at the woman, with her whining face and shifty eyes, and disliked her intensely. The phrase: What can one expect? came to the surface of her mind, and she went indoors and returned with sweets. The woman received them in open, humble palms, and promptly popped half into her own mouth. Then she said: "Dress, missus?"

"No," said Marina, with energy. Why should she?

Without a sign of disappointment, the woman twisted the necks of the sacks around her hand, and dragged them after her over the dust of the yard, and joined the group of servants who were watching this scene with interest. They exchanged greetings. The woman sat down on a log, easing her strained back, and moved the baby around under her arm pit, still in its sling, so that it could reach her breast. Charlie, the dandy, bent over her, and they began a flirtation. The others fell back. Who, indeed, could compete with that rainbow tie, the satin garters? Charlie was persuasive and assured, the woman bridling and laughing. It went on for some minutes until the baby let the nipple fall from its mouth. Then the woman got up, still laughing, shrugged the baby back into position in the small of her back, pulled the great sacks over one shoulder, and walked off, calling shrilly back to Charlie, so that all the men laughed. Suddenly they all became silent. The nurse-girl emerged from Mrs Black's flat, and sauntered slowly past them. She was a little creature, a child, in a tight pink cotton dress, her hair braided into a dozen tiny plaits that stuck out all over her head, with a childish face that was usually vivacious and mischievous. But now she looked mournful. She dragged her feet as she walked past Charlie, and gave him a long reproachful look. Jealousy, thought Marina, there was no doubt of that! And Charlie was looking uncomfortable— one could not mistake that either. But surely not! Why, she wasn't old enough for this sort of thing. The phrase, *this sort of thing*, struck Marina herself as a shameful evasion, and she examined it. Then she shrugged and said to herself: All the same, where did the girl sleep? Presumably in one of these rooms, with the men of the place?

Theresa (she had been named after Saint Theresa at the mission school where she had been educated) tossed her head in the direction of the departing seller of vegetables, gave Charlie a final supplicating glance, and disappeared into the sanitary lane.

The men began laughing again, and this time the laughter was directed at Charlie, who received it grinning self-consciously.

Now February, who had finished the ironing, came from Mrs Pond's flat and began hanging clothes over the line to air. The white things dazzled in the sun and made sharp, black shadows across the red dust. He called out to the others—what interesting events had happened since he went indoors? They laughed, shouted back. He finished pegging the clothes and went over to the others. The group stood under the big tree, talking; Marina, still watching, suddenly felt her cheeks grow hot. Charlie had separated himself off and, with a condensing, bowed movement of his body, had become the African woman, the seller of vegetables. Bent sideways with the weight of sacks, his belly thrust out to balance the heavy baby, he approached a log of wood—her own back step. Then he straightened, sprang back, stretched upward, and pulled from the tree a frond of leaves. These he balanced on his head, and suddenly

Marina saw herself. Very straight, precise, finicky, and a prim little face peering this way and that under the broad hat, hands clasped in front of her, she advanced to the log of wood and stood looking downwards.

"Peas, cabbage, potatoes," said Charlie, in a shrill female voice.

"How much?" he answered himself, in Marina's precise, nervous voice.

"Ten sheelings a pound, missus, only ten sheelings a pound!" said Charlie, suddenly writhing on the log in an ecstasy of humility.

"How ridiculous!" said Marina, in that high, alas, absurdly high voice. Marina watched herself hesitate, her face showing mixed indignation and guilt and, finally, indecision. Charlie nodded twice, said nervously: "Of course, but certainly." Then, in a hurried, embarrassed way, he retreated and came back, his arms full. He opened them and stood aside to avoid a falling shower of money. For a moment he mimed the African woman and, squatting on the ground, hastily raked in the money and stuffed it into his shirt. Then he stood up—Marina again. He bent uncertainly, with a cross, uncomfortable face, looking down. Then he bent stiffly and picked up a leaf—a single pea-pod, Marina realised— and marched off, looking at the leaf, saying: "Cheap, very very cheap?" one hand balancing the leaves on his head, his two feet set prim and precise in front of him.

As the laughter broke out from all the servants, Marina, who was not far from tears, stood by the window and said to herself. Serve you right for eavesdropping.

A clock struck. Various female voices shouted from their respective kitchens:

"February!" "Noah!" "Thursday!" "Sixpence!" "Blackbird!"

The morning lull was over. Time to prepare the midday meal for the white people. The yard was deserted, save for Theresa the nurse-girl returning disconsolately from the sanitary lane, dragging her feet through the dust. Among the stiff quills of hair on her head she had perched a half-faded yellow flower that she had found in one of the rubbish-cans. She looked hopefully at Marina's flat for a glimpse of Charlie; then slowly entered Mrs Black's.

It happened that Philip was away on one of his trips. Marina ate her lunch by herself, while Charlie, attired in his waiter's outfit, served her food. Not a trace of the cheerful clown remained in his manner. He appeared friendly, though nervous; at any moment he seemed to be thinking, this strange white woman might revert to type and start scolding and shouting.

As Marina rose from the card-table, being careful not to bump her head on the window, she happened to glance out at the yard and saw Theresa, who was standing under the tree with the youngest of her charges in her arms. The baby was reaching up to play with the leaves. Theresa's eyes were fixed on Charlie's kitchen.

"Charlie," said Marina, "where does Theresa sleep?"

Charlie was startled. He avoided her eyes and muttered: "I don't know, madam."

"But you must know, surely," said Marina, and heard her own voice climb to that high, insistent tone which Charlie had so successfully imitated.

He did not answer.

"How old is Theresa?"

"I don't know." This was true, for he did not even know his own age. As for Theresa, he saw the spindly, little-girl body, with the sharp young breasts pushing out the pink stuff of the dress she wore; he saw the new languor of her walk as she passed him. "She is nurse for Mrs Black," he said sullenly, meaning: "Ask Mrs Black. What's it got to do with me?"

Marina said: "Very well," and went out. As she did so she saw Charlie wave to Theresa through the gauze of the porch. Theresa pretended not to see. She was punishing him, because of the vegetable woman.

In the front room the light was falling full on the highland cattle, so that the glass was a square, blinding glitter. Marina shifted her seat, so that her eyes were no longer troubled by it, and contemplated those odious cattle. Why was it that Charlie, who broke a quite fantastic number of cups, saucers, and vases, never—as Mrs Skinner said he might—put that vigorously-jerking broom-handle through the glass? But it seemed he liked the picture. Marina had seen him standing in front of it, admiring it. Cattle, Marina knew from Philip, played a part in native tribal life that could only be described as religious—might it be that . . .

Some letters slapped on to the cement of the verandah, slid over its polished surface, and came to rest in the doorway. Two letters. Marina watched the uniformed postboy cycle slowly down the front of the building, flinging in the letters, eight times, slap, slap, slap, grinning with pleasure at his own skill. There was a shout of rage. One of the women yelled after him: "You lazy black bastard, can't you even get off your bicycle to deliver the letters?" The postman, without taking any notice, cycled slowly off to the next house.

This was the hour of heat, when all activity faded into somnolence. The servants were away at the back, eating their midday meal. In the eight flats, separated by the flimsy walls which allowed every sound to be heard, the women reclined. Sleeping or lazily gossiping. Marina could hear Mrs Pond, three rooms away, saying: "The fuss she made over half a pound of sugar, you would think . . ."

Marina yawned. What a lazy life this was! She decided, at that moment, that she would put an end to this nonsense of hoping, year after year, for some miracle that would provide her, Marina Giles, with a nice house, a garden, and the other vanishing amenities of life. They would buy one of those suburban houses and she would have a baby. She would have several babies. Why not? Nursemaids cost practically nothing. She would become a domestic creature and learn to discuss servants and children with women like Mrs Black and Mrs Skinner. Why not? What had she expected? Ah, what had she not expected! For a moment she allowed herself to dream of that large house, that fine exotic garden, the free and amiable life released from the tensions and pressures of modern existence. She dreamed quite absurdly—but then, if no one dreamed these dreams, no one would emigrate, continents would remain undeveloped, and then what would happen to Charlie, whose salvation was (so the statesmen and newspapers continually proclaimed) contact with Mrs Pond and Mrs Skinner—white civilization, in short.

But the phrase 'white civilization' was already coming to affect Marina as violently as it affects everyone else in that violent continent. It is a phrase like 'white man's burden,' 'way of life' or 'colour bar'—all of which are certain to touch off emotions better not classified. Marina was alarmed to find that these phrases were beginning to produce in her a feeling of fatigued distaste. For the liberal, so vociferously disapproving in the first six months, is quite certain to turn his back on the whole affair before the end of a year. Marina would soon be finding herself profoundly bored by politics.

But at this moment, having taken the momentous decision, she was quite light-hearted. After all, the house next door to this building was an eyesore, with its corrugated iron and brick and wood flung hastily together; and yet it was beautiful, covered with the yellow and purple and crimson creepers. Yes, they would buy a house in the suburbs, shroud it with greenery, and have four children; and Philip would be perfectly happy rushing violently around the country in a permanent state of moral indignation, and thus they would both be usefully occupied.

Marina reached for the two letters, which still lay just inside the door, where they had been so expertly flung, and opened the first. It was from Mrs Skinner, written from Cape Town, where she was, rather uneasily, it seemed, on holiday.

I can't help worrying if everything is all right, and the furniture. Perhaps I ought to have packed away the things, because no stranger understands. I hope Charlie is not getting cheeky, he needs a firm hand, and I forgot to tell you you must deduct one shilling from his wages because he came back late one afternoon, instead of five o'clock as I said, and I had to teach him a lesson.

Yours truly,
Emily Skinner

P.S. I hope the picture is continuing all right.

The second was from Philip.

I'm afraid I shan't be back tomorrow as Smith suggests while we are here we might as well run over to the Nwenze reserve. It's only just across the river, about seventy miles as the crow flies, but the roads are anybody's guess, after the wet season. Spent this morning as planned, trying to persuade these blacks it is better to have one fat ox than ten all skin and bone, never seen such erosion in my life, gullies twenty feet deep, and the whole tribe will starve next dry season, but you can talk till you are blue, they won't kill a beast till they're forced, and that's what it will come to, and then imagine the outcry from the people back home . . .

At this point Marina remarked to herself: Well, well; and continued:

You can imagine Screech-Jones or one of them shouting in the House: Compulsion of the poor natives. My eye. It's for their own good. Until all this mystical nonsense about cattle is driven out of their fat heads, we might as well save our breath. You should have seen where I was this morning! To get the reserve back in use, alone, would take the entire Vote this year for the whole country, otherwise the whole place will be a desert, it's all perfectly obvious, but you'll never get this damned Government to see that in a hundred years, and it'll be too late in five.

In haste.
Phil.

P.S. I do hope everything is all right, dear. I'll try not to be late.

That night Marina took her evening meal early so that Charlie might finish the washing-up and get off. She was reading in the front room when she understood that her ear was straining through the noise from the wirelesses all around her for a quite different sort of music. Yes, it was a banjo, and loud singing, coming from the servants' rooms, and there was a quality in it that was not to be heard from any wireless set. Marina went through the rooms to the kitchen window. The deserted yard, roofed high with the moss and stars, was slatted and barred with light from the eight back doors. The windows of the four servants' rooms gleamed dully; and from the room Charlie shared with February came laughter and singing and the thrumming of the banjo.

> *There's a man who comes to our house,*
> *When poppa goes away . . .*

Marina smiled. It was a maternal smile. (As Mrs Pond might remark, in a good mood: They are nothing but children.) She liked to think that these men were having a party. And women too: she could hear shrill female voices. How on earth did they all fit into that tiny room? As she returned through the back porch she heard a man's voice shouting: "Shut up there! Shut up, I say!" Mr Black from his back porch: "Don't make so much noise."

Complete silence. Marina could see Mr Black's long, black shadow poised motionless: he was listening. Marina heard him grumble: "Can't hear yourself think with these bastards . . ." He went back into his front room, and the sound of his heavy feet on the wood floor was absorbed by their wireless playing: I love you. Yes I do, I love you . . . Slam! Mr Black was in a rage.

Marina continued to read. It was not long before once more her distracted ear warned her that riotous music had begun again. They were singing: Congo Conga Conga, we do it in the Congo . . .

Steps on the verandah, a loud knock, and Mr Black entered.

"Mrs Giles, your boy's gone haywire. Listen to the din."

Marina said politely: "Do sit down Mr Black."

Mr Black who in England (from whence he had come as a child) would have been a lanky, pallid, genteel clerk, was in this country an assistant in a haberdasher's; but because of his sunfilled and energetic week-ends, he gave the impression, at first glance, of being that burly young Colonial one sees on advertisements for Empire tobacco. He was thin, bony, muscular, sunburnt; he had the free and easy Colonial manner, the back-slapping air that is always just a little too conscious. "Look," it seems to say, "in this country we are all equal (among the whites, that is—that goes without saying) and I'll fight the first person who suggests anything to the contrary." Democracy, as it were, with one eye on the audience. But alas, he was still a clerk, and felt it; and if there was one class of person he detested it was the civil servant; and if there was another, it was the person new from "Home".

Here they were, united in one person, Marina Giles, wife of Philip Giles, soil expert for the Department of Lands and Afforestation, Marina, whose mere appearance acutely irritated him, every time he saw her moving delicately through the red dust, in her straw hat, white gloves, and touch-me-not manner.

"I say!" he said aggressively, his face flushed, his eyes hot. "I say, what are you going to do about it, because if you don't, I shall."

"I don't doubt it," said Marina precisely; "but I really fail to see why these people should not have a party, if they choose, particularly as it is not yet nine o'clock, and as far as I know there is no law to forbid them."

"Law!" said Mr Black violently. "Party! They're on our premises, aren't they? It's for us to say. Anyway, if I know anything they're visiting without passes."*

"I feel you are being unreasonable," said Marina, with the intention of sounding mildly persuasive; but in fact her voice had lifted to that fatally querulous high note, and her face was as angry and flushed as his.

"Unreasonable! My kids can't sleep with that din."

"It might help if you turned down your own wireless," said Marina sarcastically.

He lifted his fists, clenching them unconsciously, "You people . . ." he began inarticulately. "If you were a man, Mrs Giles, I tell you straight . . ." He dropped his fists and looked around widly as Mrs Pond entered, her face animated with delight in the scene.

"I see Mr Black is talking to you about your boy," she began, sugarily.

"And your boy too," said Mr Black.

"Oh, if I had a husband," said Mrs Pond, putting on an appearance of helpless womanhood, "February would have got what's coming to him long ago."

"For that matter," said Marina, speaking with difficulty because of her loathing for the whole thing, "I don't think you really find a husband necessary for this purpose, since it was only yesterday I saw you hitting February yourself . . ."

"He was cheeky," began Mrs Pond indignantly.

Marina found words had failed her; but none were necessary for Mr Black had gone striding out through her own bedroom, followed by Mrs Pond, and she saw the pair of them cross the shadowy yard to Charlie's room, which was still in darkness, though the music was at a crescendo. As Mr

* *passes*: native Africans may enter the white areas of towns only if they have specially issued passes.

Black shouted: "Come out of there, you black bastards!" the noise stopped, the door swung in, and half a dozen dark forms ducked under Mr Black's extended arm and vanished into the sanitary lane. There was a scuffle, and Mr Black found himself grasping, at arm's length, two people— Charlie and his own nursemaid, Theresa. He let the girl go and she ran after the others. He pushed Charlie against the wall. "What do you mean by making all that noise when I told you not to?" he shouted.

"That's right, that's right," gasped Mrs Pond from behind him, running this way and that around the pair so as to get a good view.

Charlie, keeping his elbow lifted to shield his head, said: "I'm sorry, baas, I'm sorry, I'm sorry . . ."

"Sorry!" Mr Black, keeping firm grasp of Charlie's shoulder, lifted his other hand to hit him; Charlie jerked his arm up over his face. Mr Black's fist, expecting to encounter a cheek, met instead the rising arm and he was thrown off balance and staggered back. "How dare you hit me," he shouted furiously, rushing at Charlie but Charlie had escaped in a bound over the rubbish-cans and away into the lane.

Mr Black sent angry shouts after him; then turned and said indignantly to Mrs Pond: "Did you see that? He hit me!"

"He's out of hand," said Mrs Pond in a melancholy voice. "What can you expect? He's been spoilt."

They both turned to look accusingly at Marina.

"As a matter of accuracy," said Marina breathlessly, "he did not hit you."

"What, are you taking that nigger's side?" demanded Mr Black. He was completely taken aback. He looked, amazed, at Mrs Pond and said: "She's taking his side!"

"It's not a question of sides," said Marina in that high, precise voice. "I was standing here and saw what happened. You know quite well he did not hit you. He wouldn't dare."

"Yes," said Mr Black, "that's what a state things have

come to, with the Government spoiling them, they can hit us and get away with it, and if we touch them we get fined."

"I don't know how many times I've seen the servants hit since I've been here," said Marina angrily. "If it is the law, it is a remarkably ineffective one."

"Well, I'm going to get the police," shouted Mr Black, running back to his own flat. "No black bastard is going to hit me and get away with it. Besides, they can all be fined for visiting without passes after nine at night . . ."

"Don't be childish," said Marina, and went inside her rooms. She was crying with rage. Happening to catch a glimpse of herself in the mirror as she passed it, she hastily went to splash cold water on her face, for she looked— there was no getting away from it—rather like a particularly genteel school-marm in a temper. When she reached the front room, she found Charlie there throwing terrified glances out into the verandah for fear of Mr Black or Mrs Pond.

"Madam," he said. "Madam, I didn't hit him."

"No, of course not," said Marina; and she was astonished to find that she was feeling irritated with him, Charlie. "Really," she said, "must you make such a noise and cause all this fuss."

"But, madam . . ."

"Oh, all right," she said crossly. "All right. But you aren't supposed to . . . who were all those people?"

"My friends."

"Where from?" He was silent. "Did they have passes to be out visiting?" He shifted his eyes uncomfortably. "Well, really," she said irritably, "if the law is that you have passes, for heaven's sake . . ." Charlie's whole appearance had changed; a moment before he had been a helpless small boy; he had become a sullen young man: this white woman was like all the rest.

Marina controlled her irritation and said gently: "Listen, Charlie, I don't agree with the law and all this nonsense about passes, but I can't change it, and it does seem to me . . ." Once again her irritation rose, once again she suppressed it, and found herself without words. Which was just as well, for Charlie was gazing at her with puzzled suspicion since he saw all white people as a sort of homogeneous mass, a white layer, as it were, spread over the mass of blacks, all concerned in making life as difficult as possible for him and his kind; the idea that a white person might not agree with passes, curfew, and so on was so outrageously new that he could not admit it to his mind at once. Marina said: "Oh, well, Charlie, I know you didn't mean it, and I think you'd better go quietly to bed and keep out of Mr Black's way, if you can."

"Yes, madam," he said submissively. As he went, she asked: "Does Theresa sleep in the same room as Mr Black's boy?"

He was silent. "Does she sleep in your room perhaps?" And, as the silence persisted: "Do you mean to tell me she sleeps with you and February?" No reply. "But Charlie . . ." She was about to protest again: But Theresa's nothing but a child; but this did not appear to be an argument which appealed to him.

There were loud voices outside, and Charlie shrank back: "The police!" he said, terrified.

"Ridiculous nonsense," said Marina. But looking out she saw a white policeman; and Charlie fled out through her bedroom and she heard the back door slam. It appeared he had no real confidence in her sympathy.

The policeman entered, alone. "I understand there's been a spot of trouble," he said.

"Over nothing," said Marina.

"A tenant in this building claims he was hit by your servant."

"It's not true. I saw the whole thing."

The policeman looked at her doubtfully and said: "Well, that makes things difficult, doesn't it?" After a moment he said; "Excuse me a moment," and went out. Marina saw him talking to Mr Black outside her front steps. Soon the policeman came back. "In view of your attitude the charge has been dropped," he said.

"So I should think. I've never heard of anything so silly."

"Well, Mrs Giles, there was a row going on, and they all ran away, so they must have had guilty consciences about something, probably no passes. And you know they can't have women in their rooms."

"The woman was Mr Black's own nursemaid."

"He says the girl is supposed to sleep in the location with her father."

"It's a pity Mr Black takes so little interest in his servants not to know. She sleeps here. How can a child that age be expected to walk five miles here every morning, to be here at seven, and walk five miles back at seven in the evening?"

The policeman gave her a look: "Plenty do it," he said. "It's not the same for them as it is for us. Besides, it's the law."

"The law!" said Marina bitterly.

Again the policeman looked uncertain. He was a pleasant young man, he dealt continually with cases of this kind, he always tried to smooth things over, if he could. He decided on his usual course despite Marina's hostile manner. "I think the best thing to do," he said, "is if we leave the whole thing. We'll never catch them now, anyway—miles away by this time. And Mr Black has dropped the charge. You have a talk to your boy and tell him to be careful. Otherwise he'll be getting himself into trouble."

"And what are you going to do about the nurse? It amounts to this: It's convenient for the Blacks to have her here, so they can go out at night, and so on, so they ask no questions. It's a damned disgrace, a girl of that age expected to share a room with the men."

"It's not right, not right at all," said the policeman. "I'll have a word with Mr Black." And he took his leave, politely.

That night Marina relieved her feelings by writing a long letter about the incident to a friend of hers in England, full of phrases such as "police state", "despotism", and "fascism"; which caused that friend to reply, rather tolerantly, to the effect that she understood these hot climates were rather upsetting and she did so hope Marina was looking after herself, one must have a sense of proportion, after all.

And, in fact, by the morning Marina was wondering why she had allowed herself to be so angry about such an absurd incident. What a country this was! Unless she was very careful she would find herself flying off into hysterical states as easily, for instance, as Mr Black. If one was going to make a life here, one should adjust oneself . . .

Charlie was grateful and apologetic. He repeated: "Thank you, madam. Thank you." He brought her a present of some vegetables and said: "You are my father and my mother." Marina was deeply touched. He rolled up his eyes and made a half-rueful joke: "The police are no good, madam." She discovered that he had spent the night in a friend's room some streets away for fear the police might come and take him to prison. For, in Charlie's mind, the police meant only one thing. Marina tried to explain that one wasn't put in prison without a trial of some sort; but he merely looked at her doubtfully, as if she were making fun of him. So she left it.

And Theresa? She was still working for the Blacks. A few evenings later, when Marina went to turn off the lights before going to bed, she saw Theresa gliding into Charlie's room. She said nothing about it: what could one expect?

Charlie had accepted her as an ally. One day, as he served vegetables, reaching behind her ducked head so that they might be presented, correctly, from the left, he remarked: "That Theresa, she very nice, madam."

"Very nice," said Marina, uncomfortably helping herself to peas from an acute angle, sideways.

"Theresa says, perhaps madam give her a dress?"

"I'll see what I can find," said Marina, after a pause.

"Thank you very much, thank you, madam," he said. He was grateful: but certainly he had expected just that reply: his thanks were not perfunctory, but he thanked her as one might thank one's parents, for instance, from whom one expects such goodness, even takes it a little for granted.

Next morning, when Marina and Philip lay as usual, trying to sleep through the cheerful din of cleaning from the next room, which included a shrill and sprightly whistling, there was a loud crash.

"Oh, damn the man," said Philip, turning over and pulling the clothes over his ears.

"With a bit of luck he's broken that picture," said Marina. She put a dressing-gown on, and went next door. On the floor lay fragments of white porcelain—her favourite vase, which she had brought all the way from England. Charlie was standing over it. "Sorry, madam," he said, cheerfully contrite.

Now that vase had stood on a shelf high above Charlie's head—to break it at all was something of an acrobatic feat . . . Marina pulled herself together. After all, it was only a vase. But her favourite vase, she had had it ten years: she stood there, tightening her lips over all the angry things she would have liked to say, looking at Charlie, who was carelessly sweeping the pieces together. He glanced up, saw her her face, and said hastily, really apologetic: "Sorry madam, very, very sorry, madam." Then he added reassuringly: "But the picture is all right." He gazed admiringly up at the highland cattle which he clearly considered the main treasure of the room.

"So it is," said Marina, suppressing the impulse to say: Charlie, if you break that picture I'll give you a present "Oh, well," she said. "I suppose it doesn't matter. Just sweep the pieces up."

"Yes, missus, thank you," said Charlie cheerfully; and she left, wondering how she had put herself in a position where it became impossible to be legitimately cross with her own servant. Coming back into that room some time later to ask Charlie why the breakfast was so late, she found him still standing under the picture. "Very nice picture," he said, reluctantly leaving the room. "Six oxes. Six fine big oxes, in one picture!"

The work in the flat was finished by mid-morning. Marina told Charlie she wanted to bake; he filled the old-fashioned stove with wood for her, heated the oven and went off into the yard, whistling. She stood at the window, mixing her cake, looking out into the yard.

Charlie came out of his room, sat down on a big log under the tree, stretched his legs before him, and propped a small mirror between his knees. He took a large metal comb and began to work on his thick hair, which he endeavoured to make lie flat, whiteman's fashion. He was sitting with his back to the yard.

Soon Theresa came out with a big enamel basin filled with washing. She wore the dress Marina had given her. It was an old black cocktail dress which hung loosely around her calves, and she had tied it at the waist with a big sash of printed cotton. The sophisticated dress, treated thus, hanging full and shapeless, looked grand motherly and old-fashioned; she looked like an impish child in a matron's grab. She stood beside the washing-line gazing at Charlie's back; then slowly she began pegging the clothes, with long intervals to watch him.

It seemed Charlie did not know she was there. Then his pose of concentrated self-worship froze into a long, close inspection in the mirror, which he began to rock gently between his knees so that the sunlight flashed up from it, first into the branches over his head, then over the dust of the yard to the girl's feet, up her body: the ray of light hovered like a butterfly around her, then settled on her face. She remained still, her eyes shut, with the teasing light flickering on her lids. Then she opened them and exclaimed, indignantly: "Hau!"

Charlie did not move. He held the mirror sideways on his knees, where he could see Theresa, and pretended to be hard at work on his parting. For a few seconds they remained thus, Charlie staring into the mirror, Theresa watching him reproachfully. Then he put the mirror back into his pocket, stretched his arms back in a magnificent slow yawn, and remained there, rocking back and forth on his log.

Theresa looked at him thoughtfully; and—since now he could not see her—darted over to the hedge, plucked a scarlet hibiscus flower, and returned to the washing-line, where she continued to hang the washing, the flower held lightly between her lips.

Charlie got up, his arms still locked behind his head, and began a sort of shuffle dance in the sunny dust, among the fallen leaves and chips of wood. It was a crisp, bright morning, the sky was as blue and fresh as the sea: this idyllic scene moved Marina deeply, it must be confessed.

Still dancing Charlie let his arms fall, turned himself round, and his hands began to move in time with his feet. Jerking, lolling, posing, he slowly approached the centre of the yard, apparently oblivious of Theresa's existence.

There was a shout from the back of the building: "Theresa!" Charlie glanced around, then dived hastily into his room. The girl, left alone, gazed at the dark door into which Charlie had vanished, sighed, and blinked gently at the sunlight. A second shout: "Theresa, are you going to be all day with that washing?"

She tucked the flower among the stiff quills of hair on her head and bent to the basin that stood in the dust. The washing flapped and billowed all around her, so that the small, wiry form appeared to be wrestling with the big, ungainly sheets. Charlie ducked out of his door and ran quickly up the hedge, out of sight of Mrs Black. He stopped, watching Theresa, who was still fighting with the washing. He whistled, she ignored him. He whistled again, changing key; the long note dissolved into a dance tune, and he sauntered deliberately up the hedge, weight shifting from hip to hip with each step. It was almost a dance: the buttocks sharply protruding and then withdrawn inwards after the prancing, lifting knees. The girl stood motionless, gazing at him, tantalized. She glanced quickly over her shoulder at the building, then ran across the yard to Charlie. The two of them, safe for the moment beside the hedge, looked guiltily for possible spies. They saw Marina behind her curtain—an earnest English face, apparently wrestling with some severe moral problem. But she was a friend. Had she not saved Charlie from the police? Besides, she immediately vanished.

Hidden behind the curtain, Marina saw the couple face each other, smiling. Then the girl tossed her head and turned away. She picked a second flower from the hedge, held it to her lips, and began swinging lightly from the waist, sending Charlie provocative glances over her shoulder that were half disdain and half invitation. To Marina it was as if a mischievous black urchin was playing the part of a coquette; but Charlie was watching with a broad and appreciative smile. He followed her, strolling in an assured and masterful way, and she went before him into his room. The door closed.

Marina discovered herself to be furious. Really the whole thing was preposterous!

"Philip," she said energetically that night, "we should do something."

"What?" asked Philip, practically. Marina could not think of a sensible answer. Philip gave a short lecture on the problems of the indigenous African peoples who were half-way between the tribal society and modern industrialization. The thing, of course, should be tackled at its root. Since he was a soil expert, the root, to him, was a sensible organization of the land. (If he had been a church-man, the root would have been a correct attitude to whichever God he happened to represent; if an authority on money, a mere adjustment of currency would have provided the solution—there is very little comfort from experts these days.) To Philip, it was all as clear as daylight. These people had no idea at all how to farm. They must give up this old attitude of theirs, based on the days when a tribe worked out one piece of ground and moved on to the next; they must learn to conserve their soil and, above all, to regard cattle, not as a sort of spiritual currency, but as an organic part of farm-work. (The word *organic* occurred very frequently in these lectures by Philip.) Once these things were done, everything else would follow . . .

"But in the meantime, Philip, it is quite possible that something may *happen* to Theresa, and she can't be more than fifteen, if that . . ."

Philip looked a little dazed as he adjusted himself from the level on which he had been thinking to the level of Theresa: women always think so personally! He said, rather stiffly: "Well, old girl, in periods of transition, what can one expect?"

What one might expect did in fact occur, and quite soon. One of those long ripples of gossip and delighted indignation passed from one end to the other of 138 Cecil John Rhodes Vista. Mrs Black's Theresa had got herself into trouble; these girls had no morals; no better than savages; besides, she was a thief. She was wearing clothes that had not been given to her by Mrs Black. Marina paid a formal visit to Mrs Black in order to say that she had given Theresa various dresses. The air was not at all cleared. No one cared to what degree Theresa had been corrupted, or by whom. The feeling was: if not Theresa, then someone else. Acts of theft, adultery, and so one were necessary to preserve the proper balanced between black and white; the balance was upset, not by Theresa, who played her allotted part, but by Marina, who insisted on introducing these Fabian* scruples into a clear-cut situation.

Mrs Black was polite, grudging, distrustful. She said: "Well, if you've given her the dresses, then it's all right." She added: "But it doesn't alter what she's done, does it now?" Marina could make no reply. The white women of the building continued to gossip and pass judgement some

Fabian: the name given early in this century to a group of English socialists who believed that they could best lead people to make society more equal by cautious persuasion, thought, and discussion. .

days: one must, after all, talk about something. It was odd, however, that Mrs Black made no move at all to sack Theresa, that immoral person, who continued to look after the children with her usual good-natured efficiency, in order that Mrs Black might have time to gossip and drink tea.

So Marina, who had already made plans to rescue Theresa when she was flung out of her job, found that no rescue was necessary. From time to time Mrs Black overflowed into reproaches, and lectures about sin. Theresa wept like the child she was, her fists stuck into her eyes. Five minutes afterwards she was helping Mrs Black bath the baby, or flirting with Charlie in the yard.

For the principals of this scandal seemed the least concerned about it. The days passed, and at last Marina said to Charlie: "Well and what are you going to do now?"

"Madam?" said Charlie. He really did not know what she meant. "About Theresa," said Marina sternly.

"Theresa she going to have a baby," said Charlie, trying to look penitent, but succeeding only in looking proud.

"It's all very well," said Marina. Charlie continued to sweep the verandah, smiling to himself. "But Charlie . . ." began Marina again.

"Madam?" said Charlie, resting on his broom and waiting for her to go on.

"You can't just let things go on, and what will happen to the child when it is born?"

His face puckered, he sighed, and finally he went on sweeping rather slower than before.

Suddenly Marina stamped her foot and said: "Charlie, this really won't do!" She was really furious.

"Madam!" said Charlie reproachfully.

"Everybody has a good time," said Marina. "You and Theresa enjoy yourselves, all these females have a lovely time, gossiping and the only thing no one ever thinks about is the baby." After a pause, when he did not reply, she went on: "I suppose you and Theresa think it's quite all right for the baby to be born here, and then you two, and the baby, and February, and all the rest of your friends who have nowhere to go, will all live together in that room. It really is shocking, Charlie."

Charlie shrugged as if to say: "Well, what do you suggest?"

"Can't Theresa go and live with her father?"

Charlie's face tightened into a scowl. "Theresa's father, he no good. Theresa must work, earn money for father."

"I see." Charlie waited; he seemed to be waiting for Marina to solve this problem for him; his attitude said: I have unbounded trust and confidence in you.

"Are any of the other men working here married?"

"Yes, madam."

"Where are their wives?"

"At home." This meant, in their kraals, in the native reserves. But Marina had not meant the properly married wives, who usually stayed with the clan, and were visited by their men perhaps one month in a year, or in two years. She meant women like Theresa, who lived in town.

"Now listen, Charlie. Do be sensible. What happens to girls like Theresa when they have babies. Where do they live?"

He shrugged again, meaning: They live as they can, and is it my fault the white people don't let us have our families with us when they work? Suddenly he said grudgingly: "The nannie next door, she has her baby, she works."

"Where is her baby?"

Charlie jerked his head over at the servants' quarters of the new house.

"Does the baas know she has her baby there?"

He looked away, uncomfortably. "Well, and what happens when the police find out?"

He gave her a look which she understood. "Who is the father of that baby?"

He looked away; there was an uncomfortable silence; and then he quickly began sweeping the verandah again.

"Charlie!" said Marina, outraged. His whole body had become defensive, sullen; his face was angry. She said energetically: "You should marry Theresa. You can't go on doing this sort of thing."

"I have a wife in my kraal," he said.

"Well, there's nothing to stop you having two wives, is there?"

Charlie pointed out that he had not yet finished paying for his first wife.

Marina thought for a moment. "Theresa's a Christian, isn't she? She was educated at the mission." Charlie shrugged. "If you marry Theresa Christian-fashion, you needn't pay lobola,* need you?"

Charlie said: "The Christians only like one wife. And Theresa's father, he wants lobola."

Marina found herself delighted. At any rate he had tried to marry Theresa, and this was evidence of proper feeling. The fact that whether the position was legalized or not the baby's future was still uncertain, did not at once strike her. She was carried away by moral approval. "Well, Charlie, that's much better," she said warmly.

He gave her a rather puzzled look and shrugged again.

"How much lobola does Theresa's father want for her?"

"Plenty. He wants ten cattle."

"What nonsense!" exclaimed Marina energetically. "Where does he suppose you are going to find cattle, working in town, and where's he going to keep them?"

This seemed to annoy Charlie. "In my kraal, I have fine cattle," he pointed out. "I have six fine oxes." He swept, for a while, in silence. "Theresa's father, he mad, he mad old man. I tell him I must give three oxes this year for my own wife. Where do I find ten oxes for Theresa?"

It appeared that Charlie, no more than Theresa's father, found nothing absurd about this desire for cattle on the part of an old man living in the town location. Involuntarily

---

* *Lobola*: the native word for the present which a young man would pay to the father of the woman he was going to marry. (See Doris Lessing's *Introduction* on page 3.)

she looked over her shoulder as if Philip might be listening: this conversation would have plunged him into irritated despair. Luckily he was away on one of his trips, and was at this moment almost certain to be exhorting the Africans, in some distant reserve, to abandon this irrational attitude to "fine oxen" which in fact were bound to be nothing but skin and bone, and churning whole tracts of country to dust.

"Why don't you offer Theresa's father some money?" she suggested, glancing down at Charlie's garters which were, this morning, of cherry-coloured silk.

"He wants cattle, not money. He wants Theresa not to marry, he wants her to work for him." Charlie rapidly finished sweeping the verandah and moved off, with relief, tucking the broom under his arm, with an apologetic smile which said: I know you mean well, but I'm glad to end this conversation.

But Marina was not at all inclined to drop the thing. She interviewed Theresa who, amid floods of tears, said Yes, she wanted to marry Charlie, but her father wanted too much lobola. The problem was quite simple to her, merely a question of lobola; Charlie's other wife did not concern her; nor did she, apparently, share Charlie's view that a proper wife in the kraal was one thing, while the women of the town were another.

Marina said: "Shall I come down to the location and talk to your father?"

Theresa hung her head shyly, allowed the last big tears to roll glistening down her cheeks and go splashing to the dust. "Yes, madam," she said gratefully.

Marina returned to Charlie and said she would interview the old man. He appeared restive at this suggestion. "I'll advance you some of your wages and you can pay for Theresa in instalments," she said. He glanced down at his fine shirt, his gay socks, and sighed. If he were going to spend years of life paying five shillings a month, which was all he could afford, for Theresa, then his life as a dandy was over.

Marina said crossly: "Yes, it's all very well, but you can't have it both ways."

He said hastily: "I'll go down and see the father of Theresa, madam. I go soon."

"I think you'd better," she said sternly.

When she told Philip this story he became vigorously indignant. It presented in little, he said, the whole problem of this society. The Government couldn't see an inch in front of its nose. In the first place, by allowing the lobola system to continue, this emotional attitude towards cattle was perpetuated. In the second by making no proper arrangements for these men to have their families in the towns it made the existence of prostitutes like Theresa inevitable.

"Theresa isn't a prostitute," said Marina indignantly. "It isn't her fault."

"Of course it isn't her fault, that's what I'm saying. But she will be a prostitute, it's inevitable. When Charlie's fed up with her she'll find herself another man and have a child or two by him, and so on . . ."

"You talk about Theresa as if she were a vital statistic," said Marina, and Philip shrugged. That shrug expressed an attitude of mind which Marina would very soon find herself sharing, but she did not yet know that. She was still very worried about Theresa, and after some days she asked Charlie: "Well, and did you see Theresa's father? What did he say?"

"He wants cattle."

"Well, he can't have cattle."

"No," said Charlie brightening. "My own wife, she cost six cattles. I paid three last year. I pay three more this year, when I go home."

"When are you going home?"

"When Mrs Skinner comes back. She no good. Not like you, madam, you are my father and mother," he said, giving her his touching, grateful smile.

"And what will happen to Theresa?"

"She stay here." After a long, troubled silence, he said: "She my town wife. I come back to Theresa." This idea seemed to cheer him up.

And it seemed he was genuinely fond of the girl. Looking out of the kitchen window, Marina could see the pair of them, during lulls in the work, seated side by side on the big log under the tree—charming! A charming picture! "It's all very well . . ." said Marina to herself, uneasily.

Some mornings later she found Charlie in the front room, under the picture, and looking at it this time, not with reverent admiration, but rather nervously. As she came in he quickly returned to his work, but Marina could see he wanted to say something to her.

"Madam . . ."

"Well, what is it?"

"This picture costs plenty money?"

"I suppose it did, once."

"Cattles cost plenty money, madam."

"Yes so they do, Charlie."

"If you sell this picture, how much?"

"But it is Mrs Skinner's picture."

His body drooped with disappointment. "Yes, madam," he said politely, turning away.

"But wait, Charlie—what do you want the picture for?"

"It's all right, madam," he was going out of the room.

"Stop a moment—why do you want it? You do want it, don't you?"

"Oh, yes," he said, his face lit with pleasure. He clasped his hands tight, looking at it. "Oh, yes, yes, madam!"

"What would you do with it? Keep it in your room?"

"I give it to Theresa's father."

"Wha-a-a-t?" said Marina. Slowly she absorbed this idea. "I see," she said. And then, after a pause: "I see . . ." She looked at his hopeful face, thought of Mrs Skinner, and said suddenly, filled with an undeniably spiteful delight: "I'll give it to you, Charlie."

"Madam!" exclaimed Charlie. He even gave a couple of involuntary little steps, like a dance. "Madam, thank you, thank you."

She was as pleased as he. For a moment they stood smiling delightedly at each other. "I'll tell Mrs Skinner that I broke it," she said. He went to the picture and lifted his hands gently to the great carved frame. "You must be careful not to break it before you get it to her father." He was staggering as he lifted it down. "Wait!" said Marina suddenly. Checking himself, he stood politely: she saw he expected her to change her mind and take back the gift. "You can carry that great thing all the way to the location. I'll take it for you in the car!"

"Madam," he said. "Madam . . ." Then, looking helplessly around him for something, someone he could share his joy with, he said: "I'll tell Theresa now . . ." And he ran from the room like a schoolboy.

Marina went to Mrs Black and asked that Theresa might have the afternoon off. "She had her afternoon off yesterday," said that lady sharply.

"She's going to marry Charlie," said Marina.

"She can marry him next Thursday, can't she?"

"No, because I'm taking them both down in the car to the location, to her father, and . . ."

Mrs Black said resentfully: "She should have asked me herself."

"It seems to me," said Marina in that high, acid voice, replying not to the words Mrs Black had used, but to what she had meant. "It seems to me that if one employs a child of fifteen, and under such conditions, the very least one can do is to assume the responsibility for her; and it seems to me quite extraordinary that you never have the slightest idea what she does, where she lives, or even that she is going to get married."

"You swallowed the dictionary?" said Mrs Black, with an ingratiating smile, "I'm not saying she shouldn't get married; she should have got married before, that's what I'm saying."

Marina returned to her flat, feeling Mrs Black's resentful eyes on her back: *Who the hell does she think she is, anyway?*

When Marina and Philip reached the lorry that afternoon that was waiting outside the gate, Theresa and Charlie were already sitting in the back, carefully balancing the picture on their knees. The two white people got in the front and Marina placed anxiously through the window and said to Philip: "Do drive carefully, dear, Theresa shouldn't be bumped around."

"I'd be doing her a favour if I did bump her," said Philip grimly. He was accompanying Marina unwillingly. "Well, I don't know what you think you're going to achieve by it . . ." he had said. However, here he was, looking rather cross.

They drove down the tree-lined, shady street, through the business area that was all concrete and modernity, past the slums where the half-caste people lived, past the factory sites, where smoke poured and hung, past the cemetery where angels and crosses gleamed white through the trees—they drove five miles, which was the distance Theresa had been expected to walk every morning and evening to her work. They turned off the main road into the location, and at once everything was quite different. No tarmac road, no avenues of beautiful trees here. Dust roads, dust paths, led from all directions inwards to the centre, where the housing area was. Dust lay thick and brown on the veld trees, the great blue sky was seen through a rust-coloured haze, dust gritted on the lips and tongue, and at once the lorry began to jolt and bounce. Marina looked back and saw Charlie and Theresa jerking and sliding with the lorry, under the great picture, clinging to each other for support, and laughing because of the joy-ride. It was the first time Theresa had ridden in a white man's car; and she was waving and calling shrill greetings to the groups of black children who ran after them.

They drove fast, bumping, so as to escape from the rivers of dust that spurted up from the wheels, making a whirling red cloud behind them, from which crowds of loitering Africans ran, cursing and angry. Soon they were in an area that was like a cheap copy of the white man's town; small houses stood in blocks, intersected by dust streets. They were two-roomed shacks with tin roofs, the sun blistering off them; and Marina said angrily: "Isn't it awful, isn't it terrible?"

Had she known that these same houses represented years of campaigning by the liberals of the city, against white public opinion, which obstinately held that houses for natives were merely another manifestation of that *Fabian* spirit from England which was spoiling the fine and un-corrupted savage, she might have been more respectful. Soon they left this new area and were among the sheds and barns that housed dozens of workers each, a state of affairs which caused Marina the acutest indignation. Another glance over her shoulder showed Theresa and Charlie giggling together like a couple of children as they tried to hold the picture still on their knees, for it slid this way and that as if it had a spiteful life of its own. "Ask Charlie where we must go," said Philip; and Marina tapped on the glass till Charlie turned his head and watched her gestures till he understood and pointed onwards with his thumb. More of these brick shacks, with throngs of Africans at their doors, who watched the car indifferently until they saw it was a Government car, and then their eyes grew wary, suspicious. And now, blocking their way, was a wire fence, and Marina looked back at Charlie for instructions, and he indicated they should stop. Philip pulled the lorry up against the fence and Charlie and Theresa jumped down from the back, came forwards and Charlie said apologetically: "Now we must walk, madam." The four went through a gap in the fence and saw a slope of soiled and matted grass that ended in a huddle of buildings on the banks of a small river.

Charlie pointed at it, and went ahead with Theresa. He held the picture on his shoulders, walking bent under it.

They passed through the grass, which smelled unpleasant and was covered by a haze of flies, and came to another expanse of dust, in which were scattered buildings—no, not buildings, shacks, extraordinary huts thrown together out of every conceivable substance, with walls perhaps of sacking, or of petrol boxes, roofs of beaten tin, or bits of scrap iron.

"And what happens when it rains?" said Marina, as they wound in and out of these dwellings, among scratching chickens and snarling native mongrels. She found herself profoundly dispirited, as if something inside her said: What's the use? For this area, officially, did not exist. The law was that all the workers, the servants should live inside the location, or in one of the similar townships. But there was never enough room. People overflowed into such make-shift villages everywhere, but as they were not supposed to be there the police might at any moment swoop down and arrest them. Admittedly the police did not often swoop, as the white man must have servants, the servants must live somewhere—and so it all went on, year after year. The Government, from time to time, planned a new housing estate. On paper, all around the white man's city, were fine new townships for the blacks. One had even been built, and to this critical visitors (usually those *Fabians* from overseas) were taken, and came away impressed. They never saw these slums. And so all the time, every day, the black people came from their reserves, their kraals, drawn to the white man's city, to the glitter of money, cinemas, fine clothes; they came in their thousands, no one knew how many, making their own life, as they could, in such hovels. It was all hopeless, as long as Mrs Black, Mr Black, Mrs Pond were the voters with the power; as long as the experts and administrators such as Philip had to work behind Mrs Pond's back—for nothing is more remarkable than that democratic phenomenon, so clearly shown in this continent, where members of Parliament, civil servants (experts, in short) spend half their time and energy earnestly exhorting Mrs Pond: For heaven's sake have some sense before it is too late; if you don't let us use enough money to house and feed these people, they'll rise and cut your throats. To which reasonable plea for self-preservation, Mrs Pond merely turns a sullen and angry stare, muttering: They're getting out of hand, that's what it is, they're getting spoilt.

In a mood of grim despair, Marina found herself standing with Philip in front of a small shack that consisted of sheets of corrugated iron laid loosely together, resting in the dust, like a child's card castle. It was bound at the corners with string, and big stones held the sheet of iron that served as roof from flying away in the first gust of wind.

"Here, madam," said Charlie. He thrust Theresa forward. She went shyly to the dark oblong that was the door, leaned inwards, and spoke some words in her own language. After a moment an old man stooped his way out. He was perhaps not so old—impossible to say. He was lean and tall, with a lined and angry face, and eyes that lifted under heavy lids to peer at Marina and Philip. Towards Charlie he directed a long, deadly stare, then turned away. He wore a pair of old khaki trousers, an old, filthy singlet that left his long, sinewed arms bare: all the bones and muscles of his neck and shoulders showed taut and knotted under the skin.

Theresa, smiling bashfully, indicated Philip and Marina; the old man offered some words of greeting; but he was angry, he did not want to see them, so the two white people fell back a little.

Charlie now came forward with the picture and leaned it gently against the iron of the shack in a way which said: "Here you are, and that's all you are going to get from me." In these surroundings those fierce Scottish cattle seemed to shrink a little. The picture that had dominated a room with its expanse of shining glass, its heavy carved frame, seemed not so enormous now. The cattle seemed even

rather absurd, shaggy creatures standing in their wet
sunset, glaring with a false challenge at the group of people.
The old man looked at the picture, and then said something
angry to Theresa. She seemed afraid, and came forward,
unknotting a piece of cloth that had lain in the folds at her
waist. She handed over some small change—about three
shillings in all. The old man took the money, shaking it
contemptuously in his hand before he slid it into his pocket.
Then he spat, showing contempt. Again he spoke to Theresa,
in short, angry sentences, and at the end he flung out his
arm, as if throwing something away; and she began to cry
and shrank back to Charlie. Charlie laid his hand on her
shoulder and pressed it; then left her standing alone and
went forward to his father-in-law. He smiled, spoke
persuasively, indicated Philip and Marina. The old man
listened without speaking, his eyes lowered. Those eyes
slid sideways to the big picture, a gleam came into them;
Charlie fell silent and they all looked at the picture.

The old man began to speak, in a different voice, sad, and
hopeless. He was telling how he had wooed his second wife,
Theresa's mother. He spoke of the long courting, according
to the old customs, how, with many gifts and courtesies
between the clans, the marriage had been agreed on, how the
cattle had been chosen, ten great cattle, heavy with good
grazing; he told how he had driven them to Theresa's
mother's family, carefully across the country, so that they
might not be tired and thinned by the journey. As he spoke
to the two young people he was reminding them, and himself, of that time when every action had its ritual, its
meaning; he was asking them to contrast their graceless
behaviour with the dignity of his own marriages, symbolized
by the cattle, which were not to be thought of in terms
of money, of simply buying a woman—not at all. They
meant so much: a sign of good feeling, a token of union
between the clans, an earnest that the woman would be
looked after, an acknowledgement that she was someone
very precious, whose departure would impoverish her

family—the cattle were all these things, and many more. The old man looked at Charlie and Theresa and seemed to say: "And what about you? What are you in comparison to what we were then?" Finally he spat again, lifted the picture and went into the dark of his hut. They could see him looking at the picture. He liked it: yes, he was pleased, in his way. But soon he left it leaning against the iron and returned to his former pose—he drew a blanket over his head and shoulders and squatted down inside the door, looking out, but not as if he still saw them or intended to make any further sign towards them.

The four were left standing there, in the dust, looking at each other.

Marina was feeling very foolish. Was that all? And Philip answered by saying brusquely, but uncomfortably: "Well, there's your wedding for you."

Theresa and Charlie had linked fingers and were together looking rather awkwardly at the white people. It was an awkward moment indeed—this was the end of it, the two were married, and it was Marina who had arranged the thing. What now?

But there was a more immediate problem. It was still early in the afternoon, the sun slanted overhead, with hours of light in it still, and presumably the newly-married couple would want to be together? Marina said: "Do you want to come back with us in the lorry, or would you rather come later?"

Charlie and Theresa spoke together in their own language, then Charlie said apologetically: "Thank you, madam, we stay."

"With Theresa's father?"

Charlie said: "He won't have Theresa now. He says Theresa can go away. He not want Theresa."

Philip said: "Don't worry, Marina, he'll take her back, he'll take her money all right." He laughed, and Marina was angry with him for laughing.

"He very cross, madam," said Charlie. He even laughed himself, but in a rather anxious way.

The old man still sat quite motionless, looking past them. There were flies at the corners of his eyes; he did not lift his hand to brush them off.

"Well..." said Marina. "We can give you a lift back if you like." But it was clear that Theresa was afraid of going back now; Mrs Black might assume her afternoon off was over and make her work.

Charlie and Theresa smiled again and said "Good-bye. Thank you, madam. Thank you, baas." They went slowly off across the dusty earth, between the hovels, towards the river, where a group of tall brick huts stood like outsize sentry-boxes. There, though neither Marina nor Philip knew it, was sold illicit liquor; there they would find a tinny gramophone playing dance music from America, there would be singing, dancing, a good time. This was the place the police came first if they were in search of criminals. Marina thought the couple were going down to the river, and she said sentimentally: "Well, they have this afternoon together, that's something."

"Yes," said Philip drily. The two were angry with each other, they did not know why. They walked in silence back to the lorry and drove home, making polite, clear sentences about indifferent topics.

Next day everything was as usual. Theresa back at work with Mrs Black, Charlie whistling cheerfully in their own flat.

Almost immediately Marina bought a house that seemed passable, about seven miles from the centre of town, in a new suburb. Mrs Skinner would not be returning for two weeks yet, but it was more convenient for them to move into the new home at once. The problem was Charlie. What would he do during that time? He said he was going home to visit his family. He had heard that his first wife had a new baby and he wanted to see it.

"Then I'll pay you your wages now," said Marina. She paid him, with ten shillings over. It was an uncomfortable moment. This man had been working for them for over two months, intimately, in their home; they had influenced each other's lives—and now he was off, he disappeared, the thing was finished. "Perhaps you'll come and work for me when you come back from your family?" said Marina.

Charlie was very pleased. "Oh, yes, madam," he said. "Mrs Skinner very bad, she no good, not like you." He gave a comical grimace, and laughed.

"I'll give you our address." Marina wrote it out and saw Charlie fold the piece of paper and place it carefully in an envelope which also held his official pass, a letter from her saying he was travelling to his family, and a further letter, for which he had asked, listing various bits of clothing that Philip had given him, for otherwise, as he explained, the police would catch him and say he had stolen them.

"Well, good-bye, Charlie," said Marina. I do so hope your wife and your new baby are all right." She thought of Theresa, but did not mention her; she found herself suffering from a curious disinclination to offer further advice or help. What would happen to Theresa? Would she simply move in with the first man who offered her shelter? Almost Marina shrugged.

"Good-bye, madam," said Charlie. He went off to buy himself a new shirt with the ten shillings, and some sweets for Theresa. He was sad to be leaving Theresa. On the other hand, he was looking forward to seeing his new child and his wife; he expected to be home after about a week's walking, perhaps sooner if he could get a lift.

But things did not turn out like this.

Mrs Skinner returned before she was expected. She found the flat locked and the key with Mrs Black. Everything was very clean and tidy, but—where was her favourite picture? At first she saw only the lightish square patch on the dimming paint—then she thought of Charlie. Where was he? No sign of him. She came back into the flat and found the letter Marina had left, enclosing eight pounds for the picture "which she had unfortunately broken". The thought came to Mrs Skinner that she would not have got ten shillings for that picture if she had tried to sell it; then the phrase "sentimental value" came to her rescue, and she was furious. Where was Charlie? For, looking about her, she saw various other articles were missing. Where was her yellow earthen vase? Where was the wooden door-knocker that said *Welcome Friend*? Where was . . . she went off to talk to Mrs Black, and quite soon all the women dropped in, and she was told many things about Marina. At last she said: "It serves me right for letting to an immigrant. I should have let it to you, dear." The dear in question was Mrs Pond. The ladies were again emotionally united; the long hostilities that had led to the flat being let to Marina were forgotten; that they were certain to break out again within a week was not to be admitted in this moment of pure friendship.

Mrs Pond told Mrs Skinner that she had seen the famous picture being loaded on to the lorry. Probably Mrs Giles had sold it—but this thought was checked, for both ladies knew what the picture was worth. No, Marina must have disposed of it in some way connected with her *Fabian* outlook—what could one expect from these white kaffirs?

Fuming, Mrs Skinner went to find Theresa. She saw Charlie, dressed to kill in his new clothes, who had come to say good-bye to Theresa before setting off on his long walk. She flew out, grabbed him by the arm, and dragged him into the flat. "Where's my picture?" she demanded.

At first Charlie denied all knowledge of the picture. Then he said Marina had given it to him. Mrs Skinner dropped his arm and stared: "But it was my picture . . ." She reflected rapidly: that eight pounds was going to be very useful; she had returned from her holiday, as people do, rather short of money. She exclaimed instead: "What have you done with my yellow vase? Where's my knocker?"

Charlie said he had not seen them. Finally Mrs Skinner fetched the police. The police found the missing articles in Charlie's bundle. Normally Mrs Skinner would have cuffed him and fined him five shillings. But there was this business of the picture—she told the police to take him off.

Now, in this city in the heart of what used to be known as the Dark Continent, at any hour of the day, women shopping, typists glancing up from their work out of the window, or the business men passing in their cars, may see (if they choose to look) a file of handcuffed Africans, with two policemen in front and two behind, followed by a straggling group of African women who are accompanying their men to the courts. These are the Africans who have been arrested for visiting without passes, or owning bicycles without lights, or being in possession of clothes or articles without being able to say how they came to own them. These Africans are being marched off to explain themselves to the magistrates. They are given a small fine with the option of prison. They usually choose prison. After all, to pay a ten shilling fine when one earns perhaps twenty or thirty a month, is no joke, and it is something to be fed and housed, free, for a fortnight. This is an arrangement satisfactory to everyone concerned, for these prisoners mend roads, cut down grass, plant trees: it is as good as having a pool of free labour.

Marina happened to be turning into a shop one morning, where she hoped to buy a table for her new house, and saw, without really seeing them, a file of such handcuffed Africans passing her. They were talking and laughing among themselves, and with the black policemen who herded them, and called back loud and jocular remarks at their women. In Marina's mind the vision of that ideal table (for which she had been searching for some days, without success) was rather stronger than what she actually saw; and it was not until the prisoners had passed that she suddenly said to herself: "Good heavens, that man looks rather like Charlie— and that girl behind there, the plump girl with the spindly legs, there was something about the back view of that girl that was very like Theresa . . ." The file had in the meantime turned a corner and was out of sight. For a moment Marina thought: Perhaps I should follow and see? Then she thought: Nonsense, I'm seeing things, of course it can't be Charlie, he must have reached home by now . . . And she . . . went into the shop to buy her table.

The Second Hut

Before that season and his wife's illness, he had thought things could get no worse: until then, poverty had meant not to deviate further than snapping point from what he had been brought up to think of as a normal life.

Being a farmer (he had come to it late in life, in his forties) was the first test he had faced as an individual. Before he had always been supported, invisibly perhaps, but none the less strongly, by what his family expected of him. He had been a regular soldier, not an unsuccessful one, but his success had been at the cost of a continual straining against his own inclinations; and he did not know himself what his inclinations were. Something stubbornly un-conforming kept him apart from his fellow officers. It was an inward difference: he did not think of himself as a soldier. Even in his appearance, square, close-bitten, disciplined, there had been a hint of softness, or of strain, showing itself in his smile, which was too quick, like the smile of a deaf person afraid of showing incomprehension, and in the anxious look of his eyes. After he left the army he quickly slackened into an almost slovenly carelessness of dress and carriage. Now, in his farm clothes there was nothing left to suggest the soldier. With a loose, stained felt hat on the back of his head, khaki shorts a little too long and too wide, sleeves flapping over spare brown arms, his wispy moustache hiding a strained, set mouth, Major Carruthers looked what he was, a gentleman farmer going to seed.

The house had that brave, worn appearance of those struggling to keep up appearances. It was a four-roomed shack, its red roof dulling to streaky brown. It was the sort of house an apprentice farmer builds as a temporary shelter till he can afford better. Inside, good but battered furniture stood over worn places in the rugs; the piano was out of tune and the notes stuck; the silver tea things from the big narrow house in England where his brother (a lawyer) now lived were used as ornaments, and inside were bits of paper, accounts, rubber rings, old corks.

The room where his wife lay, in a greenish sun-lanced gloom, was a place of seedy misery. The doctor said it was her heart; and Major Carruthers knew this was true: she had broken down through heart-break over the conditions they lived in. She did not want to get better. The harsh light from outside was shut out with dark blinds, and she turned her face to the wall and lay there, hour after hour, inert and uncomplaining, in a stoicism of defeat nothing could penetrate. Even the children hardly moved her. It was as if she had said to herself: "If I cannot have what I wanted for them, then I wash my hands of life."

Sometimes Major Carruthers thought of her as she had been, and was filled with uneasy wonder and with guilt. That pleasant conventional pretty English girl had been bred to make a perfect wife for the professional soldier she had imagined him to be, but chance had wrenched her on to this isolated African farm, into a life which she submitted herself to, as if it had nothing to do with her. For the first few years she had faced the struggle humorously, courageously: it was a sprightly attitude towards life, almost flirtatious, as a woman flirts lightly with a man who means nothing to her. As the house grew shabby, and the furniture, and her clothes could not be replaced; when she looked into the mirror and saw her drying, untidy hair and roughening face, she would give a quick high laugh and say, "Dear me, the things one comes to!" She was facing this poverty as she would have faced, in England, poverty of a narrowing, but socially accepted kind. What she could not face was a different kind of fear; and Major Carruthers understood that too well, for it was now his own fear.

The two children were pale, fine-drawn creatures, almost transparent-looking in their thin nervous fairness, with the defensive and wary manners of the young who have been brought up to expect a better way of life than they enjoy.

Their anxious solicitude wore on Major Carruthers'
already over-sensitized nerves. Children had no right to
feel the aching pity which showed on their faces whenever
they looked at him. They were too polite, too careful, too
scrupulous. When they went into their mother's room she
grieved sorrowfully over them, and they submitted patiently
to her emotion. All those weeks of the school holidays
after she was taken ill, they moved about the farm like two
strained and anxious ghosts, and whenever he saw them his
sense of guilt throbbed like a wound. He was glad they were
going back to school soon, for then—so he thought—it
would be easier to manage. It was an intolerable strain,
running the farm and coming back to the neglected house
and the problems of food and clothing, and a sick wife who
would not get better until he could offer her hope.

But when they had gone back, he found that after all,
things were not much easier. He slept little, for his wife
needed attention in the night; and he became afraid for his
own health, worrying over what he ate and wore. He learnt
to treat himself as if his health was not what he was, what
made him, but something apart, a commodity like efficiency,
which could be estimated in terms of money at the end of a
season. His health stood between them and complete ruin;
and soon there were medicine bottles beside his bed, as
well as beside his wife's.

One day, while he was carefully measuring out tonics
for himself in the bedroom, he glanced up and saw his
wife's small reddened eyes staring incredulously but
ironically at him over the bedclothes. "What are you
doing?" she asked.

"I need a tonic," he explained awkwardly, afraid to
worry her by explanations.

She laughed, for the first time in weeks; then the slack
tears began welling under the lids, and she turned to the
wall again.

He understood that some vision of himself had been

destroyed, finally, for her. Now she was left with an ageing, rather fussy gentleman, carefully measuring medicine after meals. But he did not blame her; he never had blamed her; not even though he knew her illness was a failure of will. He patted her cheek uncomfortably, and said: "It wouldn't do for me to get run down, would it?" Then he adjusted the curtains over the windows to shut out a streak of dancing light that threatened to fall over her face, set a glass nearer to her hand, and went out to arrange for her tray of slops to be carried in.

Then he took, in one swift, painful movement, as if he were leaping over an obstacle, the decision he had known for weeks he must take sooner or later. With a straightening of his shoulders, an echo from his soldier past, he took on the strain of an extra burden: he must get an assistant, whether he liked it or not.

So much did he shrink from any self-exposure, that he did not even consider advertising. He sent a note by native bearer to his neighbour, a few miles off, asking that it should be spread abroad that he was wanting help. He knew he would not have to wait long. It was 1931, in the middle of a slump, and there was unemployment, which was a rare thing for this new, sparsely-populated country.

He wrote the following to his two sons at boarding-school:

I expect you will be surprised to hear I'm getting another man on the place. Things are getting a bit too much, and as I plan to plant a bigger acreage of maize this year, I thought it would need two of us. Your mother is better this week, on the whole, so I think things are looking up. She is looking forward to your next holidays, and asks me to say she will write soon. Between you and me, I don't think she's up to writing at the moment. It will soon be getting cold, I think, so if you need any clothes, let me know, and I'll see what I can do . . .

A week later, he sat on the little verandah, towards evening, smoking, when he saw a man coming through the trees on a bicycle. He watched him closely, already trying to form an estimate of his character by the tests he had used all his life: the width between the eyes, the shape of the skull, the way the legs were set on to the body. Although he had been taken in a dozen times, his belief in these methods never wavered. He was an easy prey for any trickster, lending money he never saw again, taken in by professional adventurers who (it seemed to him, measuring others by his own decency and the quick warmth he felt towards people) were the essence of gentlemen. He used to say that being a gentleman was a question of instinct: one could not mistake a gentleman.

As the visitor stepped off his bicycle and wheeled it to the verandah, Major Carruthers saw he was young, thirty perhaps, sturdily built, with enormous strength in the thick arms and shoulders. His skin was burnt a healthy orange-brown colour. His close hair, smooth as the fur of an animal, reflected no light. His obtuse, generous features were set in a round face, and the eyes were pale grey, nearly colourless.

Major Carruthers instinctively dropped his standards of value as he looked, for this man was an Afrikander, and thus came into an outside category. It was not that he disliked him for it, although his father had been killed in the Boer War, but he had never had anything to do with the Afrikaans people before, and his knowledge of them was hearsay, from Englishmen who had the old prejudice. But he liked the look of the man: he liked the honest and straightforward face.

As for Van Heerden, he immediately recognized his traditional enemy, and his inherited dislike was strong. For a moment he appeared obstinate and wary. But they needed each other too badly to nurse old hatreds, and Van Heerden sat down when he was asked, though awkwardly, suppressing reluctance, and began drawing patterns in the dust with a piece of straw he had held between his lips.

Major Carruthers did not need to wonder about the man's circumstances: his quick acceptance of what were poor terms spoke of a long search for work.

He said scrupulously: "I know the salary is low and the living quarters are bad, even for a single man. I've had a patch of bad luck, and I can't afford more. I'll quite understand if you refuse."

"What are the living quarters?" asked Van Heerden. His was the rough voice of the uneducated Afrikander: because he was uncertain where the accent should fall in each sentence, his speech had a wavering, halting sound, though his look and manner were direct enough.

Major Carruthers pointed ahead of them. Before the house the bush sloped gently down to the fields. "At the foot of the hill there's a hut I've been using as a storehouse. It's quite well-built. You can put up a place for a kitchen"

Van Heerden rose. "Can I see it?"

They set off. It was not far away. The thatched hut stood in uncleared bush. Grass grew to the walls and reached up to meet the slanting thatch. Trees mingled their branches overhead. It was round, built of poles and mud and with a stamped dung floor. Inside there was a stale musty smell because of the ants and beetles that had been at the sacks of grain. The one window was boarded over, and it was quite dark. In the confusing shafts of light from the door, a thick sheet of felted spider web showed itself, like a curtain halving the interior, as full of small flies and insects as a butcher-bird's cache. The spider crouched, vast and glittering, shaking gently, glaring at them with small red eyes, from the centre of the web. Van Heerden did what Major Carruthers would have died rather than do: he tore the web across with his bare hands, crushed the spider between his fingers, and brushed them lightly against the walls to free them from the clinging silky strands and the sticky mush of insect-body.

"It will do fine," he announced.

He would not accept the invitation to a meal, thus making it clear this was merely a business arrangement. But he asked, politely (hating that he had to beg a favour), for a month's salary in advance. Then he set off on his bicycle to the store, ten miles off, to buy what he needed for his living.

Major Carruthers went back to his sick wife with a burdened feeling, caused by his being responsible for another human being having to suffer such conditions. He could not have the man in the house: the idea came into his head and was quickly dismissed. They had nothing in common, they would make each other uncomfortable—that was how he put it to himself. Besides, there wasn't really any room. Underneath, Major Carruthers knew that if his new assistant had been an Englishman, with the same upbringing, he would have found a corner in his house and a welcome as a friend. Major Carruthers threw off these thoughts: he had enough to worry him without taking on another man's problems.

A person who had always hated the business of organization, which meant dividing responsibility with others, he found it hard to arrange with Van Heerden how the work was to be done. But as the Dutchman was good with cattle, Major Carruthers handed over all the stock on the farm to his care, thus relieving his mind of its most nagging care, for he was useless with beasts, and knew it. So they began, each knowing exactly where they stood. Van Heerden would make laconic reports at the end of each week, in the manner of an expert foreman reporting to a boss ignorant of technicalities—and Major Carruthers accepted this attitude, for he liked to respect people, and it was easy to respect Van Heerden's inspired instinct for animals.

For a few weeks Major Carruthers was almost happy. The fear of having to apply for another loan to his brother—worse, asking for the passage money to England and a job, thus justifying his family's belief in him as a failure, was pushed away; for while taking on a manager did not in itsef improve things, it was an action, a decision, and there was nothing that he found more dismaying than decisions. The thought of his family in England, and particularly his elder brother, pricked him into slow burning passions of resentment. His brother's letters galled him so that he had grown to hate mail-days. They were crisp, affectionate letters, without condesension, but about money, bank-drafts, and insurance policies. Major Carruthers did not see life like that. He had not written to his brother for over a year. His wife, when she was well, wrote once a week, in the spirit of one propitiating fate.

Even she seemed cheered by the manager's coming; she sensed her husband's irrational lightness of spirit during that short time. She stirred herself to ask about the farm; and he began to see that her interest in living would revive quickly if her sort of life came within reach again.

But some two months after Van Heerden's coming, Major Carruthers was walking along the farm road towards his lands, when he was astonished to see, disappearing into the bushes, a small flaxen-haired boy. He called, but the child froze as an animal freezes, flattening himself against the foliage. At last, since he could get no reply, Major Carruthers approached the child, who dissolved backwards through the trees, and followed him up the path to the hut. He was very angry, for he knew what he would see.

He had not been to the hut since he handed it over to Van Heerden. Now there was a clearing, and amongst the stumps of trees and the flattened grass, were half a dozen children, each as tow-headed as the first, with that bleached sapless look common to white children in the tropics who have been subjected to too much sun.

A lean-to had been built against the hut. It was merely a roof of beaten petrol tins, patched together like cloth with wire and nails and supported on two unpeeled sticks. There, holding a cooking pot over an open fire that was dangerously close to the thatch, stood a vast slatternly woman. She reminded him of a sow among her litter, as she lifted her head, the children crowding about her, and stared at him suspiciously from pale and white-lashed eyes.

"Where is your husband?" he demanded.

She did not answer. Her suspicion deepened into a glare of hate: clearly she knew no English.

Striding furiously to the door of the hut, he saw that it was crowded with two enormous native-style beds: strips of hide stretched over wooden poles embedded in the mud of the floor. What was left of the space was heaped with the stained and broken belongings of the family. Major Carruthers strode off in search of Van Heerden. His anger was now mingled with the shamed discomfort of trying to imagine what it must be to live in such squalor.

Fear rose high in him. For a few moments he inhabited the landscape of his dreams, a grey country full of sucking menace, where he suffered what he would not allow himself to think of while awake: the grim poverty that could overtake him if his luck did not turn, and if he refused to submit to his brother and return to England.

Walking through the fields, where the maize was now waving over his head, pale gold with a froth of white, the sharp dead leaves scything crisply against the wind, he could see nothing but that black foetid hut and the pathetic futureless children. That was the lowest he could bring his own children to! He felt moorless, helpless, afraid: his sweat ran cold on him. And he did not hesitate in his mind; driven by fear and anger, he told himself to be hard; he was searching in his mind for the words with which he would dismiss the Dutchman who had brought his worst nightmares to life, on his own farm, in glaring daylight, where they were inescapable.

He found him with a screaming rearing young ox that was being broken to the plough, handling it with his sure understanding of animals. At a cautious distance stood the natives who were assisting; but Van Heerden, fearless and purposeful, was fighting the beast at close range. He saw

Major Carruthers, let go the plunging horn he held, and the ox shot away backwards, roaring with anger, into the crowd of natives, who gathered loosely about it with sticks and stones to prevent it running away altogether.

Van Heerden stood still, wiping the sweat off his face, still grinning with the satisfaction of the fight, waiting for his employer to speak.

"Van Heerden," said Major Carruthers, without preliminaries, "why didn't you tell me you had a family?"

As he spoke the Dutchman's face changed, first flushing into guilt, then setting hard and stubborn. "Because I've been out of work for a year, and I knew you would not take me if I told you."

The two men faced each other, Major Carruthers tall, fly-away, shambling, bent with responsibility; Van Heerden stiff and defiant. The natives remained about the ox, to prevent its escape—for them this was a brief intermission in the real work of the farm—and their shouts mingled with the incessant bellowing. It was a hot day; Van Heerden wiped the sweat from his eyes with the back of his hand.

"You can't keep a wife and all those children here—how many children?"

"Nine."

Major Carruthers thought of his own two, and his perpetual dull ache of worry over them; and his heart became grieved for Van Heerden. Two children, with all the trouble over everything they ate and wore and thought, and what would become of them, were too great a burden; how did this man, with nine, manage to look so young?

"How old are you?" he asked abruptly, in a different tone.

"Thirty-four," said Van Heerden, suspiciously, unable to understand the direction Major Carruthers followed.

The only marks on his face were sun-creases; it was impossible to think of him as the father of nine children and the husband of that terrible broken-down woman. As Major

Carruthers gazed at him, he became conscious of the strained lines on his own face, and tried to loosen himself, because he took so badly what this man bore so well.

"You can't keep a wife and children in such conditions."

"We were living in a tent in the bush on mealie meal and what I shot for nine months, and that was through the wet season," said Van Heerden drily.

Major Carruthers knew he was beaten. "You've put me in a false position, Van Heerden," he said angrily. "You know I can't afford to give you more money. I don't know where I'm going to find my own children's school fees, as it is. I told you the position when you came. I can't afford to keep a man with such a family."

"Nobody can afford to have me either," said Van Heerden sullenly.

"How can I have you living on my place in such a fasion? Nine children! They should be at school. Didn't you know there is a law to make them go to school? Hasn't anybody been to see you about them?"

"They haven't got me yet. They won't get me unless some-one tells them."

Against this challenge, which was also unwilling appeal, Major Carruthers remained silent, until he said brusquely:

"Remember, I'm not responsible." And he walked off, with all the appearance of anger.

Van Heerden looked after him, his face puzzled. He did not know whether or not he had been dismissed. After a few moments he moistened his dry lips with his tongue, wiped his hand again over his eyes, and turned back to the ox. Looking over his shoulder from the edge of the field, Major Carruthers could see his wiry, stocky figure leaping and bending about the ox whose bellowing made the whole farm ring with anger.

Major Carruthers decided, once and for all, to put the family out of his mind. But they haunted him; he even dreamed of them; and he could not determine whether it was his own or the Dutchman's children who filled his sleep with fear.

It was a very busy time of the year. Harassed, like all his fellow-farmers, by labour difficulties, apportioning out the farm tasks was a daily problem. All day his mind churned slowly over the necessities: this fencing was urgent, that field must be reaped at once. Yet, in spite of this, he decided it was his plain duty to built a second hut beside the first. It would do no more than take the edge off the discomfort of that miserable family, but he knew he could not rest until it was built.

Just as he had made up his mind and was wondering how the thing could be managed, the bossboy came to him, saying that unless the Dutchman went, he and his friends would leave the farm.

"Why?" asked Major Carruthers, knowing what the answer would be. Van Heerden was a hard worker, and the cattle were improving week by week under his care, but he could not handle natives. He shouted at them, lost his temper, treated them like dogs. There was continual friction.

"Dutchmen are no good," said the bossboy simply, voicing the hatred of the black man for that section of the white people he considers his most brutal oppressors.

Now, Major Carruthers was proud that at a time when most farmers were forced to buy labour from the contractors, he was able to attract sufficient voluntary labour to run his farm. He was a good employer, proud of his reputation for fair dealing. Many of his natives had been with him for years, taking a few months off occasionally for a rest in their kraals, but always returning to him. His neighbours were complaining of the sullen attitude of their labourers: so far Major Carruthers had kept this side of that form of passive resistance which could ruin a farmer. It was walking on a knife-edge, but his simple human relationship with his workers was his greatest asset as a farmer, and he knew it.

He stood and thought, while his bossboy, who had been on this farm twelve years, waited for a reply. A great deal was at stake. For a moment Major Carruthers thought of dismissing the Dutchman; he realized he could not bring himself to do it: what would happen to all those children? He decided on a course which was repugnant to him. He was going to appeal to his employee's pity.

"I have always treated you square?" he asked. "I've always helped you when you were in trouble?"

The bossboy immediately and warmly assented.

"You know that my wife is ill, and that I'm having a lot of trouble just now? I don't want the Dutchman to go, just now when the work is so heavy. I'll speak to him, and if there is any more trouble with the men, then come to me and I'll deal with it myself."

It was a glittering blue day, with a chill edge on the air, that stirred Major Carruthers' thin blood as he stood, looking in appeal into the sullen face of the native. All at once, feeling the fresh air wash along his cheeks, watching the leaves shake with a ripple of gold on the trees down the slope, he felt superior to his difficulties, and able to face anything. "Come," he said, with his rare, diffident smile. "After all these years, when we have been working together for so long, surely you can do this for me. It won't be for very long."

He watched the man's face soften in response to his own; and wondered at the unconscious use of the last phrase, for there was no reason, on the face of things, why the situation should not continue as it was for a very long time.

They began laughing together; and separated cheerfully; the African shaking his head ruefully over the magnitude of the sacrifice asked of him, thus making the incident into a joke; and he dived off into the bush to explain the position to his fellow-workers.

Repressing a strong desire to go after him, to spend the lovely fresh day walking for pleasure, Major Carruthers went into his wife's bedroom, inexplicably confident and walking like a young man.

She lay as always, face to the wall, her protruding shoulders visible beneath the cheap pink bed-jacket he had bought for her illness. She seemed neither better nor worse. But as she turned her head, his buoyancy infected her a little; perhaps, too, she was conscious of the exhilarating day outside her gloomy curtains.

What kind of a miraculous release was she waiting for? he wondered, as he delicately adjusted her sheets and pillows and laid his hand gently on her head. Over the bony cage of the skull, the skin was papery and blueish. What was she thinking? He had a vision of her brain as a small frightened animal pulsating under his fingers.

With her eyes still closed, she asked in her querulous thin voice: "Why don't you write to George?"

Involuntarily his fingers contracted on her hair, causing her to start and to open her reproachful, red-rimmed eyes. He waited for her usual appeal: the children, my health, our future. But she sighed and remained silent, still loyal to the man she had imagined she was marrying; and he could feel her thinking: *the lunatic stiff pride of men.*

Understanding that for her it was merely a question of waiting for his defeat, as her deliverance, he withdrew his hand, in dislike of her, saying: "Things are not as bad as that yet." The cheerfulness of his voice was genuine, holding still the courage and hope instilled into him by the bright day outside.

"Why, what has happened?" she asked swiftly, her voice suddenly strong, looking at him in hope.

"Nothing," he said; and the depression settled down over him again. Indeed, nothing had happened; and his confidence was a trick of the nerves. Soberly he left the bedroom, thinking: I must get that well built; and when that is done, I must do the drains and then ... He was thinking, too, that all these things must wait for the second hut.

Oddly, the comparatively small problem of that hut occupied his mind during the next few days. A slow and careful man, he set milestones for himself and overtook them one by one.

Since Christmas the labourers had been working a seven-day week, in order to keep ahead in the race aganst the weeds. They resented it, of course, but that was the custom. Now that the maize was grown, they expected work to slack off, they expected their Sundays to be restored to them. To ask even half a dozen of them to sacrifice their weekly holiday for the sake of the hated Dutchman might precipitate a crisis. Major Carruthers took his time, stalking his opportunity like a hunter, until one evening he was talking with his bossboy as man to man, about farm problems; but when he broached the subject of a hut, Major Carruthers saw that it would be as he feared: the man at once turned stiff and unhelpful. Suddenly impatient, he said: "It must be done next Sunday. Six men could finish it in a day, if they worked hard."

The black man's glance became veiled and hostile. Responding to the authority in the voice he replied simply: "Yes, baas." He was accepting the order from above, and refusing responsibility: his co-operation was switched off; he had become a machine for transmitting orders. Nothing exasperated Major Carruthers more than when this happened. He said sternly: 'I'm not having any nonsense. If that hut isn't built, there'll be trouble."

"Yes, baas," said the bossboy again. He walked away, stopped some natives who were coming off the fields with their hoes over their shoulders, and transmitted the order in a neutral voice. Major Carruthers saw them glance at him in fierce antagonism; then they turned away their heads, and walked off, in a group, towards their compound.

It would be all right, he thought, in disproportionate relief. It would be difficult to say exactly what it was he feared, for the question of the hut had loomed so huge in his mind that he was beginning to feel an almost super-

stitious foreboding. Driven downwards through failure
after failure, fate was becoming real to him as a cold malig-
nant force; the careful balancing of unfriendly probabili-
ties that underlay all his planning had developed in him
an acute sensitivity to the future; and he had learned to
respect his dreams and omens. Now he wondered at the
strength of his desire to see that hut built, and whatever
danger it represented behind him.

He went to the clearing to find Van Heerden and tell him
what had been planned. He found him sitting on a candle-
box in the doorway of the hut, playing good-humouredly
with his children, as if they had been puppies, tumbling
them over, snapping his fingers in their faces, and laughing
outright with boyish exuberance when one little boy squared
up his fists at him in a moment of temper against this casual,
almost contemptuous treatment of them. Major Carruthers
heard that boyish laugh with amazement; he looked blankly
at the young Dutchman, and then from him to his wife,
who was standing, as usual, over a petrol tin that balanced
on the small fire. A smell of meat and pumpkin filled the
clearing. The woman seemed to Major Carruthers less a
human being than the expression of an elemental, irrepres-
sible force: he saw her, in her vast sagging fleshiness, with
her slow stupid face, her instinctive responses to her children, whether for affection or temper, as the symbol of
fecundity, a strong, irresistible heave of matter. She frightened him. He turned his eyes from her and explained to Van
Heerden that a second hut would be built here, beside the
existing one.

Van Heerden was pleased. He softened into quick con-
fiding friendship. He looked doubtfully behind him at the
small hut that sheltered eleven human beings, and said that
it was really not easy to live in such a small space with so
many children. He glanced at the children, cuffing them
affectionately as he spoke, smiling like a boy. He was proud
of his family, of his own capacity for making children:
Major Carruthers could see that. Almost, he smiled; then

he glanced through the doorway at the grey squalor of the interior and hurried off, resolutely preventing himself from dwelling on the repulsive facts that such close-packed living implied.

The next Saturday evening he and Van Heerden paced the clearing with tape measure and spirit level, determining the area of the new hut. It was to be a large one. Already the sheaves of thatching grass had been stacked ready for next day, shining brassily in the evening sun; and the thorn poles for the walls lay about the clearing, stripped of bark, the smooth inner wood showing white as kernels.

Major Carruthers was waiting for the natives to come up from the compound for the building before daybreak that Sunday. He was there even before the family woke, afraid that without his presence something might go wrong. He feared the Dutchman's temper because of the labourers' sulky mood.

He leaned against a tree, watching the bush come awake, while the sky flooded slowly with light, and the birds sang about him. The hut was, for a long time, silent and dark. A sack hung crookedly over the door, and he could glimpse huddled shapes within. It seemed to him horrible, a stinking kennel shrinking ashamedly to the ground away from the wide hall of fresh blue sky. Then a child came out, and another; soon they were spilling out of the doorway, in their little rags of dresses, or hitching khaki pants up over the bony jut of a hip. They smiled shyly at him, offering him friendship. Then came the woman, moving sideways to ease herself through the narrow door-frame—she was so huge it was almost a fit. She lumbered slowly, thick and stupid with sleep, over to the cold fire, raising her arms in a yawn, so that wisps of dull yellow hair fell over her shoulders and her dark slack dress lifted in creases under her neck. Then she saw Major Carruthers and smiled at him. For the first time he saw her as a human being and not as something fatally ugly. There was something shy, yet frank, in that smile; so that he could imagine the strong, laughing adolescent girl, with the frank, inviting, healthy sensuality of the young Dutchwoman—so she had been when she married Van Heerden. She stooped painfully to stir up the ashes, and soon the fire spurted up under the leaning patch of tin roof. For a while Van Heerden did not appear; neither did the natives who were supposed to be here a long while since; Major Carruthers continued to lean against a tree, smiling at the children, who nevertheless kept their distance from him unable to play naturally because of his presence there, smiling at Mrs Van Heerden who was throwing handfuls of mealie meal into a petrol tin of boiling water, to make native-style porridge.

It was just on eight o'clock, after two hours of impatient waiting, that the labourers filed up the bushy incline, with the axes and picks over their shoulders, avoiding his eyes. He pressed down his anger: after all it was Sunday, and they had had no day off for weeks; he could not blame them.

They began by digging the circular trench that would hold the wall poles. As their picks rang out on the pebbly ground, Van Heerden came out of the hut, pushing aside the dangling sack with one hand and pulling up his trousers with the other, yawning broadly, then smiling at Major Carruthers apologetically. "I've had my sleep out," he said; he seemed to think his employer might be angry.

Major Carruthers stood close over the workers, wanting it to be understood by them and by Van Heerden that he was responsible. He was too conscious of their resentment, and knew that they would scamp the work if possible. If the hut was to be completed as planned, he would need all his tact and good-humour. He stood there patiently all morning, watching the thin sparks flash up as the picks swung into the flinty earth. Van Heerden lingered nearby, unwilling to be thus publicly superseded in the responsibility for his own dwelling in the eyes of the natives.

When they flung their picks and went to fetch the poles, they did so with a side glance at Major Carruthers, challenging him to say the trench was not deep enough. He called them back, laughingly, saying: "Are you digging for a dog-kennel then, and not a hut for a man?" One smiled un-willingly in response; the others sulked. Perfunctorily they deepened the trench to the very minimum that Major Carruthers was likely to pass. By noon, the poles were leaning drunkenly in place, and the natives were stripping the binding from beneath the bark of nearby trees. Long fleshy strips of fibre, rose-coloured and apricot and yellow, lay tangled over the grass, and the wounded trees showed startling red gashes around the clearing. Swiftly the poles were laced together with this natural rope, so that when the frame was complete it showed up against green trees and sky like a slender gleaming white cage, interwoven light-ly with rosy-yellow. Two natives climbed on top to bind the roof poles into their conical shape, while the others stamped a slushy mound of sand and earth to form plaster for the walls. Soon they stopped—the rest could wait until after the midday break.

Worn out by the strain of keeping the balance between the fiery Dutchman and the resentful workers, Major Carruthers went off home to eat. He had one and a half hour's break. He finished his meal in ten minutes, longing to be able to sleep for once till he woke naturally. His wife was dozing, so he lay down on the other bed and at once dropped off to sleep himself. When he woke it was long after the time he had set himself. It was after three. He rose in a panic and strode to the clearing, in the grip of one of his premonitions.

There stood the Dutchman, in a flaring temper, shouting at the natives who lounged in front of him, laughing openly. They had only just returned to work. As Major Carruthers approached, he saw Van Heerden using his open palms in a series of quick swinging slaps against their faces, knock-ing them sideways against each other: it was as if he were cuffing his own children in a fit of anger. Major Carruthers broke into a run, erupting into the group before anything else could happen. Van Heerden fell back on seeing him.

He was beef-red with fury. The natives were bunched together, on the point of throwing down their tools and walking off the job.

"Get back to work," snapped Major Carruthers to the men: and to Van Heerden: "I'm dealing with this." His eyes were an appeal to recognize the need for tact, but Van Heerden stood squarely there in front of him, on planted legs, breathing heavily. "But Major Carruthers . . ." he began, implying that as a white man, with his employer not there, it was right that he should take the command. "Do as I say," said Major Carruthers. Van Heerden, with a deadly look at his opponents, swung on his heel and marched off into the hut. The slapping swing of the grain-bag was as if a door had been slammed. Major Carruthers turned to the natives. "Get on," he ordered briefly, in a calm decisive voice. There was a moment of uncertainty. Then they picked up their tools and went to work.

Some laced the framework of the roof; others slapped the mud on to the walls. This business of plastering was usually a festival, with laughter and raillery, for there were gaps between the poles, and a handful of mud could fly through a space into the face of a man standing behind: the thing could become a game, like children playing snowballs. Today there was no pretence at good-humour. When the sun went down the men picked up their tools and filed off into the bush without a glance at Major Carruthers. The work had not prospered. The grass was laid untidily over the roof-frame, still uncut and reaching to the ground in long swatches. The first layer of mud had been unevenly flung on. It would be a shabby building.

"His own fault," thought Major Carruthers, sending his slow, tired blue glance to the hut where the Dutchman was still cherishing the seeds of wounded pride. Next day, when Major Carruthers was in another part of the farm, the Dutchman got his own back in a fine flaming scene with the ploughboys: they came to complain to the bossboy, but not to Major Carruthers. This made him uneasy. All that week he waited for fresh complaints about the Dutch-man's behaviour. So much was he keyed up, waiting for the scene between himself and a grudging bossboy, that when nothing happened his apprehensions deepened into a deep foreboding.

The building was finished the following Sunday. The floors were stamped hard with new dung, the thatch trimm-ed, and the walls grained smooth. Another two weeks must elapse before the family could move in, for the place smelled of damp. They were weeks of worry for Major Carruthers. It was unnatural for the Africans to remain passive and sullen under the Dutchman's handling of them, and especial-ly when they knew he was on their side. There was something he did not like in the way they would not meet his eyes and in the over-polite attitude of the bossboy.

The beautiful clear weather that he usually loved so much, May weather, sharpened by cold, and crisp under deep clear skies, pungent with gusts of wind from the drying leaves and grasses of the veld, was spoilt for him this year: some-thing was going to happen.

When the family eventually moved in, Major Carruthers became discouraged because the building of the hut had represented such trouble and worry, while now things seem-ed hardly better than before: what was the use of two small round huts for a family of eleven? But Van Heerden was very pleased, and expressed his gratitude in a way that moved Major Carruthers deeply: unable to show feeling himself, he was grateful when others did, so relieving him of the burden of his shyness. There was a ceremonial atmos-phere on the evening when one of the great sagging beds was wrenched out of the floor of the first hut and its legs plastered down newly into the second hut.

That very same night he was awakened towards dawn by voices calling to him from outside his window. He start-ed up, knowing that whatever he had dreaded was here, glad that the tension was over. Outside the back door stood his bossboy, holding a hurricane lamp which momentarily blinded Major Carruthers.

"The hut is on fire."

Blinking his eyes, he turned to look. Away in the darkness flames were lapping over the trees, outlining branches so that as a gust of wind lifted them patterns of black leaves showed clear and fine against the flowing red light of the fire. The veld was illuminated with a fitful plunging glare. The two men ran off into the bush down the rough road, towards the blaze.

The clearing was lit up, as bright as morning, when they arrived. On the roof of the first hut squatted Van Heerden, lifting tins of water from a line of natives below, working from the water-butt, soaking the thatch to prevent it catching the flames from the second hut that was only a few yards off. That was a roaring pillar of fire. Its frail skeleton was still erect, but twisting and writhing incandescently within its envelope of flame, and it collapsed slowly as he came up, subsiding in a crash of sparks.

"The children," gasped Major Carruthers to Mrs Van Heerden, who was watching the blaze fatalistically from where she sat on a scattered bundle of bedding, the tears soaking down her face, her arms tight round a swathed child.

As she spoke she opened the cloths to display the smallest infant. A swathe of burning grass from the roof had fallen across its head and shoulders. He sickened as he looked, for there was nothing but raw charred flesh. But it was alive: the limbs still twitched a little.

"I'll get the car and we'll take it in to the doctor."

He ran out of the clearing and fetched the car. As he tore down the slope back again he saw he was still in his pyjamas, and when he gained the clearing for the second time, Van Heerden was climbing down from the roof, which dripped water as if there had been a storm. He bent over the burnt child.

"Too late," he said.

"But it's still alive."

Van Heerden almost shrugged; he appeared dazed. He
continually turned his head to survey the glowing heap that
had so recently sheltered his children. He licked his lips
with a quick unconscious movement, because of their burning dryness. His face was grimed with smoke and inflamed
from the great heat, so that his young eyes showed startling-
ly clear against the black skin.

"Get into the car," said Major Carruthers to the woman.
She automatically moved towards the car, without looking
at her husband, who said: "But it's too late, man."

Major Carruthers knew the child would die, but his
protest against the waste and futility of the burning expressed itself in this way: that everything must be done to save
this life, even against hope. He started the car and slid off
down the hill. Before they had gone half a mile he felt his
shoulder plucked from behind, and, turning, saw the child
was now dead. He reversed the car into the dark bush off
the road, and drove back to the clearing. Now the woman
had begun wailing, a soft monotonous, almost automatic
sound that kept him tight in his seat, waiting for the next
cry.

The fire was now a dark heap, fanning softly to a glowing
red as the wind passed over it. The children were standing
in a half-circle, gazing fascinated at it. Van Heerden stood
near them, laying his hands gently, restlessly, on their heads
and shoulders, reassuring himself of their existence there,
in the flesh and living, beside him.

Mrs Van Heerden got clumsily out of the car, still wailing,
and disappeared into the hut, clutching the bundled dead
child.

Feeling out of place among that bereaved family, Major
Carruthers went up to his house, where he drank cup after
cup of tea, holding himself tight and controlled, conscious
of overstrained nerves.

Then he stooped into his wife's room, which seemed

small and dark and airless. The cave of a sick animal, he thought, in disgust; then, ashamed of himself, he returned out of doors, where the sky was filling with light. He sent a message for the bossboy, and waited for him in a condition of tensed anger.

When the man came Major Carruthers asked immediately: "Why did that hut burn?"

The bossboy looked at him straight and said: "How should I know?" Then, after a pause, with guileful innocence: "It was the fault of the kitchen, too close to the thatch".

Major Carruthers glared at him, trying to wear down the straight gaze with his own accusing eyes.

"That hut must be rebuilt at once. It must be rebuilt today."

The bossboy seemed to say that it was a matter of indifference to him whether it was rebuilt or not. "I'll go and tell the others," he said, moving off.

"Stop" barked Major Carruthers. Then he paused, frightened, not so much at his rage, but his humiliation and guilt. He had foreseen it! He had foreseen it all! And yet, that thatch could so easily have caught alight from the small incautious fire that sent up sparks all day so close to it.

Almost, he burst out in wild reproaches. Then he pulled himself together and said: "Get away from me." What was the use? He knew perfectly well that one of the Africans whom Van Heerden had kicked or slapped or shouted at had fired that hut; no one could ever prove it.

He stood quite still, watching his bossboy move off, tugging at the long wisps of his moustache in frustrated anger.

And what would happen now?

He ordered breakfast, drank a cup of tea, and spoilt a piece of toast. Then he glanced in again at his wife, who would sleep for a couple of hours yet.

Again tugging fretfully at his moustache, Major Carruthers set off for the clearing.

Everything was just as it had been, though the pile of black débris looked low and shabby now that morning had come and heightened the wild colour of sky and bush. The children were playing nearby, their hands and faces black, their rags of clothing black—everything seemed patched and smudged with black, and on one side the trees hung withered and grimy and the soil was hot underfoot.

Van Heerden leaned against the framework of the first hut. He looked subdued and tired, but otherwise normal. He greeted Major Carruthers, and did not move.

"How is your wife?" asked Major Carruthers. He could hear a moaning sound from inside the hut.

"She's doing well."

Major Carruthers imagined her weeping over the dead child; and said: "I'll take your baby into town for you and arrange for the funeral."

Van Heerden said: "I've buried her already." He jerked his thumb at the bush behind them.

"Didn't you register its birth?"

Van Heerden shook his head. His gaze challenged Major Carruthers as if to say: Who's to know if no one tells them? Major Carruthers could not speak: he was held in silence by the thought of that charred little body, huddled into a packing-case or wrapped in a piece of cloth, thrust into the ground, at the mercy of wild animals or of white ants.

"Well, one comes and another goes," said Van Heerden at last, slowly, reaching out for philosophy as a comfort, while his eyes filled with rough tears.

Major Carruthers stared: he could not understand. At last the meaning of the words came into him, and he heard the moaning from the hut with a new understanding.

The idea had never entered his head; it had been a complete failure of the imagination. If nine children, why not ten? Why not fifteen, for that matter, or twenty? Of course there would be more children.

"It was the shock," said Van Heerden. "It should be next month."

Major Carruthers leaned back against the wall of the hut and took out a cigarette clumsily. He felt weak. He felt as if Van Heerden had struck him, smiling. This was an absurd and unjust feeling, but for a moment he hated Van Heerden for standing there and saying: this grey country of poverty that you fear so much, will take on a different look when you actually enter it. You will cease to exist: there is no energy left, when one is wrestling naked, with life, for your kind of fine feelings and scruples and regrets.

"We hope it will be a boy," volunteered Van Heerden, with a tentative friendliness, as if he thought it might be considered a familiarity to offer his private emotions to Major Carruthers. "We have five boys and four girls—three girls," he corrected himself, his face contracting.

Major Carruthers asked stiffly: "Will she be all right?"

"I do it," said Van Heerden. "The last was born in the middle of the night, when it was raining. That was when we were in the tent. It's nothing to her." he added, with pride. He was listening, as he spoke, to the slow moaning from inside. "I'd better be getting in to her," he said, knocking out his pipe against the mud of the walls. Nodding to Major Carruthers, he lifted the sack and disappeared.

After a while Major Carruthers gathered himself together and forced himself to walk erect across the clearing under the curious gaze of the children. His mind was fixed and numb, but he walked as if moving to a destination. When he reached the house, he at once pulled paper and pen towards him and wrote, and each slow difficult word was a nail in the coffin of his pride as a man.

Some minutes later he went in to his wife. She was awake, turned on her side, watching the door for the relief of his coming. "I've written for a job at Home," he said simply, laying his hand on her thin dry wrist, and feeling the slow pulse beat up suddenly against his palm.

G

He watched curiously as her face crumpled and the tears
of thankfulness and release ran slowly down her cheeks and
soaked the pillow.

The Pig

The farmer paid his labourers on a Saturday evening, when the sun went down. By the time he had finished it was always quite dark, and from the kitchen door where the lantern hung, bars of yellow light lay down the steps, across the path, and lit up the trees and the dark faces under them.

This Saturday, instead of dispersing as usual when they took their money, they retired a little way into the dark under the foliage, talking among themselves to pass the time. When the last one had been paid, the farmer said: "Call the women and the children. Everybody in the compound must be here." The boss-boy, who had been standing beside the table calling out names, stood forward and repeated the order. But in an indifferent voice, as a matter of form, for all this had happened before, every year for years past. Already there was a subdued moving at the back of the crowd as the women came in from under the trees where they had been waiting; and the light caught a bunched skirt, a copper armlet, or a bright headcloth.

Now all the dimly-lit faces showed hope that soon this ritual would be over, and they could get back to their huts and their fires. They crowded closer without being ordered.

The farmer began to speak, thinking as he did so of his lands that lay all about him, invisible in the darkness, but sending on the wind a faint rushing noise like the sea; and although he had done this before so often, and was doing it now half-cynically, knowing it was a waste of time, the memory of how good those fields of strong young plants looked when the sun shone on them put urgency and even anger into his voice.

The trouble was that every year black hands stripped the cobs from the stems in the night, sacks of cobs; and he could never catch the thieves. Next morning he would see the prints of bare feet in the dust between the rows. He had tried everything; had warned, threatened, docked rations, even fined the whole compound collectively—it made no difference. The lands lying next to the compound would be cheated of their yield, and when the harvesters bought in their loads, everyone knew there would be less than what had been expected.

And if everyone knew it, why put on this display for the tenth time? That was the question the farmer saw on the faces in front of him; polite faces turning this way and that over impatient bodies and shifting feet. They were thinking only of the huts and the warm meal waiting for them. The philosophic politeness, almost condescension, with which he was being treated infuriated the farmer; and he stopped in the middle of a sentence, banging on the table with his fist, so that the faces centred on him and the feet stilled.

"Jonas," said the farmer. Out on to the lit space stepped a tall elderly man with a mild face. But now he looked sombre. The farmer saw that look and braced himself for a fight. This man had been on the farm for several years. An old scoundrel, the farmer called him, but affectionately: he was fond of him, for they had been together for so long. Jonas did odd jobs for half the year; he drew water for the garden, cured hides, cut grass. But when the growing season came he was an important man.

"Come here, Jonas," the farmer said again; and picked up the .33 rifle that had been leaning against his chair until now. During the rainy season, Jonas slept out his days in his hut, and spent his nights till the cold dawns came guarding the fields from the buck and the pigs that attacked the young plants. They could lay waste whole acres in one night, a herd of pigs. He took the rifle, greeting it, feeling its familiar weight on his arm. But he looked reluctant nevertheless.

"This year, Jonas, you will shoot everything you see—understand?"

"Yes, baas."

"Everything, buck, baboons, pig. And everything you hear. You will not stop to look. If you hear a noise, you will shoot."

There was a movement among the listening people, and soft protesting noises.

"And if it turns out to be a human pig, then so much the worse. My lands are no place for pigs of any kind."

Jonas said nothing, but he turned towards the others, holding the rifle uncomfortably on his arm, appealing that they should not judge him.

"You can go," said the farmer. After a moment the space in front of him was empty, and he could hear the sound of bare feet feeling their way along dark paths, the sound of loudening angry talk. Jonas remained beside him.

"Well, Jonas?"

"I do not want to shoot this year."

The farmer waited for an explanation. He was not disturbed at the order he had given. In all the years he had worked this farm no one had been shot, although every season the thieves moved at night along the mealie rows, and every night Jonas was out with a gun. For he would shout, or fire the gun into the air, to frighten intruders. It was only when dawn came that he fired at something he could see. All this was a bluff. The threat might scare off a few of the more timid; but both sides knew, as usual, that it was a bluff. The cobs would disappear; nothing could prevent it.

"And why not?" asked the farmer at last.

"It's my wife. I wanted to see you about it before," said Jonas, in dialect.

"Oh, your wife!" The farmer had remembered. Jonas was old-fashioned. He had two wives, an old one who had borne him several children, and a young one who gave him a good deal of trouble. Last year, when this wife was new, he had not wanted to take on this job which meant being out all night.

"And what is the matter with the day-time?" asked the farmer with waggish good-humour, exactly as he had the year before. He got up, and prepared to go inside.

Jonas did not reply. He did not like being appointed

official guardian against theft by his own people, but even
that did not matter so much, for it never once occurred to
him to take the order literally. This was only the last straw.
He was getting on in years now, and he wanted to spend his
nights in peace in his own hut, instead of roaming the bush.
He had disliked it very much last year, but now it was even
worse. A younger man visited his pretty young wife when
he was away.

Once he had snatched up a stick, in despair, to beat her
with; then he had thrown it down. He was old, and the other
man was young, and beating her could not cure his heartache.
Once he had come up to his master to talk over the situation,
as man to man; but the farmer had refused to do anything.
And, indeed, what could he do? Now, repeating what he had
said then, the farmer spoke from the kitchen steps, holding
the lamp high in one hand above his shoulder as he turned
to go in, so that it sent beams of light swinging across the
bush: "I don't want to hear anything about your wife, Jonas.
You should look after her yourself. And if you are not too
old to take a young wife, then you aren't too old to shoot.
You will take the gun as usual this year. Good night." And
he went inside, leaving the garden black and pathless. Jonas
stood quite still, waiting for his eyes to accustom themselves
to the dark; then he started off down the path, finding his
way by the feel of the loose stones under his feet.

He had not yet eaten, but when he came to within sight
of the compound, he felt he could not go farther. He halted,
looking at the little huts silhouetted black against cooking
fires that sent up great drifting clouds of illuminated smoke.
There was his hut, he could see it, a small conical shape.
There his wives were, waiting with his food prepared and
ready.

But he did not want to eat. He felt he could not bear to
go in and face his old wife, who mocked him with her tongue,
and his young wife who answered him submissively but
mocked him with her actions. He was sick and tormented,
cut off from his friends who were preparing for an evening

by the fires, because he could see the knowledge of his betrayal in their eyes. The cold pain of jealousy that had been gnawing at him for so long, felt now like an old wound, aching as an old wound aches before the rains set in.

He did not want to go into the fields, either to perch until he was stiff in one of the little cabins on high stilts that were built at the corners of each land as shooting platforms, or to walk in the dark through the hostile bush. But that night, without going for his food, he set off as usual on his long vigil.

The next night, however, he did not go; nor the next, nor the nights following. He lay all day dozing in the sun on his blanket, turning himself over and over in the sun, as if its rays could cauterize the ache from the hearth. When evening came, he ate his meal early before going off with the gun. And then he stood with his back to a tree, within sight of the compound; indeed, within a stone's throw of his own hut, for hours, watching silently. He felt numb and heavy. He was there without purpose. It was as if his legs had refused an order to march away from the place. All that week the lands lay unguarded, and if the wild animals were raiding the young plants, he did not care. He seemed to exist only in order to stand at night watching his hut. He did not allow himself to think of what was happening inside. He merely watched; until the fires burned down, and the bush grew cold and he was so stiff that when he went home, at sunrise, he had the appearance of one exhausted after a night's walking.

The following Saturday there was a beer drink. He could have got leave to attend it, had he wanted; but at sundown he took himself off as usual and saw that his wife was pleased when he left.

As he leaned his back to the tree trunk that gave him its support each night, and held the rifle lengthwise to his chest, he fixed his eyes steadily on the dark shape that was his hut, and remembered that look on his young wife's face. He allowed himself to think steadily of it, and of many

similar things. He remembered the young man, as he had
seen him only a few days before, bending over the girl as
she knelt to grind meal, laughing with her; then the way
they both looked up, startled, at his approach, their faces
growning blank.

He could feel his muscles tautening against the rifle as
he pictured that scene, so that he set it down on the ground,
for relief, letting his arms fall. But in spite of the pain, he
continued to think, for tonight things were changed in him,
and he no longer felt numb and purposeless. He stood erect
and vigilant, letting the long cold barrel slide between his
fingers, the hardness of the tree at his back like a second
spine. And as he thought of the young man another picture
crept into his mind again and again, that of a young water-
buck he had shot last year, lying soft at his feet, its tongue
slipping out into the dust as he picked it up, so newly dead
that he imagined he felt the blood still pulsing under the
warm skin. And from the small wet place under its neck a
few sticky drops rolled over glistening fur. Suddenly, as he
stood there thinking of the blood, and the limp dead body
of the buck, and the young man laughing with his wife, his
mind grew clear and cool and the oppression on him lifted.

He sighed deeply, and picked up the rifle again, holding
it close, like a friend, against him, while he gazed in through
the trees at the compound.

It was early, and the flush from sunset had not yet quite
gone from the sky, although where he stood among the
undergrowth it was night. In the clear spaces between the
huts groups of figures took shape, talking and laughing
and getting ready for the dance. Small cooking fires were
being lit; and a big central fire blazed, sending up showers
of sparks into the clouds of smoke. The tomtoms were
beating softly; soon the dance would begin. Visitors were
coming in through the bush from other farm compounds
miles away: it would be a long wait.

Three times he heard soft steps along the path close to
him before he drew back and turned his head to watch the

young man pass, as he had passed every night that week, with a jaunty eager tread and eyes directed towards Jonas's hut. Jonas stood as quiet as a tree struck by lightning, holding his breath, although he could not be seen, because the thick shadows from the trees were black around him. He watched the young man thread his way through the huts into the circle of firelight, and pass cautiously to one side of the groups of waiting people, like someone uncertain of his welcome, before going in through the door of his own hut.

Hours passed, and he watched the leaping dancing people, and listened to the drums as the stars swung over his head and the night birds talked in the bush around him. He thought steadily now, as he had not previously allowed himself to think, of what was happening inside the small dark hut that gradually became invisible as the fires died and the dancers went to their blankets. When the moon was small and high and cold behind his back, and the trees threw sharp black shadows on the path, and he could smell morning on the wind, he saw the young man coming towards him again. Now Jonas shifted his feet a little, to ease the stiffness out of them, and moved the rifle along his arm, feeling for the curve of the trigger on his finger.

As the young man lurched past, for he was tired, and moved carelessly, Jonas slipped out into the smooth dusty path a few paces behind, shrinking back as the released branches swung wet into his face and scattered large drops of dew on to his legs. It was cold; his breath misted into a thin pearly steam dissolving into the moonlight.

He was so close to the man in front that he could have touched him with the raised rifle; had he turned there would have been no concealment; but Jonas walked confidently, though carefully, and thought all the time of how he had shot down from ten paces away that swift young buck as it started with a crash out of a bush into a cold moony field.

When they reached the edge of the land where acres of mealies sloped away, dimly green under a dome of stars, Jonas began to walk like a cat. He wanted now to be sure; and he was only fifty yards from the shooting platform in the corner of the field, that looked in this light like a crazy fowl-house on stilts. The young man was staggering with tiredness and drink, making a crashing noise at each step as he snapped the sap-full mealies under heavy feet.

But the buck had shot like a spear from the bush, had caught the lead in its chest as it leaped, had fallen as a spear curves to earth; it had not blundered and lurched and swayed. Jonas began to feel a disgust for this man, and the admiration and fascination he felt for his young rival vanished. The tall slim youth who had laughed down at his wife had nothing to do with the ungainly figure crashing along before him, making so much noise that there could be no game left unstartled for miles.

When they reached the shooting platform, Jonas stopped dead, and let the youth move on. He lifted the rifle to his cheek and saw the long barrel slant against the stars, which sent a glint of light back down the steel. He waited, quite still, watching the man's back sway above the mealies. Then, at the right moment, he squeezed his finger close, holding the rifle ready to fire again.

As the sound of the shot reverberated, the round dark head jerked oddly, blotting out fields of stars; the body seemed to crouch, and one hand went out as if he were going to lean sideways to the ground. Then he disappeared into the mealies with a startled thick cry. Jonas lowered the rifle and listened. There was threshing noise, a horrible grunting, and half-words muttered, like someone talking in sleep.

Jonas picked his way along the rows, feeling the sharp leaf edges scything his legs, until he stood above the body that now jerked softly among the stems. He waited until it stilled, then bent to look, parting the chilled, moon-green leaves so that he could see clearly.

It was no clean small hole: raw flesh gaped, blood poured

black to the earth, the limbs were huddled together shapeless and without beauty, the face was pressed into the soil.

"A pig" said Jonas aloud to the listening moon, as he kicked the side gently with his foot, "nothing but a pig."

He wanted to hear how it would sound when he said it again, telling how he had shot blind into the grunting, invisible herd.

The Antheap

Beyond the plain rose the mountains, blue and hazy in a strong blue sky. Coming closer they were brown and grey and green, ranged heavily one beside the other, but the sky was still blue. Climbing up through the pass the plain flattened and diminished behind, and the peaks rose sharp and dark grey from lower heights of heaped granite boulders, and the sky overhead was deeply blue and clear and the heat came shimmering off in waves from every surface. "Through the range, down the pass, and into the plain the other side—let's go quickly, there it will be cooler, the walking easier." So thinks the traveller. So the traveller has been thinking for many centuries, walking quickly to leave the stifling mountains, to gain the cool plain where the wind moves freely. But there is no plain. Instead, the pass opens into a hollow which is closely surrounded by kopjes: the mountains clench themselves into a fist here, and the palm is a mile-wide reach of thick bush, where the heat gathers and clings, radiating from boulders, rocking off the trees, pouring down from a sky which is not blue, but thick and low and yellow, because of the smoke that rises, and has been rising so long from this mountain-imprisoned hollow. For though it is hot and close and arid half the year, and then warm and steamy and wet in the rains, there is gold here, so there are always people, and everywhere in the bush are pits and slits where the prospectors have been, or shallow holes, or even deep shafts. They say that the Bushmen were here, seeking gold, hundreds of years ago. Perhaps, it is possible. They say that trains of Arabs came from the coast, with slaves and warriors, looking for gold to enrich the courts of the Queen of Sheba. No one has proved they did not.

But it is at least certain that at the turn of the century there was a big mining company which sunk half a dozen fabulously deep shafts, and found gold going ounces to the ton sometimes, but it is a capricious and chancy piece of ground, with the reefs all broken and unpredictable, and so this company loaded its heavy equipment into lorries and off they went to look for gold somewhere else, and in a place where the reefs lay more evenly.

For a few years the hollow in the mountains was left silent, no smoke rose to dim the sky, except perhaps for an occasional prospector, whose fire was a single column of wavering blue smoke, as from the cigarette of a giant, rising into the blue, hot sky.

Then all at once the hollow was filled with violence and noise and activity and hundreds of people. Mr Macintosh had bought the rights to mine this gold. They told him he was foolish, that no single man, no matter how rich, could afford to take chances in this place.

But they did not reckon with the character of Mr Macintosh who had already made a fortune and lost it, in Australia, and then made another in New Zealand, which he still had. He proposed to increase it here. Of course, he had no intention of sinking those expensive shafts which might or might not reach gold and hold the dipping, chancy reefs and seams. The right course was quite clear to Mr Macintosh, and this course he followed, though it was against every known rule of proper mining.

He simply hired hundreds of African labourers and set them to shovel up the soil in the centre of that high, enclosed hollow in the mountains, so that there was soon a deeper hollow, then a vast pit, then a gulf like an inverted mountain. Mr Macintosh was taking great swallows of the earth, like a gold-eating monster, with no fancy ideas about digging shafts or spending money on roofing tunnels. The earth was hauled, at first, up the shelving sides of the gulf in buckets, and these were suspended by ropes made of twisted bark fibre, for why spend money on steel ropes when this fibre was offered free to mankind on every tree? And if it got brittle and broke and the buckets went plunging into the pit, then they were not harmed by the fall, and there was plenty of fibre left on the trees. Later, when the gulf grew too deep, there were trucks on rails, and it was not unkown for these, too, to go sliding and plunging to the bottom, because in all Mr Macintosh's dealings there was a fine, easy good-humour, which meant he was more likely to laugh at such an accident than grow angry. And if someone's head got in the way of falling buckets or trucks, then there were plenty of black heads and hands for the hiring. And if the loose, sloping bluffs of soil fell in landslides, or if a tunnel, narrow as an antbear's hole, that was run off sideways from the main pit like a tentacle exploring for new reefs, caved in suddenly, swallowing half a dozen men—well, one can't make an omelette without breaking eggs. This was Mr Macintosh's favourite motto.

The Africans who worked this mine called it "the pit of death", and they called Mr Macintosh "The Gold Stomach". Nevertheless, they came in their hundreds to work for him, thus providing free arguments for those who said: "The native doesn't understand good treatment, he only appreciates the whip, look at Macintosh, he's never short of labour."

Mr Macintosh's mine, raised high in the mountains, was far from the nearest police station, and he took care that there was always plenty of kaffir beer brewed in the compound, and if the police patrols came searching for criminals, these could count on Mr Macintosh facing the police for them and assuring them that such and such a native, Registration Number Y2345678, had never worked for him. Yes, of course they could see his books.

Mr Macintosh's books and records might appear to the simple-minded as casual and ineffective, but these were not the words used of his methods by those who worked for him, and so Mr Macintosh kept his books himself. He, employed no book-keeper, no clerk. In fact, he employed only one white man, an engineer. For the rest he had six overseers or boss-boys whom he paid good salaries and treated like important people.

The engineer was Mr Clarke, and his house and Mr

Macintosh's house were on one side of the big pit, and the compound for the Africans was on the other side. Mr Clarke earned fifty pounds a month, which was more than he would earn anywhere else. He was a silent, hardworking man, except when he got drunk, which was not often. Three or four times in the year he would be off work for a week, and then Mr Macintosh did his work for him till he recovered, when he greeted him with the good-humoured words: "Well, laddie, got that off your chest?"

Mr Macintosh did not drink at all. His not drinking was a passionate business, for like many Scots people he ran to extremes. Never a drop of liquor could be found in his house. Also, he was religious, in a reminiscent sort of way, because of his parents, who had been very religious. He lived in a two-roomed shack, with a bare wooden table in it, three wooden chairs, a bed and a wardrobe. The cook boiled beef and carrots and potatoes three days a week, roasted beef three days, and cooked a chicken on Sundays.

Mr Macintosh was one of the richest men in the country, he was more than a millionaire. People used to say of him: But for heaven's sake, he could do anything, go anywhere, what's the point of having so much money if you live in the back of beyond with a parcel of blacks on top of a big hole in the ground?

But to Mr Macintosh it seemed quite natural to live so, and when he went for a holiday to Cape Town, where he lived in the most expensive hotel, he always came back again long before he was expected. He did not like holidays. He liked working.

He wore old, oily khaki trousers, tied at the waist with an old red tie, and he wore a red handkerchief loose around his neck over a white cotton singlet. He was short and broad and strong, with a big square head tilted back on a thick neck. His heavy brown arms and neck sprouted thick black hair around the edges of the singlet. His eyes were small and grey and shrewd. His mouth was thin, pressed tight in the middle. He wore an old felt hat on the back of his head, and carried a stick cut from the bush, and he went strolling around the edge of the pit, slashing the stick at bushes and grass or sometimes at lazy Africans, and he shouted orders to his boss-boys, and watched the swarms of workers far below him in the bottom of the pit, and then he would go to his little office and make up his books, and so he spent his day. In the evenings he sometimes asked Mr Clarke to come over and play cards.

Then Mr Clarke would say to his wife: "Annie, he wants me," and she nodded and told her cook to make supper early.

Mrs Clarke was the only white woman on the mine. She did not mind this, being a naturally solitary person. Also, she had been profoundly grateful to reach this haven of fifty pounds a month with a man who did not mind her husband's bouts of drinking. She was a woman of early middle age, with a thin, flat body, a thin, colourless face, and quiet blue eyes. Living here, in this destroying heat, year after year, did not make her ill, it sapped her slowly, leaving her rather numbed and silent. She spoke very little, but then she roused herself and said what was necessary.

For instance, when they first arrived at the mine it was to a two-roomed house. She walked over to Mr Macintosh and said: "You are alone, but you have four rooms. There are two of us and the baby, and we have two rooms. There's no sense in it." Mr Macintosh gave her a quick, hard look his mouth tightened, and then he began to laugh. "Well, yes, that is so," he said, laughing, and he made the change at once, chuckling every time he remembered how the quiet Annie Clarke had put him in this place.

Similarly, about once a month Annie Clarke went to his house and said: "Now get out of my way, I'll get things straight for you." And when she'd finished tidying up she said: "You're nothing but a pig, and that's the truth." She was referring to his habit of throwing his clothes everywhere, or wearing them for weeks unwashed, and also to other matters which no one else dared to refer to, even as indirectly as this. To this he might reply, chuckling with the pleasure of teasing her: "You're a married woman, Mrs Clarke," and she said: "Nothing stops you getting married that I can see." And she walked away very straight, her cheeks burning with indignation.

She was very fond of him, and he of her. And Mr Clarke liked and admired him, and he liked Mr Clarke. And since Mr Clarke and Mrs Clarke lived amiably together in their four-roomed house, sharing bed and board without ever quarrelling, it was to be presumed they like each other too. But they seldom spoke. What was there to say?

It was to this silence, to these understood truths, that little Tommy had to grow up and adjust himself.

Tommy Clarke was three months when he came to the mine, and day and night his ears were filled with noise, every day and every night for years, so that he did not think of it as noise, rather, it was a different sort of silence. The mine-stamps thudded *gold*, gold, *gold,* gold, *gold,* on and on, never changing, never stopping. So he did not hear them. But there came a day when the machinery broke, and it was when Tommy was three years old, and the silence was so terrible and so empty that he went screeching to his mother: "It's stopped, it's stopped," and he wept, shivering, in a corner until the thudding began again. It was as if the heart of the world had gone silent. But when it started to beat, Tommy heard it, and he knew the difference between silence and sound, and his ears acquired a new sensitivity, like a conscience. He heard the shouting and the singing from the swarms of working Africans, reckless, noisy people because of the danger they always must live with. He heard the picks ringing on stone, the softer, deeper thud of picks on thick earth. He heard the clang of the trucks, and the roar of falling earth, and the rumbling of trolleys on rails. And at night the owls hooted and the night-jars screamed, and the crickets chirped. And when it stormed it seemed the sky itself was flinging down bolts of noise against the mountains, for the thunder rolled and crashed, and the lightning darted from peak to peak around him. It was never silent, never, save for that awful moment when the big heart stopped beating. Yet later he longed for it to stop again, just for an hour, so that he might hear a true silence. That was when he was a little older, and the quietness of his parents was beginning to trouble him. There they were, always so gentle, saying so little, only: That's how things are; or: You ask so many questions; or: You'll understand when you grow up.

It was a false silence, much worse than that real silence had been.

He would play beside his mother in the kitchen, who never said anything but Yes, and No, and—with a patient, sighing voice, as if even his voice tired her: You talk so much, Tommy!

And he was carried on his father's shoulders around the big, black working machines, and they couldn't speak because of the din the machines made. And Mr Macintosh would say: Well, laddie? and give him sweets from his pocket, which he always kept there, especially for Tommy. And once he saw Mr Macintosh and his father playing cards in the evening, and they didn't talk at all, except for the words that the game needed.

So Tommy escaped to the friendly din of the compound across the great gulf, and played all day with the black children, dancing in their dances, running through the bush after rabbits, or working wet clay into shapes of bird or beast. No silence there, everything noisy and cheerful, and at evening he returned to his equable, silent parents, and after the meal he lay in bed listening to the *thud,* thud, *thud,* thud, *thud,* thud, of the stamps. In the compound across the gulf they were drinking and dancing, the drums made a quick beating against the slow thud of the stamps, and the dancers around the fires yelled, a high, undulating sound like a big wind coming fast and crooked through a cap in the mountains. That was a different world, to which he belonged as much as to this one, where people said:

Finish your pudding; or: It's time for bed; and very little else.

When he was five years old he got malaria and was very sick. He recovered, but in the rainy season of the next year he got it again. Both times Mr Macintosh got into his big American car and went streaking across the thirty miles of bush to the nearest hospital for the doctor. The doctor said quinine, and be careful to screen for mosquitoes. It was easy to give quinine, but Mrs Clarke, that tired, easy-going woman, found it hard to say: Don't, and Be in by six; and Don't go near water; and so, when Tommy was seven, he got malaria again. And now Mrs Clarke was worried, because the doctor spoke severely, mentioning blackwater.

Mr Macintosh drove the doctor back to his hospital and then came home, and at once went to see Tommy, for he loved Tommy very deeply.

Mrs Clarke said: "What do you expect, with all these holes everywhere, they're full of water all the wet season."

"Well, lassie, I can't fill in all the holes and shafts, people have been digging up here since the Queen of Sheba."

"Never mind about the Queen of Sheba. At least you could screen our house properly."

"I pay your husband fifty pounds a month," said Mr Macintosh, conscious of being in the right.

"Fifty pounds and a proper house," said Annie Clarke.

Mr Macintosh gave her that quick, narrow look, and then laughed loudly. A week later the house was encased in fine wire mesh all round from roof-edge to verandah-edge, so that it looked like a new meat safe, and Mrs Clarke went over to Mr Macintosh's house and gave it a grand cleaning, and when she left she said: "You're nothing but a pig, you're as rich as the Oppenheimers, why don't you buy yourself some new vests at least. And you'll be getting malaria, too, the way you go traipsing about at nights."

She returned to Tommy, who was seated on the verandah behind the grey-glistening wire-netting, in a big deck-chair. He was very thin and white after the fever. He was a long child, bony, and his eyes were big and black, and his mouth full and pouting from the petulances of the illness. He had a mass of richly-brown hair, like caramels, on his head. His mother looked at this pale child of hers, who was yet so brightly coloured and full of vitality, and her tired will-power revived enough to determine a new régime for him. He was never to be out after six at night, when the mosquitoes were abroad. He was never to be out before the sun rose.

"You can get up," she said, and he got up, thankfully throwing aside his covers.

"I'll go over to the compound," he said at once.

She hesitated, and then said: "You mustn't play there any more."

"Why not?" he asked, already fidgeting on the steps outside the wire-netting cage.

Ah, how she hated these Whys, and Why nots! They tired her utterly. "Because I say so," she snapped.

But he persisted: "I always play there."

"You're getting too big now, and you'll be going to school soon."

Tommy sank on to the steps and remained there, looking away over the great pit to the busy, sunlit compound. He had known this moment was coming, of course. It was a knowledge that was part of the silence. And yet he had not known it. He said: "Why, why, why, why?" singing it out in a persistent wail.

"Because I say so." Then, in tired desperation: "You get sick from the Africans, too."

At this, he switched his large black eyes from the scenery to his mother, and she flushed a little. For they were derisively scornful. Yet she half-believed it herself, or rather, must believe it, for all through the wet season the bush would lie waterlogged and festering with mosquitoes, and nothing could be done about it, and one has to put the blame on something.

She said: "Don't argue. You're not to play with them.

You're too big now to play with a lot of dirty kaffirs. When you were little it was different, but now you're a big boy."

Tommy sat on the steps in the sweltering afternoon sun that came thick and yellow through the haze of dust and smoke over the mountains, and he said nothing. He made no attempt to go near the compound, now that his growing to manhood depended on his not playing with the black people. So he had been made to feel. Yet he did not believe a word of it, not really.

Some days later, he was kicking a football by himself around the back of the house when a group of black children called to him from the bush, and he turned away as if he had not seen them. They called again and then ran away. And Tommy wept bitterly, for now he was alone.

He went to the edge of the big pit and lay on his stomach looking down. The sun blazed through him so that his bones ached, and he shook his mass of hair forward over his eyes to shield them. Below, the great pit was so deep that the men working on the bottom of it were like ants. The trucks that climbed up the almost vertical sides were like matchboxes. The system of ladders and steps cut in the earth, which the workers used to climb up and down, seemed so flimsy across the gulf that a stone might dislodge it. Indeed, falling stones often did. Tommy sprawled, gripping the earth tight with tense belly and flung limbs, and stared down. They were all like ants and flies. Mr Macintosh, too, when he went down, which he did often, for no one could say he was a coward. And his father, and Tommy himself, they were all no bigger than little insects.

It was like an enormous ant-working, as brightly tinted as a fresh antheap. The levels of earth around the mouth of the pit were reddish, then lower down grey and gravelly, and lower still, clear yellow. Heaps of the inert, heavy yellow soil, brought up from the bottom, lay all around him. He stretched out his hand and took some of it. It was unresponsive, lying lifeless and dense on his fingers, a little damp from the rain. He clenched his fist, and loosened it, and now the mass of yellow earth lay shaped on his palm, showing the marks of his fingers. A shape like—what? A bit of root? A fragment of rock rotted by water? He rolled his plams vigorously around it, and it became smooth like a water-ground stone. Then he sat up and took more earth, and formed a pit, and up the sides flying ladders with bits of stick, and little kips of wetted earth for the trucks. Soon the sun dried it, and it all cracked and fell apart. Tommy gave the model a kick and went moodily back to the house. The sun was going down. It seemed that he had left a golden age of freedom behind, and now there was a new country of restrictions and time-tables.

His mother saw how he suffered, but thought: Soon he'll go to school and find companions.

But he was only just seven, and very young to go all the way to the city to boarding-school. She sent for school-books, and taught him to read. Yet this was for only two or three hours in the day, and for the rest he mooned about, as she complained, gazing away over the gulf to the compound, from where he could hear the noise of the playing children. He was stoical about it, or so it seemed, but underneath he was suffering badly from this new knowledge which was much more vital than anything he had learned from the school-books. He knew the word loneliness, and lying at the edge of the pit he formed the yellow clay into little figures which he called Betty and Freddy and Dirk. Playmates. Dirk was the name of the boy he liked best among the children in the compound over the gulf.

One day his mother called him to the back door. There stood Dirk, and he was holding between his hands a tiny duiker, the size of a thin cat. Tommy ran forward, and was about to exclaim with Dirk over the little animal, when he remembered his new status. He stopped, stiffened himself, and said: "How much?"

Dirk, keeping his eyes evasive, said: "One shilling, Baas."

Tommy glanced at his mother and then said, proudly, his voice high: "Damned cheek, too much."

Annie Clarke flushed. She was ashamed and flustered. She came forward and said quickly: "It's all right, Tommy, I'll give you the shilling." She took the coin from the pocket of her apron and gave it to Tommy, who handed it at once to Dirk. Tommy took the little animal gently in his hands, and his tenderness for this frightened and lonely creature rushed up to his eyes and he turned away so that Dirk couldn't see—he would have been bitterly ashamed to show softness in front of Dirk, who was so tough and fearless.

Dirk stood back, watching, unwilling to see the last of the buck. Then he said: "It's just born, it can die".

Mrs Clarke said, dismissingly: "Yes, Tommy will look after it." Dirk walked away slowly, fingering the shilling in his pocket, but looking back at where Tommy and his mother were making a nest for the little buck in a packing-case. Mrs Clarke made a feeding-bottle with some linen stuffed into the neck of a tomato sauce bottle and filled it with milk and water and sugar. Tommy knelt by the buck and tried to drip the milk into its mouth.

It lay trembling lifting its delicate head from the crumpled, huddled limbs, too weak to move, the big eyes dark and forlorn. Then the trembling became a spasm of weakness and the head collapsed with a soft thud against the side of the box, and then slowly, and with a trembling effort, the neck lifted the head again. Tommy tried to push the wad of linen into the soft mouth, and the milk wetted the fur and ran down over the buck's chest, and he wanted to cry.

"But it'll die, mother, it'll die," he shouted, angrily.

"You mustn't force it," said Annie Clarke, and she went away to her household duties. Tommy knelt there with the bottle, stroking the trembling little buck and suffering every time the thin neck collapsed with weakness, and tried again and again to interest it in the milk. But the buck wouldn't drink at all.

"Why?" shouted Tommy, in the anger of his misery. 'Why won't it drink? Why? Why?"

"But it's only just born," said Mrs Clarke. The cord was still on the creature's navel, like a shrivelling, dark stick.

That night Tommy took the little buck into his room, and secretly in the dark lifted it, folded in a blanket, into his bed. He could feel it trembling fitfully against his chest, and he cried into the dark because he knew it was going to die.

In the morning when he woke, the buck could not lift its head at all, and it was a weak, collapsed weight on Tommy's chest, a chilly weight. The blanket in which it lay was messed with yellow stuff like a scrambled egg. Tommy washed the buck gently, and wrapped it again in new coverings, and laid it on the verandah where the sun could warm it.

Mrs Clarke gently forced the jaws open and poured down milk until the buck choked. Tommy knelt beside it all morning, suffering as he had never suffered before. The tears ran steadily down his face and he wished he could die too, and Mrs Clarke wished very much she could catch Dirk and give him a good beating, which would be unjust, but might do something to relieve her feelings. "Besides," she said to her husband, "it's nothing but cruelty, taking a tiny thing like that from its mother."

Late that afternoon the buck died, and Mr Clarke, who had not seen his son's misery over it, casually threw the tiny, stiff corpse to the cookboy and told him to go and bury it. Tommy stood on the verandah, his face tight and angry, and watched the cookboy shovel his little buck hastily under some bushes, and return whistling.

Then he went into the room where his mother and father were sitting and said: "Why is Dirk yellow and not dark brown like the other kaffirs?"

Silence. Mr Clarke and Annie Clarke looked at each other. Then Mr Clarke said: "They come different colours." Tommy looked forcefully at his mother, who said: "He's a half-caste."

"What's a half-caste?"

"You'll understand when you grow up."

Tommy looked from his father, who was filling his pipe, his eyes lowered to the work, then at his mother, whose cheekbones held that proud, bright flush.

"I understand now," he said, defiantly.

"Then why do you ask?" said Mrs Clarke, with anger. Why, she was saying, do you infringe the rule of silence?

Tommy went out, and to the brink of the great pit. There he lay, wondering why he had said he understood when he did not. Though in a sense he did. He was remembering, though he had not noticed it before, that among the gang of children in the compound were two yellow children. Dirk was one, and Dirk's sister another. She was a tiny child, who came toddling on the fringe of the older children's games. But Dirk's mother was black, or rather, dark-brown like the others. And Dirk was not really yellow, but light copper-colour. The colour of this earth, were it a little darker. Tommy's fingers were fiddling with the damp clay. He looked at the little figures he had made, Betty and Freddy. Idly, he smashed them. Then he picked up Dirk and flung him down. But he must have flung him down too carefully, for he did not break, and so he set the figure against the stalk of a weed. He took a lump of clay, and as his fingers experimentally pushed and kneaded it, the shape grew into the shape of a little duiker. But not a sick duiker, which had died because it had been taken from its mother. Not at all, it was a fine strong duiker, standing with one hoof raised and its head listening, ears pricked forward.

Tommy knelt on the verge of the great pit, absorbed, while the duiker grew into its proper form. He became dissatisfied—it was too small. He impatiently smashed what he had done, and taking a big heap of the yellowish, dense soil, shook water on it from an old rusty railway sleeper that had collected rainwater, and made the mass soft and workable. Then he began again. The duiker would be half life-size.

And so his hands worked and his mind worried along its path of questions: Why? Why? Why? And finally: If Dirk is half black, or rather half white and half dark-brown, then who is his father?

For a long time his mind hovered on the edge of the answer, but did not finally reach it. But from time to time he looked across the gulf to where Mr Macintosh was strolling, swinging his big cudgel, and he thought: There are only two white men on this mine.

The buck was now finished, and he wetted his fingers in rusty rainwater, and smoothed down the soft clay to make it glisten like the surfaces of fur, but at once it dried and dulled, and as he knelt there he thought how the sun would crack it and it would fall to pieces, and an angry dissatisfaction filled him and he hung his head and wanted very much to cry. And just as the first tears were coming he heard a soft whistle from behind him, and turned, and there was Dirk, kneeling behind a bush and looking out through the parted leaves.

"Is the buck all right?" asked Dirk.

Tommy said: "It's dead," and he kicked his foot at his model duiker so that the thick clay fell apart in lumps.

Dirk said: "Don't do that, it's nice," and he sprang forward and tried to fit the pieces together.

"It's no good, the sun'll crack it," said Tommy, and he began to cry, although he was so ashamed to cry in front of Dirk. "The buck's dead," he wept, "it's dead."

"I can get you another," said Dirk, looking at Tommy rather surprised. "I killed its mother with a stone. It's easy."

Dirk was seven, like Tommy. He was tall and strong, like Tommy. His eyes were dark and full, but his mouth was not full and soft, but long and narrow, clenched in the middle. His hair was very black and soft and long, falling uncut around his face, and his skin was a smooth, yellowish copper. Tommy stopped crying and looked at Dirk. He said: "It's cruel to kill a buck's mother with a stone." Dirk's mouth parted in surprised laughter over his big white teeth. Tommy watched him laugh, and he thought: Well, now I know who his father is.

He looked away to his home, which was two hundred yards off, exposed to the sun's glare among low bushes of hibiscus and poinsettia. He looked at Mr Macintosh's house, which was a few hundred yards farther off. Then he looked at Dirk. He was full of anger, which he did not understand, but he did understand that he was also defiant, and this was a moment of decision. After a long time he said: "They can see us from here," and the decision was made.

They got up, but as Dirk rose he saw the little clay figure laid against a stem, and he picked it up. "This is me," he said at once. For crude as the thing was, it was unmistakably Dirk, who smiled with pleasure. "Can I have it?" he asked, and Tommy nodded, equally proud and pleased.

They went off into the bush between the two houses, and then on for perhaps half a mile. This was the deserted part of the hollow in the mountains, no one came here, all the bustle and noise was on the other side. In front of them rose a sharp peak, and low at its foot was a high anthill, draped with Christmas fern and thick with shrub.

The two boys went inside the curtains of fern and sat down. No one could see them here. Dirk carefully put the little clay figure of himself inside a hole in the roots of a tree. Then he said: "Make the buck again." Tommy took his knife and knelt beside a fallen tree, and tried to carve the buck from it. The wood was soft and rotten, and was easily carved, and by night there was the clumsy shape of the buck coming out of the trunk. Dirk said: "Now we've both got something."

The next day the two boys made their way separately to

the antheap and played there together, and so it was every day.

Then one evening Mrs Clarke said to Tommy just as he was going to bed: "I thought I told you not to play with the kaffirs?"

Tommy stood very still. Then he lifted his head and said to her, with a strong look across at his father: "Why shouldn't I play with Mr Macintosh's son?"

Mrs Clarke stopped breathing for a moment, and closed her eyes. She opened them in appeal at her husband. But Mr Clarke was filling his pipe. Tommy waited and then said good night and went to his room.

There he undressed slowly and climbed into the narrow iron bed and lay quietly, listening to the thud, thud, gold, gold, thud, thud, of the mine-stamps. Over in the compound they were dancing, and the tom-toms were beating fast, like the quick beat of the buck's heart that night as it lay on his chest. They were yelling like the wind coming through gaps in a mountain and through the window he could see the high, flaring light of the fires, and the black figures of the dancing people were wild and active against it.

Mrs Clarke came quickly in. She was crying. "Tommy," she said, sitting on the edge of his bed in the dark.

"Yes?" he said, cautiously.

"You mustn't say that again. Not ever."

He said nothing. His mother's hand was urgently pressing his arm. "Your father might lose his job," said Mrs Clarke, wildly. "We'd never get this money anywhere else. Never. You must understand, Tommy."

"I do understand," said Tommy, stiffly, very sorry for his mother, but hating her at the same time. "Just don't say it, Tommy, don't ever say it." Then she kissed him in a way that was both fond and appealing, and went out, shutting the door. To her husband she said it was time Tommy went to school, and next day she wrote to make the arrangements.

And so now Tommy made the long journey by car and train into the city four times a year, and four times a year he came back for the holidays. Mr Macintosh always drove him to the station and gave him ten shillings pocket money, and he came to fetch him in the car with his parents, and he always said: "Well, laddie, and how's school?" And Tommy said: "Fine, Mr Macintosh." And Mr Macintosh said: "We'll make a college man of you yet."

When he said this, the flush came bright and proud on Annie Clarke's cheeks, and she looked quickly at Mr Clarke, who was smiling and embarrassed. But Mr Macintosh laid his hands on Tommy's shoulders and said: "There's my laddie, there's my laddie," and Tommy kept his shoulders stiff and still. Afterwards, Mrs Clarke would say, nervously: "He's fond of you, Tommy, he'll do right by you." And once she said: "It's natural, he's got no children of his own." But Tommy scowled at her and she flushed and said: "There's things you don't understand yet, Tommy, and you'll regret it if you throw away your chances." Tommy turned away with an impatient movement. Yet it was not so clear at all, for it was almost as if he were a rich man's son, with all that pocket money, and the parcels of biscuits and sweets that Mr Macintosh sent into school during the term, and being fetched in the great rich car. And underneath it all he felt as if he were dragged along by the nose. He felt as if he were part of a conspiracy of some kind that no one ever spoke about. Silence. His real feelings were growing up slow and complicated and obstinate underneath that silence.

At school it was not at all complicated, it was the other world. There Tommy did his lessons and played with his friends and did not think of Dirk. Or rather, his thoughts of him were proper for that world. A half-caste, ignorant, living in the kaffir location—he felt ashamed that he played with Dirk in the holidays, and he told no one. Even on the train coming home he would think like that of Dirk, but the nearer he reached home the more his thoughts wavered and darkened. On the first evening at home he would speak of the school, and how he was first in the class, and he played with this boy or that, or went to such fine houses in the city as a guest. The very first morning he would be standing on the verandah looking at the big pit and at the compound away beyond it, and his mother watched him, smiling in nervous supplication. And then he walked down the steps, away from the pit, and into the bush to the antheap. There Dirk was waiting for him. So it was every holiday. Neither of the boys spoke at first of what divided them. But, on the eve of Tommy's return to school after he had been there a year, Dirk said: "You're getting educated, but I've nothing to learn." Tommy said: "I'll bring back books and teach you." He said this in a quick voice, as if ashamed, and Dirk's eyes were accusing and angry. He gave his sarcastic laugh and said: "That's what you say, white boy."

It was not pleasant, but what Tommy said was not pleasant either, like a favour wrung out of a condescending person.

The two boys were sitting on the antheap under the fine lacy curtains of Christmas fern, looking at the rocky peak soaring into the smoky yellowish sky. There was the most unpleasant sort of annoyance in Tommy, and he felt ashamed of it. And on Dirk's face there was an aggressive but ashamed look. They continued to sit there, a little apart, full of dislike for each other, and knowing that the dislike came from the pressure of the outside world. "I said I'd teach you, didn't I?" said Tommy, grandly, shying a stone at a bush so that leaves flew off in all directions. "You white bastard," said Dirk, in a low voice, and he let out that sudden ugly laugh, showing his white teeth. "What did you say?" said Tommy, going pale and jumping to his feet. "You heard," said Dirk, still laughing. He too got up. Then Tommy flung himself on Dirk and they overbalanced and rolled off into the bushes, kicking and scratching. They rolled apart and began fighting properly, with fists. Tommy was better-fed and more healthy. Dirk was tougher. They were a match, and they stopped when they were too tired and battered to go on. They staggered over to the antheap and sat there side by side, panting, wiping the blood off their faces. At last they lay on their backs on the rough slant of the anthill and looked up at the sky. Every trace of dislike had vanished, and they felt easy and quiet. When the sun went down they walked together through the bush to a point where they could not be seen from the houses, and there they said, as always: "See you tomorrow."

When Mr Macintosh gave him the usual ten shillings, he put them into his pocket thinking he would buy a football, but he did not. The ten shillings stayed unspent until it was nearly the end of term, and then he went to the shops and bought a reader and some exercise books and pencils, and an arithmetic. He hid these at the bottom of his trunk and whipped them out before his mother could see them.

He took them to the antheap next morning, but before he could reach it he saw there was a little shed built on it, and the Christmas fern had been draped like a veil across the roof of the shed. The bushes had been cut on the top of the anthill, but left on the sides, so that the shed looked as if it rose from the tops of the bushes. The shed was of unbarked poles pushed into the earth, the roof was of thatch, and the upper half of the front was left open. Inside there was a bench of poles and a table of planks on poles. There sat Dirk, waiting hungrily, and Tommy went and sat beside him, putting the books and pencils on the table.

"This shed is fine," said Tommy, but Dirk was already looking at the books. So he began to teach Dirk how to read. And for all that holiday they were together in the shed while Dirk pored over the books. He found them more difficult than Tommy did, because they were full of words for things Dirk did not know, like curtains or carpet, and teaching Dirk to read the word carpet meant telling him all about carpets and the furnishings of a house. Often Tommy felt bored and restless and said: "Let's play," but Dirk said fiercely: "No, I want to read." Tommy grew fretful, for after all he had been working in the term and now he felt entitled to play. So there was another fight. Dirk said Tommy was a lazy white bastard, and Tommy said Dirk was a dirty half-caste. They fought as before, evenly matched and to no conclusion, and afterwards felt fine and friendly, and even made jokes about the fighting. It was arranged that they should work in the mornings only and leave the afternoons for play. When Tommy went back home that evening his mother saw the scratches on his face and the swollen nose, and said hopefully: "Have you and Dirk been fighting?" But Tommy said no, he had hit his face on a tree.

His parents, of course, knew about the shed in the bush, but did not speak of it to Mr Macintosh. No one did. For Dirk's very existence was something to be ignored by everyone, and none of the workers, not even the overseers, would dare to mention Dirk's name. When Mr Macintosh asked Tommy what he had done to his face, he said he had slipped and fallen.

And so their eighth year and their ninth went past. Dirk could read and write and do all the sums that Tommy could do. He was always handicapped by not knowing the different way of living, and soon he said, angrily, it wasn't fair, and there was another fight about it, and then Tommy began another way of teaching. He would tell how it was to go to a cinema in the city, every detail of it, how the seats were arranged in such a way, and one paid so much, and the lights were like this, and the picture on the screen worked like that. Or he would describe how at school they ate such things for breakfast and other things for lunch. Or tell how the man had come with picture slides talking about China. The two boys got out an atlas and found China, and Tommy told Dirk every word of what the lecturer had said. Or it·might be Italy or some other country. And they would argue that the lecturer should have said this or that, for Dirk was always hotly scornful of the white man's way of looking at things, so arrogant, he said. Soon Tommy saw things through Dirk; he saw the other life in town clear and brightly-coloured and a little distorted, as Dirk did.

Soon, at school, Tommy would involuntarily think: I must remember this to tell Dirk. It was impossible for him to do anything, without being very conscious of just how it happened, as if Dirk's black, sarcastic eye had got inside him, Tommy, and never closed. And a feeling of unwillingness grew in Tommy, because of the strain of fitting these two worlds together. He found himself swearing at niggers or kaffirs like the other boys, and more violently than they did, but immediately afterwards he would find himself thinking: I must remember this so as to tell Dirk. Because of all this thinking, and seeing everything clear all the time, he was very bright at school, and found the the work easy. He was two classes ahead of his age.

That was the tenth year, and one day Tommy went to the shed in the bush and Dirk was not waiting for him. It was the first day of the holidays. All the term he had been remembering things to tell Dirk, and now Dirk was not there. A dove was sitting on the Christmas fern, cooing lazily in the hot morning, a sleepy, lonely sound. When Tommy came pushing through the bushes it flew away. The mine-stamps thudded heavily, gold, gold, and Tommy saw that the shed was empty even of books, for the case where they were usually kept was hanging open.

He went running to his mother: "Where's Dirk?" he asked.

"How should I know?" said Annie Clarke, cautiously. She really did not know.

"You do know, you do!" he cried, angrily. And then he went racing off to the big pit. Mr Macintosh was sitting on an upturned truck on the edge, watching the hundreds of workers below him, moving like ants on the yellow bottom. "Well, laddie?" he asked, amiably, and moved over for Tommy to sit by him.

"Where's Dirk?" asked Tommy, accusingly, standing in front of him.

Mr Macintosh tipped his old felt hat even further back and scratched at his front hair and looked at Tommy.

"Dirk's working," he said, at last.

"Where?"

Mr Macintosh pointed at the bottom of the pit. Then he said again: "Sit down, laddie, I want to talk to you."

"I don't want to," said Tommy, and he turned away and went blundering over the veld to the shed. He sat on the bench and cried and when dinner-time came he did not go home. All that day he sat in the shed, and when he had finished crying he remained on the bench, leaning his back against the poles of the shed, and stared into the bush. The doves cooed and cooed, kru-kruuuu, kru-kruuuuu, and a woodpecker tapped, and the mine-stamps thudded. Yet it was very quiet, a hand of silence gripped the bush, and he could hear the borers and the ants at work in the poles of the bench he sat on. He could see that although the anthill seemed dead, a mound of hard, peaked, baked earth, it was very much alive, for there was a fresh outbreak of wet, damp earth in the floor of the shed. There was a fine crust of reddish, lacey earth over the poles of the walls. The shed would have to be built again soon, because the ants and borers would have eaten it through. But what was the use of a shed without Dirk?

All that day he stayed there, and did not return until dark, and when his mother said: "What's the matter with you, why are you crying?" he said angrily, "I don't know," matching her dishonesty with his own. The next day, even before breakfast, he was off to the shed, and did not return until dark, and refused his supper although he had not eaten all day.

And the next day it was the same, but now he was bored and lonely. He took his knife from his pocket and whittled at a stick, and it became a boy, bent and straining under the weight of a heavy load, his arms clenched up to support it. He took the figure home at supper-time and ate with it on the table in front of him.

"What's that?" asked Annie Clarke, and Tommy answered: "Dirk."

He took it to his bedroom, and sat in the soft lamp-light, working away with his knife, and he had it in his hand the following morning when he met Mr Macintosh at the brink of the pit. "What's that laddie?" asked Mr Macintosh, and Tommy said: "Dirk."

Mr Macintosh's mouth went thin, and then he smiled and said "Let me have it."

"No, it's for Dirk."

Mr Macintosh took out his wallet and said: "I'll pay you for it."

"I don't want any money," said Tommy, angrily, and Mr Macintosh, greatly disturbed, put back his wallet. Then Tommy, hesitating, said: "Yes, I do." Mr Macintosh, his values confirmed, was relieved, and he took out his wallet again and produced a pound note, which seemed to him very generous. "Five pounds," said Tommy, promptly. Mr Macintosh first scowled, then laughed. He tipped back his head and roared with laughter. "Well, laddie, you'll make a business man yet. Five pounds for a little bit of wood!"

"Make it for yourself then, if it's just a bit of wood."

Mr Macintosh counted out five pounds and handed them over. "What are you going to do with that money?" he asked, as he watched Tommy buttoning them carefully into his shirt pocket "Give them to Dirk," said Tommy, triumphantly, and Mr Macintosh's heavy old face went purple. He watched while Tommy walked away from him, sitting on the truck, letting the heavy cudgel swing lightly against his shoes. He solved his immediate problem by thinking. He's a good laddie, he's got a good heart.

That night Mrs Clarke came over while he was sitting over his roast beef and cabbage, and said: "Mr Macintosh, I want a word with you." He nodded at a chair, but she did not sit. "Tommy's upset," she said, delicately, "he's been used to Dirk, and now he's got no one to play with."

For a moment Mr Macintosh kept his eyes lowered, then he said: "It's easily fixed, Annie, don't worry yourself." He spoke heartily, as it was easy for him to do, speaking of a worker, who might be released at his whim for other duties.

That bright protesting flush came on to her cheeks, in spite of herself, and she looked quickly at him, with real indignation. But he ignored it and said: "I'll fix it in the morning, Annie."

She thanked him and went back home, suffering because she had not said those words which had always soothed her conscience in the past: You're nothing but a pig, Mr Macintosh . . .

As for Tommy, he was sitting in the shed, crying his eyes out. And then, when there were no more tears, there came such a storm of anger and pain that he would never forget it as long as he lived. What for? He did not know, and that was the worst of it. It was not simply Mr Macintosh, who loved him, and who thus so blackly betrayed his own flesh and blood, nor the silences of his parents. Something deeper, felt working in the substance of life as he could hear those ants working away with those busy jaws at the roots of the poles he sat on, to make new material for their different forms of life. He was testing those words which were used, or not used—merely suggested—all the time, and for a ten-year-old boy it was almost too hard to bear. A child may say of a companion one day that he hates so and so, and the next: He is my friend. That is how a relationship is, shifting and changing, and children are kept safe in their hates and loves by the fabric of social life their parents make over their heads. And middle-aged people say: This is my friend, this is my enemy, including all the shifts and changes of feeling in one word, for the sake of an easy mind. In between these ages, at about twenty perhaps, there is a time when the young people test everything, and accept many hard and cruel truths about living, and that is because they do not know how hard it is to accept them finally, and for the rest of their lives. It is easy to be truthful at twenty.

But it is not easy at ten, a little boy entirely alone, looking at words like friendship. What, then, was friendship? Dirk was his friend, that he knew, but did he like Dirk? Did he love him? Sometimes not at all. He remembered how Dirk had said: "I'll get you another baby buck. I'll kill its mother with a stone." He remembered his feeling of revulsion at the cruelty. Dirk was cruel. But—and here Tommy unexpectedly laughed, and for the first time he understood Dirk's way of laughing. It was really funny to say that Dirk was cruel, when his very existence was a cruelty. Yet Mr Macintosh laughed in exactly the same way, and his skin was white, or rather, white browned over by the sun. Why was Mr Macintosh also entitled to laugh, with that same abrupt ugliness? Perhaps somewhere in the beginnings of the rich Mr Macintosh there had been the same cruelty, and that had worked its way through the life of Mr Macintosh until it turned into the cruelty of Dirk, the coloured boy, the half-caste? If so, it was all much deeper than differently coloured skins, and much harder to understand.

And then Tommy thought how Dirk seemed to wait always, as if he, Tommy, were bound to stand by him, as if this were a justice that was perfectly clear to Dirk; and he, Tommy, did in fact fight with Mr Macintosh for Dirk, and he could behave in no other way. Why? Because Dirk was his friend? Yet there were times when he hated Dirk, and certainly Dirk hated him, and when they fought they could have killed each other easily, and with joy.

Well, then? Well, then? What was friendship, and why were they bound so closely, and by what? Slowly the little boy, sitting alone on his antheap came to an understanding which is proper to middle-aged people, that resignation in knowledge which is called irony. Such a person may know, for instance, that he is bound most deeply to another

person, although he does not like that person, in the way
the word is ordinarily used, or the way he talks, or his
politics, or anything else. And yet they are friends and
will always be friends, and what happens to this bound
couple affects each most deeply, even though they may be
in different continents, or may never see each other again.
Or after twenty years they may meet, and there is no need
to say a word, everything is understood. This is one of the
ways of friendship, and just as real as amiability or being
alike.

Well, then? For it is a hard and difficult knowledge for
any little boy to accept. But he accepted it, and knew that
he and Dirk were closer than brothers and always be so.
He grew many years older in that day of painful struggle,
while he listened to the mine-stamps saying gold, gold, and
to the ants working away with their jaws to destroy the bench
he sat on, to make food for themselves.

Next morning Dirk came to the shed, and Tommy,
looking at him, knew that he, too, had grown years older
in the months of working in the great pit. Ten years old—
but he had been working with men and he was not a child.

Tommy took out the five pound notes and gave them
to Dirk.

Dirk pushed them back. "What for?" he asked.

"I got them from *him*," said Tommy, and at once Dirk
took them as if they were his right.

And at once, inside Tommy, came indignation, for he
felt he was being taken for granted, and he said: "Why
aren't you working?"

"He said I needn't. He means, while you are having your
holidays."

"I got you free," said Tommy, boasting.

Dirk's eyes narrowed in anger. "He's my father," he
said, for the first time.

"But he made you work," said Tommy, taunting him.
And then: "Why do you work? I wouldn't. I should say
no."

"So you would say no?" said Dirk in angry sarcasm.

"There's no law to make you."

"So there's no law, white boy, no law . . ." But Tommy had sprung at him, and they were fighting again, rolling over and over, and this time they fell apart from exhaustion and lay on the ground panting for a long time.

Later Dirk said: "Why do we fight, it's silly?"

"I don't know," said Tommy, and he began to laugh, and Dirk laughed too. They were to fight often in the future, but never with such bitterness, because of the way they were laughing now.

It was the following holidays before they fought again. Dirk was waiting for him in the shed.

"Did he let you go?" asked Tommy at once, putting down new books on the table for Dirk.

"I just came," said Dirk, "I didn't ask."

They sat together on the bench, and at once a leg gave way and they rolled off on to the floor laughing, "We must mend it," said Tommy. "Let's build the shed again."

"No," said Dirk at once, "don't let's waste time on the shed. You can teach me while you're here, and I can make the shed when you're gone back to school."

Tommy slowly got up from the floor, frowning. Again he felt he was being taken for granted. "Aren't you going to work on the mine during the term?"

"No, I'm not going to work on the mine again. I told him I wouldn't."

"You've got to work," said Tommy, grandly.

"So I've got to work," said Dirk, threateningly. "You can go to school, white boy, but I've got to work, and in the holidays I can just take time off to please you."

They fought until they were tired, and five minutes afterwards they were seated on the anthill talking. "What did you do with the five pounds?" asked Tommy.

"I gave them to my mother."

"What did you do with them?"

"She bought herself a dress, and then food for us all, and

bought me these trousers, and she put the rest away to keep."

A pause. Then, deeply ashamed, Tommy asked: "Doesn't he give her any money?"

"He doesn't come any more. Not for more than a year."

"Oh, I thought he did still," said Tommy casually, whistling.

"No." Then, fiercely, in a low voice: "There'll be some more half-castes in the compound soon."

Dirk sat crouching, his fierce black eyes on Tommy, ready to spring at him. But Tommy was sitting with his head bowed, looking at the ground. "It's not fair," he said. "It's not fair."

"So you've discovered that, white boy?" said Dirk. It was said good-naturedly, and there was no need to fight. They went to their books and Tommy taught Dirk some new sums.

But they never spoke of what Dirk would do in the future, how he would use all this schooling. They did not dare.

That was the eleventh year.

When they were twelve, Tommy returned from school to be greeted by the words: "Have you heard the news?"

"What news?"

They were sitting as usual on the bench. The shed was newly built, with strong thatch, and good walls, plastered this time with mud, so as to make it harder for the ants.

"They are saying you are going to be sent away."

"Who says so?"

"Oh, everyone," said Dirk, stirring his feet about vaguely under the table. This way because it was the first few minutes after the return from school, and he was always cautious, until he was sure Tommy had not changed towards him. And that "everyone" was explosive. Tommy nodded, however, and asked apprehensively: "Where to?"

"To the sea."

"How do they know?" Tommy scarcely breathed the word *they*.

"Your cook heard your mother say so . . ." And then Dirk

added with a grin, forcing the issue: "Cheek, dirty kaffirs talking about white men."

Tommy smiled obligingly, and asked: "How, to the sea, what does it mean?"

"How should we know, dirty kaffirs."

"Oh, shut up," said Tommy, angrily. They glared at each other their muscles tensed. But they sighed and looked away. At twelve it was not easy to fight, it was all too serious.

That night Tommy said to his parents: "They say I'm going to sea. Is it true?"

His mother asked quickly: "Who said so?"

"But is it true?" Then, derisively: "Cheek, dirty kaffirs talking about *us*."

"Please don't talk like that, Tommy, it's not right."

"Oh, mother, please, how am I going to sea?"

"But be sensible Tommy, it's not settled, but Mr Macintosh . . ."

"So it's Mr Macintosh!"

Mrs Clarke looked at her husband; who came forward and sat down and settled his elbows on the table. A family conference. Tommy also sat down.

"Now listen, son. Mr Macintosh has a soft spot for you. You should be grateful to him. He can do a lot for you."

"But why should I go to sea?"

"You don't have to. He suggested it—he was in the Merchant Navy himself once."

"So I've got to go just because he did."

"He's offered to pay for you to go to college in England, and give you money until you're in the Navy."

"But I don't want to be a sailor. I've never even seen the sea."

"But you're good at your figures, and you have to be, so why not?"

"I won't," said Tommy, angrily. "I won't, I won't." He glared at them through tears. "You just want to get rid of me, that's all it is. You want me to go away from here, from . . ."

The parents looked at each other and sighed.

"Well, if you don't want to, you don't have to. But it's not every boy who has a chance like this."

"Why doesn't he send Dirk?" asked Tommy, aggressively.

"Tommy," cried Annie Clarke, in great distress.

"Well, why doesn't he? He's much better than me at figures."

"Go to bed," said Mr Clarke suddenly, in a fit of temper. "Go to bed."

Tommy went out of the room, slamming the door hard. He must be grown-up. His father had never spoken to him like that. He sat on the edge of the bed in stubborn rebellion, listening to the thudding of the stamps. And down in the compound they were dancing, the lights of the fires flickered red on his window-pane.

He wondered if Dirk were there, leaping around the fires with the others.

Next day he asked him: "Do you dance with the others?" At once he knew he had blundered. When Dirk was angry, his eyes darkened and narrowed. When he was hurt, his mouth set in a way which made the flesh pinch, thinly under his nose. So he looked now.

"Listen, white boy. White people don't like us half-castes. Neither do the blacks like us. No one does. And so I don't dance with them."

"Let's do some lessons," said Tommy, quickly. And they went to their books, dropping the subject.

Later Mr Macintosh came to the Clarkes' house and asked for Tommy. The parents watched Mr Macintosh and their son walk together along the edge of the great pit. They stood at the window and watched, but they did not speak.

Mr Macintosh was saying easily: "Well, laddie, and so you don't want to be sailor."

"No, Mr Macintosh."

"I went to sea when I was fifteen. It's hard, but you aren't afraid of that. Besides, you'd be an officer."

Tommy said nothing.

"You don't like the idea?"

"No."

Mr Macintosh stopped and looked down into the pit. The earth at the bottom was as yellow as it had been when Tommy was seven, but now, was much deeper. Mr Macintosh did not know how deep, because he had not measured it. Far below, in the man-made valley, the workers were moving and shifting like black seeds tilted on a piece of paper.

"Your father worked on the mines and he became an engineer working at nights, did you know that?"

"Yes."

"It was very hard for him. He was thirty before he was qualified, and then he earned twenty-five pounds a month until he came to this mine."

"Yes."

"You don't want to do that, do you?"

"I will if I have to," muttered Tommy, defiantly.

Mr Macintosh's face was swelling and purpling. The veins along nose and forehead were black. Mr Macintosh was asking himself why this lad treated him like dirt, when he was offering to do him an immense favour. And yet, in spite of the look of sullen indifference which was so ugly on that young face, he could not help loving him. He was a fine boy, tall, strong, and his hair was the soft, bright brown, and his eyes clear and black. A much better man than his father, who was rough and marked by the long struggle of his youth. He said: "Well, you don't have to be a sailor, perhaps you'd like to go to university and be a scholar."

"I don't know," said Tommy, unwillingly, although his heart had moved suddenly. Pleasure—he was weakening. Then he said suddenly: "Mr Macintosh, why do you want to send me to college?"

And Mr Macintosh fell right into the trap. "I have no children," he said, sentimentally. "I feel for you like my own son." He stopped. Tommy was looking away towards the compound, and his intention was clear.

"Very well then," said Mr Macintosh, harshly. "If you want to be a fool."

Tommy stood with his eyes lowered and he knew quite well he was a fool. Yet he could not have behaved in any other way.

"Don't be hasty," said Mr Macintosh, after a pause. "Don't throw away your chances, laddie. You're nothing but a lad, yet. Take your time." And with this tone, he changed all the emphasis of the conflict, and made it simply a question of waiting. Tommy did not move, so Mr Macintosh went on quickly: "Yes, that's right, you just think it over.' He hastily slipped a pound note from his pocket and put it into the boy's hand.

"You know what I'm going to do with it?" said Tommy, laughing suddenly, and not at all pleasantly.

"Do what you like, do just as you like, it's your money," said Mr Macintosh, turning away so as not to have to understand.

Tommy took the money to Dirk, who received it as if it were his right, a feeling in which Tommy was now an accomplice, and they sat together in the shed. "I've got to be something," said Tommy angrily. "They're going to make me be something."

"They wouldn't have to *make* me be anything," said Dirk, sardonically, "I know what I'd be."

"What?" asked Tommy, enviously.

"An engineer."

"How do you know what you've got to do?"

"That's what I want," said Dirk, stubbornly.

After a while Tommy said: "If you went to the city, there's a school for coloured children."

"I wouldn't see my mother again."

"Why not?"

"There's laws, white boy, laws. Anyone who lives with and after the fashion of the natives is a native. Therefore I'm a native, and I'm not entitled to go to school with the half-castes."

"If you went to the town, you'd not be living with the natives so you'd be classed as a coloured."

"But then I couldn't see my mother, because if she came to town she'd still be a native."

There was a triumphant conclusiveness in this that made Tommy think: He intends to get what he wants another way . . . And then: Through me . . . But he had accepted that justice a long time ago, and now he looked at his own arm that lay on the rough plank of the table. The outer side was burnt dark and dry with the sun, and the hair glinted on it like fine copper. It was no darker than Dirk's brown arm, and no lighter. He turned it over. Inside, the skin was smooth, dusky white, the veins running blue and strong across the wrist. He looked at Dirk, grinning, who promptly turned his own arm over, in a challenging way. Tommy said, unhappily: "You can't go to school properly because the inside of your arm is brown. And that's that!" Dirk's tight and bitter mouth expanded into the grin that was also his father's and he said: "That is so, white boy, that is so."

"Well, it's not my fault," said Tommy, aggressively, closing his fingers and banging the fist down again and again.

"I didn't say it was your fault," said Dirk at once.

Tommy said, in that uneasy, aggressive tone: "I've never even seen your mother."

To this, Dirk merely laughed, as if to say: You have never wanted to.

Tommy said, after a pause: "Let me come and see her now."

Then Dirk said in a tone which was uncomfortable, almost like compassion: "You don't have to."

"Yes," insisted Tommy. "Yes, now." He got up, and Dirk rose too. "She won't know what to say," warned Dirk. "She doesn't speak English." He did not really want Tommy to go to the compound; Tommy did not really want to go. Yet they went.

In silence they moved along the path between the trees, in silence skirted the edge of the pit, in silence entered the trees on the other side, and moved along the paths to the compound. It was big, spread over many acres, and the huts were in all stages of growth and decay, some new, with shining thatch, some tumble-down, with dulled and sagging thatch, some in the process of being built, the peeled wands of the roof-frames gleaming like milk in the sun.

Dirk led the way to a big square hut. Tommy could see people watching him walking with the coloured boy, and turning to laugh and whisper. Dirk's face was proud and tight, and he could feel the same look on his own face. Outside the square hut sat a little girl of about ten. She was bronze, Dirk's colour. Another little girl, quite black, perhaps six years old, was squatted on a log, finger in mouth, watching them. A baby, still unsteady on its feet, came staggering out of the doorway and collapsed, chuckling, against Dirk's knees. Its skin was almost white. Then Dirk's mother came out of the hut after the baby, smiled when she saw Dirk, but went anxious and bashful when she saw Tommy. She made a little bobbing curtsey, and took the baby from Dirk, for the sake of something to hold in her awkward and shy hands.

"This is Baas Tommy," said Dirk. He sounded very embarrassed.

She made another little curtsey and stood smiling.

She was a large woman, round and smooth all over, but her legs were slender, and her arms, wound around the child, thin and knotted. Her round face had a bashful curiosity, and her eyes moved quickly from Dirk to Tommy and back, while she smiled and smiled, biting her lips with strong teeth, and smiled again.

Tommy said: "Good morning," and she laughed and said "Good morning."

Then Dirk said: "Enough now, let's go." He sounded very angry. Tommy said: "Good-bye." Dirk's mother said: "Good-bye," and made her little bobbing curtsey, and she moved her child from one arm to another and bit her lip anxiously over her gleaming smile.

Tommy and Dirk went away from the square mud hut where the variously-coloured children stood staring after them.

"There now," said Dirk, angrily. "You've seen my mother."

"I'm sorry," said Tommy uncomfortably, feeling as if the responsibility for the whole thing rested on him. But Dirk laughed suddenly and said: "Oh, all right, all right, white boy, it's not your fault."

All the same, he seemed pleased that Tommy was upset.

Later, with an affection of indifference, Tommy asked, thinking of those new children: "Does Mr Macintosh come to your mother again now?"

And Dirk answered "Yes," just one word.

In the shed Dirk studied from a geography book, while Tommy sat idle and thought bitterly that they wanted him to be a sailor. Then his idle hands protested, and he took a knife and began slashing at the edge of the table. When the gashes showed a whiteness from the core of the wood, he took a stick lying on the floor and whittled at it, and when it snapped from thinness he went out to the trees, picked up a lump of old wood from the ground, and brought it back to the shed. He worked on it with his knife, not knowing what it was he made, until a curve under his knife reminded him of Dirk's sister squatting at the hut door, and then he directed his knife with a purpose. For several days he fought with the lump of wood, while Dirk studied. Then he brought a tin of boot polish from the house, and worked the bright brown wax into the creamy white wood, and soon there was a bronze-coloured figure of the little girl, staring with big, curious eyes while she squatted on spindly legs.

Tommy put it in front of Dirk, who turned it around, grinning a little. "It's like her," he said at last. "You can have it if you like." said Tommy. Dirk's teeth flashed, he hesitated, and then reached into his pocket and took out a bundle of dirty cloth. He undid it, and Tommy saw the little clay figure he had made of Dirk years ago. It was crumbling, almost worn to a lump of mud, but in it was still the vigorous challenge of Dirk's body. Tommy's mind signalled recognition—for he had forgotten he had ever made it—and he picked it up. "You kept it?" he asked shyly, and Dirk smiled. They looked at each other, smiling. It was a moment of warm, close feeling, and yet in it was the pain that neither of them understood, and also the cruelty and challenge that made them fight. They lowered their eyes unhappily. "I'll do your mother," said Tommy, getting up and running away into the trees, in order to escape from the challenging closeness. He searched until he found a thorn tree, which is so hard it turns the edge of an axe, and then he took an axe and worked at the felling of the tree until the sun went down. A big stone near him was kept wet to sharpen the axe, and next day he worked on until the tree fell. He sharpened the worn axe again, and cut a length of tree about two feet, and split off the tough bark, and brought it back to the shed. Dirk had fitted a shelf against the logs of the wall at the back. On it he had set the tiny, crumbling figure of himself, and the new bronze shape of his little sister. There was a space left for the new statue. Tommy said, shyly: "I'll do it as quickly as I can so that it will be done before the term starts." Then, lowering his eyes, which suffered under this new contract of shared feeling, he examined the piece of wood. It was not pale and gleaming like almonds, as was the softer wood. It was a gingery brown, a close-fibred, knotted wood, and down its centre, as he knew, was a hard black spine. He turned it between his hands and thought that this was more difficult than anything he had ever done. For the first time he studied a piece of wood before starting on it, with a desired shape in his mind, trying to see how what he wanted would grow out of the dense mass of material he held.

Then he tried his knife on it and it broke. He asked Dirk for his knife. It was a long piece of metal, taken from a pile of scrap mining machinery, sharpened on stone until it was razor-fine. The handle was cloth wrapped tight around.

With this new and unwieldy tool Tommy fought with the wood for many days. When the holidays were ending, the shape was there, but the face was blank. Dirk's mother was full-bodied, with soft, heavy flesh and full, naked shoulders above a tight, sideways draped cloth. The slender legs were planted firm on naked feet, and the thin arms, knotted with work, were lifted to the weight of a child who, a small, helpless creature swaddled in cloth, looked out with large, curious eyes. But the mother's face was not yet there.

"I'll finish it next holidays," said Tommy, and Dirk set it carefully beside the other figures on the shelf. With his back turned he asked cautiously: "Perhaps you won't be here next holidays?"

Yes I will," said Tommy, after a pause. "Yes I will."

It was a promise, and they gave each other that small, warm, unwilling smile, and turned away, Dirk back to the compound and Tommy to the house, where his trunk was packed for school.

That night Mr Macintosh came over to the Clarkes' house and spoke with the parents in the front room. Tommy, who was asleep, woke to find Mr Macintosh beside him. He sat on the foot of the bed and said: "I want to talk to you, laddie." Tommy turned the wick of the oil-lamp, and now he could see in the shadowy light that Mr Macintosh had a look of uneasiness about him. He was sitting with his strong old body balanced behind the big stomach, hands laid on his knees, and his grey Scots eyes were watchful.

"I want you to think about what I said," said Mr Macintosh, in a quick, bluff good-humour. "Your mother says in two years' time you will have matriculated,* you're doing fine at school. And after that you can go to college."

Tommy lay on his elbow, and in the silence the drums came tapping from the compound, and he said: "But Mr Macintosh, I'm not the only one who's good at his books."

Mr Macintosh stirred, but said bluffly: "Well, but I'm talking about you."

---

* *matriculated*: passed the school examinations which qualify a pupil for university entrance.

Tommy was silent, because as usual these opponents were so much stronger than was reasonable, simply because of their ability to make words mean something else. And then, his heart, painfully beating, he said: "Why don't you send Dirk to college? You're so rich, and Dirk knows everything I know. He's better than me at figures. He's a whole book ahead of me, and he can do sums I can't."

Mr Macintosh crossed his legs impatiently, uncrossed them, and said: "Now why should I send Dirk to college?" For now Tommy would have to put into precise words what he meant, and this Mr Macintosh was quite sure he would not do. But to make certain, he lowered his voice and said: "Think of your mother, laddie, she's worrying about you, and you don't want to make her worried, do you?"

Tommy looked towards the door, under it came a thick yellow streak of light: in that room his mother and his father were waiting in silence for Mr Macintosh to emerge with news of Tommy's sure and wonderful future.

"You know why Dirk should go to college," said Tommy in despair, shifting his body unhappily under the sheets, and Mr Macintosh chose not to hear it. He got up, and said quickly: "You just think it over, laddie. There's no hurry, but by next holidays I want to know." And he went out of the room. As he opened the door, a brightly-lit, painful scene was presented to Tommy: his father and mother sat, smiling in embarrassed entreaty at Mr Macintosh. The door shut, and Tommy turned down the light, and there was darkness.

He went to school next day. Mrs Clarke, turning out Mr Macintosh's house as usual, said unhappily: "I think you'll find everything in its proper place," and slipped away, as if she were ashamed.

As for Mr Macintosh, he was in a mood which made others, besides Annie Clarke, speak to him carefully. His cook-boy, who had worked for him twelve years, gave notice that month. He had been knocked down twice by that powerful, hairy fist, and he was not a slave, after all, to remain bound to a bad-tempered master. And when a load of rock slipped and crushed the skulls of two workers, and the police came out for an investigation, Mr Macintosh met them irritably, and told them to mind their own business. For the first time in that mine's history of scandalous recklessness, after many such accidents, Mr Macintosh heard the indignant words from the police officer: "You speak as if you were above the law, Mr Macintosh. If this happens again, you'll see . . ."

Worst of all, he ordered Dirk to go back to work in the pit, and Dirk refused.

"You can't make me," said Dirk.

"Who's the boss on this mine?" shouted Mr Macintosh.

"There's no law to make children work," said the thirteen-year-old who stood as tall as his father, a straight, lithe youth against the bulky strength of the old man.

The word *law* whipped the anger in Mr Macintosh to the point where he could feel his eyes go dark, and the blood pounding in that hot darkness in his head. In fact, it was the power of this anger that sobered him, for he had been very young when he had learned to fear his own temper. And above all, he was a shrewd man. He waited until his sight was clear again, and then asked, reasonably: "Why do you want to loaf around the compound, why not work and earn money?"

Dirk said: "I can read and write, and I know my figures better than Tommy— Baas Tommy," he added, in a way which made the anger rise again in Mr Macintosh, so that he had to make a fresh effort to subdue it.

But Tommy was a point of weakness in Mr Macintosh, and it was then that he spoke the words which afterwards made him wonder if he'd gone suddenly crazy. For he said: "Very well, when you're sixteen you can come and do my books and write the letters for the mine."

Dirk said: "All right," as if this were no more than his due, and walked off, leaving Mr Macintosh impotently furious with himself. For how could anyone but himself

see the books? Such a person would be his master. It was
impossible, he had no intention of ever letting Dirk, or
anyone else, see them. Yet he had made the promise. And so
he would have to find another way of using Dirk, or—and
the words came involuntarily—getting rid of him.

From a mood of settled bad temper, Mr Macintosh
dropped into one of sullen thoughtfulness, which was
entirely foreign to his character. Being shrewd is quite
different from the processes of thinking. Shrewdness, particularly the money-making shrewdness, is a kind of instinct.
While Mr Macintosh had always known what he wanted
to do, and how to do it, that did not mean he had known
why he wanted so much money, or why he had chosen
these ways of making it. Mr Macintosh felt like a cat whose
nose has been rubbed into its own dirt, and for many
nights he sat in the hot little house, that vibrated continually
from the noise of the minestamps, most uncomfortably
considering himself and his life. He reminded himself, for
instance, that he was sixty, and presumably had not more
than ten or fifteen years to live. It was not a thought that
an unreflective man enjoys, particularly when he had never
considered his age at all. He was so healthy, strong, tough.
But he was sixty nevertheless, and what would be his
monument? An enormous pit in the earth, and a million
pounds' worth of property. Then how should he spend ten
or fifteen years? Exactly as he had the preceding sixty, for
he hated being away from this place, and this gave him a
caged and useless sensation, for it had never entered his
head before that he was not as free as he felt himself to be.

Well, then—and this thought gnawed most closely to Mr
Macintosh's pain—why had he not married? For he considered himself a marrying sort of man, and had always
intended to find himself the right sort of woman and marry
her. Yet he was already sixty. The truth was that Mr
Macintosh had no idea at all why he had not married and got
himself sons; and in these slow, uncomfortable ponderings
the thought of Dirk's mother intruded itself only to be

hastily thrust away. Mr Macintosh, the sensualist, had a taste for dark-skinned women; and now it was certainly too late to admit as a permanent feature of his character something he had always considered as a sort of temporary whim, or makeshift, like someone who learns to enjoy an inferior brand of tobacco when better brands are not available.

He thought of Tommy, of whom he had been used to say: "I've taken a fancy to the laddie." Now it was not so much a fancy as a deep, grieving love. And Tommy was the son of his employee, and looked at him with contempt, and he, Mr Macintosh, reacted with angry shame as if he were guilty of something. Of what? It was ridiculous.

The whole situation was ridiculous, and so Mr Macintosh allowed himself to slide back into his usual frame of mind. Tommy's only a boy, he thought, and he'll see reason in a year or so. And as for Dirk, I'll find him some kind of a job when the time comes . . .

At the end of the term, when Tommy came home, Mr Macintosh asked, as usual, to see the school report, which usually filled him with pride. Instead of heading the class with approbation from the teachers and high marks in all subjects, Tommy was near the bottom, with such remarks as Slovenly, and Lazy, and Bad-mannered. The only subject in which he got any marks at all was that called Art, which Mr Macintosh did not take into account.

When Tommy was asked by his parents why he was not working, he replied, impatiently: "I don't know," which was quite true; and at once escaped to the anthill. Dirk was there, waiting for the books Tommy always brought for him. Tommy reached at once up to the shelf where stood the figure of Dirk's mother, lifted it down and examined the unworked space which would be the face. "I know how to do it," he said to Dirk, and took out some knives and chisels he had brought from the city.

That was how he spent the three weeks of that holiday, and when he met Mr Macintosh he was sullen and uncomfortable. "You'll have to be working a bit better,"

he said, before Tommy went back, to which he received no
answer but an unwilling smile.

During that term Tommy distinguished himself in two
ways besides being steadily at the bottom of the class he
had so recently led. He made a fiery speech in the debating
society on the iniquity of the colour bar, which rather
pleased his teachers, since it is a well-known fact that the
young must pass through these phases of rebellion before
settling down to conformity. In fact, the greater the verbal
rebellion, the more settled was the conformity likely to be.
In secret Tommy got books from the city library such as are
not usually read by boys of his age, on the history of Africa,
and on comparative anthropology, and passed from there to
the history of the moment—he ordered papers from the
Government Stationery Office, the laws of the country. Most
particularly those affecting the relations between black
and white and coloured. These he bought in order to take
back to Dirk. But in addition to all this ferment, there
was that subject Art, which in this school meant a drawing
lesson twice a week, copying busts of Julius Caesar, or it
might be Nelson, or shading in fronds of fern or leaves,
or copying a large vase or a table standing diagonally to the
class, thus learning what he was told were the laws of
Perspective. There was no modelling, nothing approaching
sculpture in this school, but this was the nearest thing to
it, and that mysterious prohibition which forbade him to
distinguish himself in Geometry or English, was silent when
it came to using the pencil.

At the end of the term his Report was very bad, but it
admitted that he had An Interest in Current Events, and
a Talent for Art.

And now this word Art, coming at the end of two succes-
sive terms, disturbed his parents and forced itself on Mr
Macintosh. He said to Annie Clarke: "It's a nice thing to
make pictures, but the lad won't earn a living by it." And
Mrs Clarke said reproachfully to Tommy: "It's all very well,

Tommy, but you aren't going to earn a living drawing pictures."

"I didn't say I wanted to earn a living with it," shouted Tommy, miserably. "Why have I got to *be* something, you're always wanting me to *be* something."

That holidays Dirk spent studying the Acts of Parliament and the Reports of Commissions and Sub-Committees which Tommy had brought him, while Tommy attempted something new. There was a square piece of soft white wood which Dirk had pilfered from the mine, thinking Tommy might use it. And Tommy set it against the walls of the shed, and knelt before it and attempted a frieze or engraving—he did not know the words for what he was doing. He cut out a great pit, surrounded by mounds of earth and rock, with the peaks of great mountains beyond, and at the edge of the pit stood a big man carrying a stick, and over the edge of the pit wound a file of black figures, tumbling into the gulf. From the pit came flames and smoke. Tommy took green ooze from leaves and mixed clay to colour the mountains and edges of the pit, and he made the little figures black with charcoal, and he made the flames writhing up out of the pit red with the paint used for parts of the mining machinery.

"If you leave it here, the ants'll eat it," said Dirk, looking with grim pleasure at the crude but effective picture.

To which Tommy shrugged. For while he was always solemnly intent on a piece of work in hand, afraid of anything that might mar it, or even distract his attention from it, once it was finished he cared for it not at all.

It was Dirk who had painted the shelf which held the other figures with a mixture that discouraged ants, and it was now Dirk who set the piece of square wood on a sheet of tin smeared with the same mixture, and balanced it in a way so it should not touch any part of the walls of the shed, where the ants might climb up.

And so Tommy went back to school, still in that mood

of obstinate disaffection, to make more copies of Julius Caesar and vases of flowers, and Dirk remained with his books and his Acts of Parliament. They would be fourteen before they met again, and both knew that crises and decisions faced them. Yet they said no more than the usual: Well, so long, before they parted. Nor did they ever write to each other, although this term Tommy had a commission to send certain books and other Acts of Parliament for a purpose which he entirely approved.

Dirk had built himself a new hut in the compound, where he lived alone, in the compound but not of it, affectionate to his mother, but apart from her. And to this hut at night came certain of the workers who forgot their dislike of the half-caste, that cuckoo in their nest, in their common interest in what he told them of the Acts and Reports. What he told them was what he had learnt himself in the proud loneliness of his isolation. "Education," he said, "Education, that's the key"—and Tommy agreed with him, although he had, or so one might suppose from the way he was behaving, abandoned all idea of getting an education for himself. All that term parcels came to "Dirk, c/o Mr Macintosh", and Mr Macintosh delivered them to Dirk without any questions.

In the dim and smoky hut every night, half a dozen of the workers laboured with stubs of pencil and the exercise books sent by Tommy, to learn to write and do sums and understand the Laws.

One night Mr Macintosh came rather late out of that other hut, and saw the red light from a fire moving softly on the rough ground outside the door of Dirk's hut. All the others were dark. He moved cautiously among them until he stood in the shadows outside the door, and looked in. Dirk was squatting on the floor, surrounded by half a dozen men, looking at a newspaper.

Mr Macintosh walked thoughtfully home in the starlight. Dirk, had he known what Mr Macintosh was thinking, would have been very angry, for all his flaming rebellion, his words of resentment were directed against Mr Macintosh and his tyranny. Yet for the first time Mr Macintosh was thinking of Dirk with a certain rough, amused pride. Perhaps it was because he was a Scot, after all, and in every one of his nation is an instinctive respect for learning and people with the determination to "get on". A chip off the old block, thought Mr Macintosh, remembering how he, as a boy, had laboured to get a bit of education. And if the chip was the wrong colour—well, he would do something for Dirk. Something, he would decide when the time came. As for the others who were with Dirk, there was nothing easier than to sack a worker and engage another. Mr Macintosh went to his bed, dressed as usual in vest and pyjama trousers, unwashed and thrifty in candlelight.

In the morning he gave orders to one of the overseers that Dirk should be summoned. His heart was already soft with thinking about the generous scene which would shortly take place. He was going to suggest that Dirk should teach all the overseers to read and write—on a salary from himself, of course—in order that these same overseers should be more useful in the work. They might learn to mark pay-sheets, for instance.

The overseer said that Baas Dirk spent his days studying in Baas Tommy's hut—with the suggestion in his manner that Baas Dirk could not be disturbed while so occupied, and that this was on Tommy's account.

The man, closely studying the effect of his words, saw how Mr Macintosh's big, veiny face swelled, and he stepped back a pace. He was not one of Dirk's admirers.

Mr Macintosh, after some moments of heavy breathing, allowed his shrewdness to direct his anger. He dismissed the man, and turned away.

During that morning he left his great pit and walked off into the bush in the direction of the towering blue peak. He had heard vaguely that Tommy had some kind of a hut, but imagined it as a child's thing. He was still very angry because of that calculated "Baas Dirk". He walked for a

while along a smooth path through the trees, and came to
a clearing. On the other side was an anthill, and on the
anthill a well-built hut, draped with Christmas fern around
the open front, like curtains. In the opening sat Dirk. He
wore a clean white shirt, and long smooth trousers. His
head, oiled and brushed close, was bent over books. The
hand that turned the pages of the books had a brass ring on
the little finger. He was the very image of an aspiring clerk:
that form of humanity which Mr Macintosh despised most.

Mr Macintosh remained on the edge of the clearing for
some time, vaguely waiting for something to happen, so that
he might fling himself, armoured and directed by his contemptuous anger, into a crisis which would destroy Dirk
for ever. But nothing did happen. Dirk continued to turn
the pages of the book, so Mr Macintosh went back to his
house, where he ate boiled beef and carrots for his dinner.

Afterwards he went to a certain drawer in his bedroom,
and from it took an object carelessly wrapped in cloth which,
exposed, showed itself as that figure of Dirk the boy Tommy
had made and sold for five pounds. And the Macintosh
turned and handled and pored over that crude wooden
image of Dirk in a passion of curiosity, just as if the boy
did not live on the same square mile of soil with him,
fully available to his scrutiny at most hours of the day.

If one imagines a Judgement Day with the graves giving
up their dead impartially, black, white, bronze, and yellow,
to a happy reunion, one of the pleasures of that reunion
might well be that people who have lived on the same acre
or street all their lives will look at each other with incredulous recognition. "So that is what you were like," might
be the gathering murmur around God's heaven. For the
glass wall between colour and colour is not only a barrier
against touch, but has become thick and distorted, so that
black men, white men, see each other through it, but see—
what? Mr Macintosh examined the image of Dirk as if
searching for some final revelation, but the thought that
came persistently to his mind was that the statue might be

of himself as a lad of twelve. So after a few moments he rolled it again in the cloth and tossed it back into the corner of a drawer, out of sight, and with it the unwelcome and tormenting knowledge.

Late that afternoon he left his house again and made his way towards the hut on the antheap. It was empty, and he walking through the knee-high grass and bushes till he could climb up the hard, slippery walls of the antheap and so into the hut.

First he looked at the books in the case. The longer he looked, the faster faded that picture of Dirk as an oiled and mincing clerk, which he had been clinging to ever since he threw the other image into the back of a drawer. Respect for Dirk was reborn. Complicated mathematics, much more advanced than he had ever done. Geography. History. "The Development of the Slave Trade in the Eighteenth Century." "The Growth of Parliamentary Institutions in Great Britain." This title made Mr Macintosh smile— the freebooting buccaneer examining a coastguard's notice perhaps. Mr Macintosh lifted down one book after another and smiled. Then, beside these books, he saw a pile of slight, blue pamphlets, and he examined them. "The Natives Employment Act." "The Natives Juvenile Employment Act." "The Native Passes Act." And Mr Macintosh flipped over the leaves and laughed, and had Dirk heard that laugh it would have been worse to him than any whip.

For as he patiently explained these laws and others like them to his bitter allies in the hut at night, it seemed to him that every word he spoke was like a stone thrown at Mr Macintosh, his father. Yet Mr Macintosh laughed, since he despised these laws, although in a different way, as much as Dirk did. When Mr Macintosh, on his rare trips to the city, happened to drive past the House of Parliament, he turned on it a tolerant and appreciative gaze. "Well, why not?" he seemed to be saying. "It's an occupation, like any other."

So to Dirk's desperate act of retaliation he responded with a smile, and tossed back the books and pamphlets on

the shelf. And then he turned to look at the other things in
the shed, and for the first time he saw the high shelf where the
statuettes were arranged. He looked, and felt his face
swelling with that fatal rage. There was Dirk's mother,
peering at him in bashful sensuality from over the baby's
head, there the little girl, his daughter, squatting on spindly
legs and staring. And there, on the edge of the shelf, a small,
worn shape of clay which still held the vigorous strength
of Dirk. Mr Macintosh, breathing heavily, holding down
his anger, stepped back to gain a clearer view of those
figures, and his heel slipped on a slanting piece of wood.
He turned to look, and there was the picture Tommy had
carved and coloured of his mine. Mr Macintosh saw the great
pit, the black little figures tumbling and sprawling over into
the flames, and he saw himself, stick in hand, astride on his
two legs at the edge of the pit, his hat on the back of his head.

And now Mr Macintosh was so disturbed and angry that
he was driven out of the hut and into the clearing, where
he walked back and forth through the grass, looking at the
hut while his anger growled and moved inside him. After
some time he came close to the hut again and peered in. Yes,
there was Dirk's mother, peering bashfully from her shelf,
as if to say: Yes, it's me, remember? And there on the floor
was the square tinted piece of wood which said what Tommy
thought of him and his life. Mr Macintosh took a box of
matches from his pocket. He lit a match. He understood he
was standing in the hut with a lit match in his hand to
no purpose. He dropped the match and ground it out with
his foot. Then he put a pipe in his mouth, filled it and lit
it, gazing all the time at the shelf and at the square carving.
The second match fell to the floor and lay spurting a small
white flame. He ground his heel hard on it. Anger heaved
up in him beyond all sanity, and he lit another match,
pushed it into the thatch of the hut, and walked out of it
and so into the clearing and away into the bush. Without
looking behind him he walked back to his house where his
supper of boiled beef and carrots was waiting for him. He

was amazed, angry, resentful. Finally he felt aggrieved, and wanted to explain to someone what a monstrous injustice was Tommy's view of him. But there was no one to explain it to; and he slowly quietened to a steady dulled sadness, and for some days remained so, until time restored him to normal. From this condition he looked back at his behaviour and did not like it. Not that he regretted burning the hut, it seemed to him unimportant. He was angry at himself for allowing his anger to dictate his actions. Also he knew that such an act brings its own results.

So he waited, and thought mainly of the cruelty of fate in denying him a son who might carry on his work—for he certainly thought of his work as something to be continued. He thought sadly of Tommy, who denied him. And so his affection for Tommy was sprung again by thinking of him, and he waited, thinking of reproachful things to say to him.

When Tommy returned from school he went straight to the clearing and found a mound of ash on the antheap that was already sifted and swept by the wind. He found Dirk, sitting on a tree trunk in the bush waiting for him.

"What happened?" asked Tommy. And then, at once: "Did you save your books?"

Dirk said: "*He* burnt it."

"How do you know?"

"I know."

Tommy nodded. "All your books have gone," he said, very grieved, and as guilty as if he had burnt them himself.

"Your carvings and your statues are burnt too."

But at this Tommy shrugged since he could not care about his things once they were finished. "Shall we build the hut again now?" he suggested.

"My books are burnt," said Dirk, in a low voice, and Tommy looking at him, saw how his hands were clenched He instinctively moved a little aside to give his friend's anger space.

"When I grow up I'll clear you all out, all of you, there won't be one white man left in Africa, not one."

Tommy's face had a small, half-scared smile on it. The hatred Dirk was directing against him was so strong he nearly went away. He sat beside Dirk on the tree trunk and said: "I'll try and get you more books."

"And then he'll burn them again."

"But you've already got what was in them inside your head," said Tommy, consolingly. Dirk said nothing, but sat like a clenched fist, and so they remained on the tree trunk in the quiet bush while the doves cooed and the mine-stamps thudded, all that hot morning. When they had to separate at midday to return to their different worlds, it was with deep sadness, knowing that their childhood was finished, and their playing, and something new was ahead.

And at that meal Tommy's mother and father had his school report on the table, and they were reproachful. Tommy was at the foot of his class, and he would not matriculate that year. Or any year if he went on like this.

"You used to be such a clever boy," mourned his mother, "and now what's happened to you?"

Tommy, sitting silent at the table, moved his shoulders in a hunched, irritable way, as if to say: Leave me alone. Nor did he feel himself to be stupid and lazy, as the report said he was.

In his room were drawing blocks and pencils, hammers and chisels. He had never said to himself he had exchanged one purpose for another, for he had no purpose. How could he, when he had never been offered a future he could accept? Now, at this time, in his fifteenth year, with his reproachful parents deepening their reproach, and the knowledge that Mr Macintosh would soon see that report, all he felt was a locked stubbornness, and a deep strength.

In the afternoon he went back to the clearing, and he took his chisels with him. On the old, soft, rotted tree trunk that he sat on that morning, he sat again, waiting for Dirk. But Dirk did not come. Putting himself in his friend's place he understood that Dirk could not endure to be with a white-skinned person—a white face, even that of his oldest friend, was too much the enemy. But he waited, sitting on the tree trunk all through the afternoon, with his chisels and hammers in a little box at his feet in the grass, and he fingered the soft, warm wood he sat on, letting the shape and texture of it come into the knowledge of his fingers.

Next day, there was still no Dirk.

Tommy began walking around the fallen tree, studying it. It was very thick, and its roots twisted and slanted into the air to the height of his shoulder. He began to carve the root. It would be Dirk again.

That night Mr Macintosh came to the Clarkes' house and read the report. He went back to his own, and sat wondering why Tommy was set so bitterly against him. The next day he went to the Clarkes' house again to find Tommy, but the boy was not there.

He therefore walked through the thick bush to the ant-heap, and found Tommy kneeling in the grass working on the tree root.

Tommy said: "Good morning," and went on working, and Mr Macintosh sat on the trunk and watched.

"What are you making?" asked Mr Macintosh.

"Dirk," said Tommy, and Mr Macintosh went purple and almost sprang up and away from the tree trunk. But Tommy was not looking at him. So Mr Macintosh remained, in silence. And then the useless vigour of Tommy's concentration on that rotting bit of root goaded him, and his mind moved naturally to a new decision.

"Would you like to be an artist?" he suggested.

Tommy allowed his chisel to rest, and looked at Mr Macintosh as if this were a fresh trap. He shrugged, and with the appearance of anger, went on with his work.

"If you've a real gift, you can earn money by that sort of thing! I had a cousin back in Scotland who did it. He made souvenirs, you know, for travellers." He spoke in a soothing and jolly way.

Tommy let the souvenirs slide by him, as another of these impositions on his independence. He said: "Why did you burn Dirk's books?"

But Mr Macintosh laughed in relief. "Why should I burn the books?" It really seemed ridiculous to him, his rage had been against Tommy's work, not Dirk's.

"I know you did," said Tommy. "I know it. And Dirk does too."

Mr Macintosh lit his pipe in good humour. For now things seemed much easier. Tommy did not know why he had set fire to the hut, and that was the main thing. He puffed smoke for a few moments and said: "Why should you think I don't want Dirk to study? It's a good thing, a bit of education."

Tommy stared disbelievingly at him.

"I asked Dirk to use his education, I asked him to teach some of the others. But he wouldn't have any of it. Is that my fault?"

Now Tommy's face was completely incredulous. Then he went scarlet, which Mr Macintosh did not understand. Why should the boy be looking so foolish? But Tommy was thinking: We were on the wrong track . . . And then he imagined what his offer must have done to Dirk's angry, rebellious pride, and he suddenly understood. His face still crimson, he laughed. It was a bitter, ironical laugh, and Mr Macintosh was upset— it was not a boy's laugh at all.

Tommy's face slowly faded from crimson, and he went back to work with his chisel. He said, after a pause: "Why don't you send Dirk to college instead of me? He's much more clever than me. I'm not clever, look at my report."

"Well, laddie . . ." began Mr Macintosh reproachfully— he had been going to say: "Are you being lazy at school simply to force my hand over Dirk?" He wondered at his own impulse to say it; and slid off into the familiar obliqueness which Tommy ignored: "But you know how things are, or you ought to by now. You talk as if you didn't understand."

But Tommy was kneeling with his back to Mr Macintosh, working at the root, so Mr Macintosh continued to smoke. Next day he returned and sat on the tree trunk and watched. Tommy looked at him as if he considered his presence an unwelcome gift, but he did not say anything.

Slowly, the big fanged root which rose from the trunk was taking Dirk's shape. Mr Macintosh watched with uneasy loathing. He did not like it, but he could not stop watching. Once he said: "But if there's a veld fire, it'll get burnt. And the ants'll eat it in any case." Tommy shrugged. It was the making of it that mattered, not what happened to it afterwards, and this attitude was so foreign to Mr Macintosh's accumulating nature that it seemed to him that Tommy was touched in the head. He said: "Why don't you work on something that'll last? Or even if you studied like Dirk it would be better."

Tommy said: "I like doing it."

"But look, the ants are already at the trunk—by the time you get back from your school next time there'll be nothing left of it."

"Or someone might set fire to it," suggested Tommy. He looked steadily at Mr Macintosh's reddening face with triumph. Mr Macintosh found the words too near the truth. For certainly, as the days passed, he was looking at the new work with hatred and fear and dislike. It was nearly finished. Even if nothing more were done to it, it could stand as it was, complete.

Dirk's long, powerful body came writhing out of the wood like something struggling free. The head was clenched back, in the agony of the birth, eyes narrowed and desperate, the mouth—Mr Macintosh's mouth—tightened in obstinate purpose. The shoulders were free, but the hands were held; they could not pull themselves out of the dense wood, they were imprisoned. His body was free to the knees, but below them the human limbs were uncreated, the natural shapes of the wood swelled to the perfect muscled knees.

Mr Macintosh did not like it. He did not know what art

was, but he knew he did not like this at all, it disturbed him deeply, so that when he looked at it he wanted to take an axe and cut it to pieces. Or burn it, perhaps . . .

As for Tommy, the uneasiness of this elderly man who watched him all day was a deep triumph. Slowly, and for the first time, he saw that perhaps this was not a sort of game that he played, it might be something else. A weapon—he watched Mr Macintosh's reluctant face, and a new respect for himself and what he was doing grew in him.

At night, Mr Macintosh sat in his candle-lit room and he thought or rather *felt*, his way to a decision.

There was no denying the power of Tommy's gift. Therefore, it was a question of finding the way to turn it into money. He knew nothing about these matters, however, and it was Tommy himself who directed him, for towards the end of the holidays he said: "When you're so rich you can do anything. You could send Dirk to college and not even notice it."

Mr Macintosh, in the reasonable and persuasive voice he now always used, said, "But you know these coloured people have nowhere to go."

Tommy said: "You could send him to the Cape. There are coloured people in the university there. Or Johannesburg." And he insisted against Mr Macintosh's silence: "You're so rich you can do anything you like."

But Mr Macintosh, like most rich people, thought not of money as things to buy, things to do, but rather how it was tied up in buildings and land.

"It would cost thousands," he said. "Thousands for a coloured boy."

But Tommy's scornful look silenced him, and he said hastily: "I'll think about it." But he was thinking not of Dirk, but of Tommy. Sitting alone in his room he told himself it was simply a question of paying for knowledge.

So next morning he made his preparations for a trip to town. He shaved, and over his cotton singlet he put a striped jacket, which half concealed his long, stained khaki trousers. This was as far as he ever went in concessions to the city life he despised. He got into his big American car and set off.

In the city he took the simplest route to knowledge.

He went to the Education Department, and said he wanted to see the Minister of Education. "I'm Macintosh," he said, with perfect confidence; and the pretty secretary who had been patronizing his clothes, went at once to the Minister and said: "There is a Mr Macintosh to see you." She described him as an old, fat, dirty man with a large stomach, and soon the doors opened and Mr Macintosh was with the spring of knowledge.

He emerged five minutes later with what he wanted, the name of a certain expert. He drove through the deep green avenues of the city to the house he had been told to go to, which was a large and well-kept one, and comforted Mr Macintosh in his faith that art properly used could make money. He parked his car in the road and walked in.

On the verandah, behind a table heaped with books, sat a middle-aged man with spectacles. Mr Tomlinson was essentially a scholar with working hours he respected, and he lifted his eyes to see a big, dirty man with black hair showing above the dirty whiteness of his vest, and he said sharply: "What do you want?"

"Wait a minute, laddie," said Mr Macintosh easily, and he held out a note from the Minister of Education, and Mr Tomlinson took it and read it, feeling reassured. It was worded in such a way that his seeing Mr Macintosh could be felt as a favour he was personally doing the Minister.

"I'll make it worth your while," said Mr Macintosh, and at once distaste flooded Mr Tomlinson, and he went pink, and said: "I'm afraid I haven't the time."

"Damn it, man, it's your job, isn't it? Or so Wentworth said".

"No," said Mr Tomlinson, making each word clear, "I advise on ancient Monuments."

Mr Macintosh stared, then laughed, and said: "Went-worth said you'd do, but it doesn't matter, I'll get someone else." And he left.

Mr Tomlinson watched this hobo go off the verandah and into a magnificent car, and his thought was: "He must have stolen it." Then puzzled and upset, he went to the telephone. But in a few moments he was smiling. Finally he laughed. Mr Macintosh was *the* Mr Macintosh, a genuine specimen of the old-timer. It was the phrase "old-timer" that made it possible for Mr Tomlinson to relent. He therefore rang the hotel at which Mr Macintosh, as a rich man, would be bound to be staying, and he said he had made an error, he would be free the following day to accompany Mr Macintosh.

And so next morning, Mr Macintosh, not at all surprised that the expert was at his service after all, with Mr Tomlinson, who preserved a tolerant smile, drove out to the mine.

They drove very fast in the powerful car, and Mr Tomlinson held himself steady while they jolted and bounced, and listened to Mr Macintosh's tales of Australia and New Zealand, and thought of him rather as he would of an ancient Monument.

At last the long plain ended, and foothills of greenish scrub heaped themselves around the car, and then high mountains piled with granite boulders, and the heat came in thick, slow waves into the car, and Mr Tomlinson thought: I'll be glad when we're through the mountains into the plain. But instead they turned into a high, enclosed place with mountains all around, and suddenly there was an enormous gulf in the ground, and on one side of it were two tiny tin-roofed houses, and on the other acres of kaffir huts. The mine-stamps thudded regularly, like a pulse of the heart, and Mr Tomlinson wondered how anybody, white or black, could bear to live in such a place.

He ate boiled beef and carrots and greasy potatoes with one of the richest men in the sub-continent, and thought

how well and intelligently he would use such money if he
had it—which is the only consolation left to the cultivated
man of moderate income. After lunch, Mr Macintosh said:
"And now, let's get it over."

Mr Tomlinson expressed his willingness, and smiling to
himself, followed Mr Macintosh off into the bush on a kaffir
path. He did not know what he was going to see. Mr
Macintosh had said: "Can you tell if a youngster has got
any talent just by looking at a piece of wood he has carved?"

Mr Tomlinson said he would do his best.

Then they were beside a fallen tree trunk, and in the grass
knelt a big lad, with untidy brown hair falling over his face,
labouring at the wood with a large chisel.

"This is a friend of mine," said Mr Macintosh to Tommy,
who got to his feet and stood uncomfortably, wondering
what was happening. "Do you mind if Mr Tomlinson sees
what you are doing?"

Tommy made a shrugging movement and felt that
things were going beyond his control. He looked in awed
amazement at Mr Tomlinson, who seemed to him rather like
a teacher or professor, and certainly not at all what he
imagined an artist to be.

"Well?" said Mr Macintosh to Mr Tomlinson, after a
space of half a minute.

Mr Tomlinson laughed in a way which said: "Now don't
be in such a hurry." He walked around the carved tree root,
looking at the figure of Dirk from this angle and that.

Then he asked Tommy: "Why do you make these
carvings?"

Tommy very uncomfortably shrugged, as if to say: "What
a silly question;" and Mr Macintosh hastily said: "He gets
high marks for Art at School."

Mr Tomlinson smiled again and walked around to the
other side of the trunk. From here he could see Dirk's face,
flattened back on the neck, eyes half-closed and strained, the
muscles of the neck shaped from natural veins of the wood.

"Is this someone you know?" he asked Tommy in an easy, intimate way, one artist to another.

"Yes," said Tommy, briefly; he resented the question.

Mr Tomlinson looked at the face and then at Mr Macintosh. "It has a look of you," he observed dispassionately, and coloured himself as he saw Mr Macintosh grow angry. He walked well away from the group, to give Mr Macintosh space to hide his embarrassment. When he returned, he asked Tommy: "And so you want to be a sculptor?"

"I don't know," said Tommy, defiantly.

Mr Tomlinson shrugged rather impatiently, and with a nod at Mr Macintosh suggested it was enough. He said good-bye to Tommy, and went back to the house with Mr Macintosh.

There he was offered tea and biscuits, and Mr Macintosh asked: "Well, what do you think?"

But by now Mr Tomlinson was certainly offended at this casual cash-on-delivery approac.ı to art, and he said: "Well, that rather depends, doesn't it?"

"On what?" demanded Mr Macintosh.

"He seems to have talent," conceded Mr Tomlinson.

"That's all I want to know," said Mr Macintosh, and suggested that now he could run Mr Tomlinson back to town.

But Mr Tomlinson did not feel it was enough, and he said: "It's quite interesting, that statue. I suppose he's seen pictures in magazines. It has quite a modern feeling."

"Modern?" said Mr Macintosh, "what do you mean?"

Mr Tomlinson shrugged again, giving it up. "Well," he said, practically, "what do you mean to do?"

"If you say he has talent, I'll send him to the University and he can study art."

After a long pause, Mr Tomlinson murmured: "What a fortunate boy he is." He meant to convey depths of disillusionment and irony, but Mr Macintosh said: "I always did have a fancy for him."

He took Mr Tomlinson back to the city, and as he dropped him on his verandah, presented him with a cheque for fifty pounds, which Mr Tomlinson most indignantly returned. "Oh, give it to charity," said Mr Macintosh impatiently, and went to his car, leaving Mr Tomlinson to heal his susceptibilities in any way he chose.

When Mr Macintosh reached his mine again it was midnight, and there were no lights in the Clarkes' house, and so his need to be generous must be stifled until the morning.

Then he went to Annie Clarke and told her he would send Tommy to university, where he could be an artist, and Mrs Clarke wept gratitude, and said that Mr Macintosh was much kinder than Tommy deserved, and perhaps he would learn sense yet and go back to his books.

As far as Mr Macintosh was concerned it was all settled.

He set off through the trees to find Tommy and announce his future to him.

But when he arrived at seeing distance there were two figures. Dirk and Tommy, seated on the trunk talking, and Mr Macintosh stopped among the trees, filled with such bitter anger at this fresh check to his plans that he could not trust himself to go on. So he returned to his house, and brooded angrily—he knew exactly what was going to happen when he spoke to Tommy, and now he must make up his mind, there was no escape from a decision.

And while Mr Macintosh mused bitterly in his house, Tommy and Dirk waited for him; it was now all as clear to them as it was to him.

Dirk had come out of the trees to Tommy the moment the two men left the day before. Tommy was standing by the fanged root, looking at the shape of Dirk in it, trying to understand what was going to be demanded of him. The word "artist" was on his tongue, and he tasted it, trying to make the strangeness of it fit that powerful shape struggling out of the wood. He did not like it. He did not want—but what did he want? He felt pressure on himself, the faint beginnings of something that would one day be like a tunnel

of birth from which he must fight to emerge; he felt the
obligations working within himself like a goad which would
one day be a whip perpetually falling behind him so that
he must perpetually move onwards.

His sense of fetters and debts was confirmed when
Dirk came to stand by him. First he asked: "What did they
want?"

"They want me to be an artist, they always want me to
be something," said Tommy sullenly. He began throwing
stones at the tree and shying them off along the tops of
the grass. Then one hit the figure of Dirk, and he stopped.

Dirk was looking at himself. "Why do you make me like
that?" he asked. The narrow, strong face expressed nothing
but that familiar, sardonic antagonism, as if he said: "You,
too—just like the rest!"

"Why, what's the matter with it?" challenged Tommy
at once.

Dirk walked around it, then back. "You're just like all
the rest," he said.

"Why? Why don't you like it?" Tommy was really
distressed. Also, his feeling was: What's it got to do with
him? Slowly he understood that his emotion was that belief
in his right to freedom which Dirk always felt immediately,
and he said in a different voice: "Tell me what's wrong with
it?"

"Why do I have to come out of the wood? Why haven't
I any hands or feet?"

"You have, but don't you see. . . " But Tommy looked
at Dirk standing in front of him and suddenly gave an
impatient movement: "Well, it doesn't matter, it's only
a statue."

He sat on the trunk and Dirk beside him. After a while
he said: "How should you be, then?"

"If you made yourself, would you be half wood?"

Tommy made an effort to feel this, but failed. "But it's
not me, it's you." He spoke with difficulty, and thought:

But it's important, I shall have to think about it later. He almost groaned with the knowledge that here it was, the first debt, presented for payment.

Dirk said suddenly: "Surely it needn't be wood. You could do the same thing if you put handcuffs on my wrists." Tommy lifted his head and gave a short, astonished laugh. "Well, what's funny?" said Dirk, aggressively. "You can't do it the easy way, you have to make me half wood, as if I was more a tree than a human being."

Tommy laughed again, but unhappily. "Oh, I'll do it again," he acknowledged at last. "Don't fuss about that one, it's finished. I'll do another."

There was a silence.

Dirk said: "What did that man say about you?"

"How do I know?"

"Does he know about art?"

"I suppose so."

"Perhaps you'll be famous," said Dirk at last. "In that book you gave me, it said about painters. Perhaps you'll be like that."

"Oh, shut up," said Tommy, roughly. "You're just as bad as *he* is."

"Well, what's the matter with it?"

"Why have I got to *be* something? First it was a sailor, and then it was a scholar, and now it's an artist."

"They wouldn't *have* to make me be anything," said Dirk sarcastically.

"I know," admitted Tommy grudgingly. And then, passionately: "I shan't go to university unless he sends you too."

"I know," said Dirk at once, "I know you won't."

They smiled at each other, that small, shy, revealed smile, which was so hard for them because it pledged them to such a struggle in the future.

Then Tommy asked: "Why didn't you come near me all this time?"

"I get sick of you," said Dirk. "I sometimes feel I don't want to see a white face again, not ever. I feel that I hate you all, every one."

"I know," said Tommy, grinning. Then they laughed, and the last strain of dislike between them vanished.

They began to talk, for the first time, of what their lives would be.

Tommy said: "But when you've finished training to be an engineer, what will you do? They don't let coloured people be engineers."

"Things aren't always going to be like that," said Dirk.

"It's going to be very hard," said Tommy, looking at him questioningly, and was at once reassured when Dirk said, sarcastically: "Hard, it's *going* to be hard? Isn't it hard now, white boy?"

Later that day Mr Macintosh came towards them from his house.

He stood in front of them, that big, shrewd, rich man, with his small, clever grey eyes, and his narrow, loveless mouth; and he said aggressively to Tommy: "Do you want to go to the University and be an artist."

"If Dirk comes too," said Tommy immediately.

"What do you want to study?" Mr Macintosh asked Dirk, direct.

"I want to be an engineer," said Dirk at once.

"If I pay your way through the university then at the end of it I'm finished with you. I never want to hear from you and you are never to come back to this mine once you leave it."

Dirk and Tommy both nodded, and the instinctive agreement between them fed Mr Macintosh's bitter unwillingness in the choice, so that he ground out viciously: "Do you think you two can be together in the University? You don't understand. You'll be living separate, and you can't go around together just as you like."

The boys looked at each other, and then as if some sort of pact had been made between them, simply nodded.

"You can't go to university anyway, Tommy, until you've done a bit better at school. If you go back for another year and work you can pass your matric, and go to university, but you can't go now, right at the bottom of the class."

Tommy said: "I'll work." He added at once: "Dirk'll need more books to study here till we can go."

The anger was beginning to swell Mr Macintosh's face, but Tommy said: "It's only fair. You burnt them, and now he hasn't any at all."

"Well," said Mr Macintosh heavily. "Well, so that's how it is!"

He looked at the two boys, seated together on the tree trunk. Tommy was leaning forward, eyes lowered, a troubled but determined look on his face. Dirk was sitting erect, looking straight at his father with eyes filled with hate.

"Well," said Mr Macintosh, with an effort at raillery which sounded harsh to them all: "Well, I send you both to university and you don't give me so much as a thank you!"

At this, both faced towards him, with such bitter astonishment that he flushed.

"Well, well," he said. "Well, well. . . ." And then he turned to leave the clearing, and cried out as he went, so as to give the appearance of dominance: "Remember, laddie, I'm not sending you unless you do well at school this year . . ."

And so he left them and went back to his house, an angry old man, defeated by something he did not begin to understand.

As for the boys, they were silent when he had gone.

The victory was entirely theirs, but now they had to begin again, in the long and difficult struggle to understand what they had won and how they would use it.

Questions for Discussion

No Witchcraft for Sale

1 What impression do we get of the way in which the young Teddy is growing up before the accident?

2 What do you feel was the most amazing thing about Gideon's action after the snake bite?

3 Why was Gideon so stubborn about refusing to find the root?

4 Why did Gideon look "sadly" at Teddy in the last paragraph of the story (*page 19*)?

5 Do we learn enough about the Farquars in the story to judge what sort of people they are?

The Old Chief Mshlanga

6 How has the young girl gathered her impressions of the black people, and what are her feelings towards them?

7 Why did the news which the white policeman gives (*page 25*) make the girl's mother change her attitude towards the cook?

8 Why was Chief Mshlanga not pleased to see the girl in the village (*page 29*)?

9 "I had learnt that if one cannot call a country to heel like a dog, neither can one dismiss the past with a smile in an easy gush of feeling saying: I could not help it, I am also a victim." (*page 31*) What does the girl mean when she says this?

10 How do you feel when you read the son's translation of the father's final remark: "All this land, this land that you call yours, is his land, and belongs to our people"? (*page 32*) Does it in any way change what the reader thinks of the characters?

A Sunrise on the Veld

11   The author describes the boy's early morning journey through the veld. What picture of the boy and his character do we get?

12   What are the boy's feelings when he says (*page 40*): "I can't stop it. I can't stop it. There is nothing I can do."?

13   "Even as he himself had done." (*page 41*) The author is suggesting a likeness between the buck and the boy. What is the likeness?

14   What has the boy come to realize when we read (*page 42*): "For a moment he would not face it"?

Little Tembi

15   Jane was good at feeding and looking after the natives. What qualities did she have that made her so good at this?

16   When she is losing touch with Tembi, Jane remarks (*page 49*): "Oh dear, it's such a pity when they grow up, isn't it?" What does this tell us about Jane?

17   What do you feel about the two beatings which Willie gives (*pages 52 and 58*)?

18   Do you see any link between the following quotations, and can you answer Jane's final question?
"Tembi behaves as if he had some sort of claim on us." (*page 61*).
"What thanks do I get? They aren't grateful for anything we do for them." (*page 64*)
"What did he *want*, Willie? What is it he was *wanting*, all this time?" (*page 72*)

The Nuisance

19   In what ways was the drawing of water by "the cross-

eyed one" different from the rest of the village women?
(*page 74*)

20   What do we gather about the attitudes of the white
      farmers towards the natives from the question on page
      76?
      "And what has the Long One been up to now, with his
      harem?"

21   What does the writer think of her father's approach
      to the natives? Look at her way of describing him in
      the paragraph on page 77 starting "My father re-
      ferred....".

22   Explain whether the story is mainly about the Long
      One and his missing wife, or about the relationship
      between the family and the natives. What, in particular,
      do we get from the last two short paragraphs?

A Home for the Highland Cattle

23   In what ways did Marina and Philip differ in their
      thoughts about the country?

24   All the white people in 138 Cecil John Rhodes Vista
      had coloured servants. How did their use of these ser-
      vants tell us about them as people and the problems of
      relationships between white and coloured?

25   Looking back over the story, do you consider that
      Marina, with her carefully thought-out attitudes to
      "the colour question" actually did more good for her
      servant than, say, Mrs Pond or Mr Black?

The Second Hut

26   Why did Major Carruthers's wife cry after she noticed
      his taking medicine (*page 148*)?

27   When Major Carruthers discovers Van Heerden's fa-
      mily is living in such squalid conditions in the hut, he

is very put out (*page 153–154*). What are his feelings, and why does he feel so strongly? (Look not only at the description of his discovery of the hut, but also his meeting with Van Heerden on page 155: "The only marks on his face were sun creases . . .")

28   Most readers find the burning of the second hut very disturbing and upsetting. What is it about the event which you find *most* disturbing, and why?

29   Major Carruthers and Van Heerden are both white men struggling to make a life in unfamiliar and difficult surroundings. Yet they are very different. Compare their differences, and try to decide what is the central and most important difference between them. Which of the two men seems the more sensible? For which have you most sympathy?

The Pig

30   Was it worth the farmer's trouble calling all the compound together? Why did he do it?

31   Both the farmer and, eventually, Jonas speak of shooting people as if they were pigs:
"And if it turns out to be a human pig, then so much the worse. My lands are no place for pigs of any kind." (*page 175*)

"A pig" said Jonas aloud to the listening moon, as he kicked the side gently with his foot, "nothing but a pig." (*page 181*).
What are they thinking of, and how do their uses of the description "pig" differ?

The Antheap

32   What draws the two boys together?

33   What does the author mean when she writes that Tommy "grew many years older" on the day that he found Dirk working (*page 208*)?

34   Tommy started modelling casually and completely by
      chance. Why did he take to it so fully? In what ways
      were the carvings of Dirk's mother (*page 218*) and the
      later carving of Dirk himself (*page 233*) such important
      steps in his growth as an artist?

35   It would have been possible to have mentioned Mr
      Tomlinson's visit and his judgment (*page 238*) very
      briefly and without describing Mr Macintosh's visit to
      town or their drive back together. What would be lost
      to the story if these descriptions were cut?

36   Both Dirk and Tommy hate Mr Macintosh, and we
      are shown many unpleasant sides to his character. Is
      he, nevertheless, in any way likeable? Have you any
      sympathy for him?

37   The story ends: "The victory was entirely theirs, but
      now they had to begin again, in the long and difficult
      struggle to understand what they had won and how
      they would use it." (*page 245*) What *had* they won, and
      how might they use it?

Looking Back over the Stories

38   Here are three remarks by Doris Lessing. Discuss each
      one in connection with the stories in this volume. Do
      you find any evidence of what she says in the stories
      themselves?

(*a*)   "It is a monstrous society." (*Introduction, page 7*)

(*b*)   "And while the cruelties of the white man towards the
      black man are among the heaviest counts in the in-
      dictment against humanity, colour prejudice is not
      our original fault, but only one aspect of the atrophy
      of the imagination that prevents us from seeing our-
      selves in every creature that breathes beneath the sun."
      (*African Stories*, Michael Joseph, 1964, page 8)

(*c*)   "I believe that the chief gift from Africa to writers,
      white and black, is the continent itself, its presence

which for some people is like an old fever, latent always in their blood; or like an old wound throbbing in the bones as the air changes. This is not a place to visit unless one chooses to be an exile ever afterwards from an inexplicable majestic silence lying just over the border of memory or of thought." (*African Stories*, page 8)

The Author

Doris Lessing was born on a farm in Southern Rhodesia in 1919. She spent her childhood there, coming to England only when she was thirty. By that time she had written her first novel, *The Grass is Singing*. This was published soon after her arrival in England and was very successful.

She followed this with a collection of short stories from which some of those in this volume have been selected: *This was the Old Chief's Country*. The short story has always attracted her as a form of writing, and she has published four other collections. She has said: "I enjoy writing short stories very much. . . . Some writers I know have stopped writing short stories because, as they say, 'there is no market for them'. Others like myself, the addicts, go on, and I suggest would go on even if there really wasn't any home for them but a private drawer." One of these volumes, *Five*, was of rather long stories, halfway between novels and short stories as we usually think of them. Two of those are included in the present volume: 'A Home for the Highland Cattle' and 'The Antheap'. Doris Lessing has said that she particularly likes writing this length of story: "There is space in them to take one's time, to think aloud, to follow, for a paragraph or two, on a side-trail—none of which is possible in a short story."

Of Doris Lessing's other fiction, readers of the present collection are very likely to enjoy these:
The Grass is Singing, a novel;
Short stories included in the volumes *The Habit of Living* (Michael Joseph) and *A Man and Two Women* (MacGibbon and Kee).

THE RHODESIAN SCENE

a sequence of photographs

These photographs are not illustrations of particular moments in the stories, but provide a background which may help the reader to imagine the Rhodesian setting.

254